SHE IS

BEHIND

ENEMY LINES

SHE IS BEHIND ENEMY LINES

Janina Clarke

This is a work of fiction. Names, characters, places, incidents, and dialogues are products of the author's imagination or are used fictitiously. Any resemblance to actual people, living or dead, events or locales is entirely coincidental.

ISBN-13:9798525973930

Thirty-nine women were sent to France by 'F' section of the Special Operations Executive from 1941- 45. They were acting as organisers, radio operators and courier secret agents working behind enemy lines. They volunteered or were chosen because they spoke fluent French, came from all walks of life and different nationalities. They knew it was unlikely they would see their countries again but accepted the risk. Some of them were captured and tortured and died in concentration camps.

Only twenty-two survived the war. There were others who were not recorded.

This book is dedicated to all of them.

PROLOGUE

September 1943, Saint Just, Normandy, France.

Jean-Pierre hurriedly dresses while two Gestapo men are banging on his front door. Giselle pulls her gown around her, and she looks sick with worry.

'I'll let them in.'

'Slowly.' He tries not to look at her worried face. They know why the Gestapo are here. It's too late to run.

'All right. All right. Wait!' She gets to the door as the Gestapo in long coats and narrow-brimmed trilby hats burst in. One man dashes up the stairs, taking them two at a time.

'Sacre bleu! What is it this time?' she demands.

'We've come to take him for his *Service du Travail Obligatoire*. His time is up.'

'He has an exclusion permit.'

'Not anymore,' the other man tells her. She watches him rub his hands together with excitement. She can only imagine what will happen to her lover if she ever sees him alive again. He will end up in a German camp, in a munition's factory, or hauling fossil fuel down German mines. The Gestapo follows the other man up the stairs and she hears banging and scuffles as they arrest Jean-Pierre. She closes her eyes and prays they don't hurt him.

'For God's sake!' Her tears start to fall. They drag Jean-Pierre down the stairs, his shirt hanging out as he's trying to button up his trousers.

'Wait!' She puts his shoes on his feet. He can't go to work in German mines without shoes.

'You wouldn't care if he had no clothes on,' she sobs. Jean-Pierre tries to bend down and kiss her.

'Giselle...' He tries to look at her face for the last time. She goes to touch his cheek which has stubble, and his hair is tousled. The Gestapo pull him back up roughly by his arms, they push him towards the open door and down the steps into the black Citroen Traction Avant, leaving her breathing hard and tears running down her face.

She knows the routine, she's part of the local résistance movement and so is Jean-Pierre. Many of her friends have been taken in the night even though they weren't part of the résistance movement. If he's not starved to death, he'll be bullied into submission by the brutality she's seen handed out by the Gestapo. And if he resists, he'll most likely be shot. Either way, he and other young men like him will be supporting the German Reich, while the German soldiers are fighting at the front. The only good news they've had recently in occupied France is that the German army has been defeated at Stalingrad.

Giselle slowly picks up the clothes from the floor in the bedroom and wipes her tears away with the back of her hand. She opens the window blinds as the early dawn light starts to fill the sky. The floorboard below her clicks. She looks down and realises that for Jean-Pierre's sake she must move the illegal radio hidden under the floorboards beneath her feet.

If the Gestapo come back, they might search and find it and realise he's a radio operator for the local *résistance*. Then they would be tortured and shot as spies. She gathers some clothes and shoves them into a bag and retrieves the radio from under the floorboards, putting it under some clothes in her bicycle basket to cover it up, in case she gets stopped by the soldiers. Taking care not to make a sound, she lets herself out into the gloom of early dawn. Her nerves are tense as she cycles along the quiet street, the heavy basket dragging on the handlebars. She catches the twitch of a curtain out of the corner of her eye as she senses someone watching her cycle into the distance.

Chapter 1

February 21st, 1944, Normandy

A Royal Air Force Halifax is flying under cover of darkness towards northern France. I'm ensconced in the aircraft next to the parachute exit cone in the rear fuselage, it's cramped and uncomfortable. The smell of engine oil and metal reminds me of the military life I left in England. First, I was in the Women's Auxiliary Air Force, now in Churchill's Secret Army, and I'm here on a secret mission for the Special Operations Executive, otherwise known as SOE.

We're flying over the English Channel, missing the enemy's flak, but the aircraft drops suddenly every now and then before climbing rapidly, making me feel sick and anxious.

It's going to be a short flight for me – I'll be the one to parachute first. The crew will fly on to a secret destination further south to drop off much-needed guns and ammunition for another *résistance* group. It's a dangerous mission, one I've been trained and waiting for, for the past six months.

The wind is picking up, which isn't good. It's not what I wanted as the Halifax bobs up and down. I hold my stomach, as if that's going to stop the nausea. My heart's beating fast and I've forgotten about the freezing cold for the moment, while I try not to bring up my last meal I ate in England. At Tangmere, there's a special cottage where Vera, assistant to Maurice Buckmaster 'F section' head of SOE, said *au revoir* and gave me a compact as a good-bye present. The men get a pen. We all get a suicide pill - just in case we get caught by the Gestapo, that's if we have time to take it.

Even with layers of clothes underneath my big overalls, I'm shivering, but it's probably more from fright than cold. I am wearing most of my winter clothes for my mission in France, as it's February and the middle of winter.

We start to descend – we're not far from my designated drop zone, Saint Just. I'm being dropped behind enemy lines to replace the local *résistance* radio operator who's gone missing.

It's 1944 and, with the lead up to D-Day, I have a mountain of responsibility to try and revitalise a small *résistance* cell in the area to train and build up resources of guns and ammunition, so that we can sabotage enemy sites on the lead up to our day of reckoning, or D-Day. The French call it 'Liberation Day' which is more apt, I think. London and the SOE haven't heard from this circuit in a long time. There is supposed to be two of us parachuting into northern France, but I am the only one who turned up. I guess the other agent changed his mind, leaving me even more nervous to be dropped in. I am hoping a friendly résistance group is there to pick me up.

The RAF despatcher opens the bay door, and the cold air comes rushing in. The noise is so loud I put my hands over my ears. I swallow. It's now or never. I hope the parachute opens. My heart beats against my ribs.

I can see houses below, although blacked out: a town, then trees and fields, looking like shadowy ghosts. A light shines up into the darkness suddenly, out of nowhere: it's probably the local baker firing up the oven. The despatcher first empties box after box of flitter paper, they get caught in the wind and blow around in the air like a snowstorm. I catch the tail end of one of the messages as it flies back at me:

...liberty and freedom from oppression. The people of Great Britain support you. We will conquer the oppressors and France will be free again!

The despatcher leaves the bay door open, and I know my time has come. I hold my breath.. He hooks me up and indicates to sit on the edge. I know the routine.

He shouts above the noise, 'Ready love?'

As ready as I'll ever be. This is the worst bit, waiting for the green light to go on. He can tell how nervous I am, he's done this dozens of times before with other SOE agents. How long did they say a radio operator lasts? On average, six weeks in enemy territory.

Suddenly the moon appears from behind a cloud and the trees tops below look as if they're beckoning. I sit on the edge of a precipice in my thick padded flying suit and helmet. There are other items attached to my leg, which will parachute down with me; a suitcase with a radio in it, and thousands in French francs.

We wait for the signal from the pilot. If the *résistance* below doesn't flash the correct Morse letter, we fly off and all of this will be wasted. There are strict protocols, just in case the Gestapo are lying in wait for us because it could be a trap. Many an agent has previously parachuted into the hands of the Gestapo.

The despatcher signals me with thumbs up to go. I freeze, so he pushes me off, roughly. He thought I wouldn't go.

The cold wind takes my breath away. Within seconds, my parachute opens.

The constant drum of the Halifax engines revs up as the aeroplane sails off and up into the night. It's peaceful as I drift on the wind, until I realise the wind is sending me off target towards some taller trees on the edge of a forest. I hold my breath and my heart is racing as my parachute catches on the tallest tree. With a sudden jerk on my straps, I am caught, suspended in mid-air, I gasp and gulp the freezing cold air into my lungs as I struggle trying to free the straps from the branches. They're too taught with my weight to be freed. I panic for a moment as the blood pumps in my ears and I can't hear any sounds in the forest. Everything seems to be frozen in time. The parachute straps are cutting into my thighs. I pause to think. My hands are free, so I stretch my left arm down to my leg strap and take my knife out of it. I could cut the straps. How far is it to fall? What would I fall on? I can't risk it and get a broken leg now.

It's pitch black as the moon has disappeared. I am so grateful to have landed without breaking any bones, so I don't struggle and try and steady my breathing and decide to just wait for the local *résistance* group to rescue me. If there *are* people around to rescue me, I am all right.

Still, no one comes.

I try and cut one of the harnesses holding me up by sawing on the strap with my SOE standard issue Fairburn and Sykes knife. I'd forgotten how sharp the knife is, I haven't used it before. It cuts straight through it, and I instantly drop and jolt as I dangle from one harness hanging lopsided like a puppet. The sharp intake of breath of cold air again heightens my senses. At last, the parachute rips and I fall bit by bit through the dark mass of branches sticking out, they scratch me on the way down and rip my padded suit.

For once, I am thankful I am dressed like a padded bear. I'm not sure where I am. The white parachute above me is caught amongst the bare twigs and branches of the tree. I hang precariously a few feet off the ground. I feel as if my insides are stretched up to my armpits. My laboured breathing blows out clouds of condensation. I don't want the Gestapo to find me hanging from a tree. This isn't exactly 'setting Europe ablaze' which Winston Churchill expects of his trained agents in his Special Operations Executive.

Chapter 2

I hang there, listening for any sound. I hear a small noise, almost imperceptible. Is it a small mammal at my feet?

I look down and I see a man in a cap at my feet. It's only about five feet to the ground. I catch my breath. He looks up, his cap shading his face and he puts his finger to his lips. He climbs the tree like a gazelle above me, and after a few minutes, I unceremoniously drop three feet, then yoyo back and forth, as the lines strain to hold me. Then suddenly I drop and roll onto the wet grass. My breath is knocked out of me as I lay there winded on the ground and trying to get my brain and body working. I lay there a moment fascinated, watching the young man above me try to disconnect my parachute from the bare branches.

In French, he exclaims, 'This will make good material to sell.'

I hear someone rushing up behind me – I hope it's the people I'm supposed to be meeting.

Another male voice says, 'Mon Dieu! He's here. And still alive.'

A deeper male voice exclaims, 'Gaston, check for his case, while I check him out.'

I am seeing stars, literally, as I look up through to the canopy of trees above me. The people tread quietly around my body as if I'm dead. I wonder if I'm in Heaven, it's so peaceful.

Someone pulls my helmet off and says, 'It's a woman. Well!'

It's hard to sit up, I feel battered and bruised, but at least there are no bones broken. I won't be good for anybody if I have broken bones. My eyes look up and as I try to steady my breath, I see five men, and the youngest man helps me to sit up.

'Comment vous appelez-vous?'

'Bonjour, J'mappelle Emilie,' I answer. 'Et vous?'

'Pierre.'

'Bonjour Pierre.'

'I know I am not what you expected,' I tell them, continuing in French. The small group of men gathers around me. 'There was supposed to be two of us, he was the weapons expert, but he was unable to drop with me.'

I see faces now as the moonlight emerges from behind a cloud. A man with raven black hair, a square jaw and a prominent nose acts like he's the leader. The men gather around me. Aside from Pierre, he's not as old as the others, he's tall with a deep but surprisingly soft voice. They're all dressed in dark clothes which helps to camouflage them. I struggle to get to my feet in my padded suit, I feel I must look as big as a bear. The leader sticks a hand under my arm and helps me up.

11

'We expected one man, not a woman. You speak French very well. Are you all right? You went off target.'

'Je vais bien.' I'm fine. I try to look unperturbed and brush leaves and twigs off my clothes and trying to ignore the scratches on my face from the branches. The two older men look like ex-army the way they defer to their leader. They look me up and down, as if they haven't seen a woman before dressed like a padded bear.

'I've been sent to support you as a wireless operator but I'm not sure of your circuit name.' There is a moment of quiet as everyone pauses to listen. 'The wind blew me off course. Are you the *chef de réseau*?'

'Yes, my codename is Cesar,' says the leader. 'We're all part of the Boulanger circuit.'

'Good evening. My code name is Emily. We only heard about your *réseau* last week.' I smile and nod at everyone. The moonlight is lighting up this gap in the woods, so I can see the men's faces of the *résistance*, they nod back at me, curious but serious. Another *réseau* in Bayeux had contacted London HQ on their behalf when the contact had realised they were running a circuit without help of money or equipment from the Special Operations Executive, Baker Street, London. A small circuit but an essential one to combat the Nazi activity in this area.

The light of the moon catches the side of Robert's face, so he's not as young as I first thought, perhaps forty. He has solid shoulders and pulls me to my feet as if I'm as light as a feather, even with my padded suit on.

'We're glad you're here. Whether you're a man or a woman I don't care, you're here to help us get some guns and equipment from London.' He smiles at me as if to give encouragement. Can he sense I feel I'm out of my depth? I have parachuted into the unknown. I must trust these men, so that we can help each other.

'We thought you would be a man,' says one of the men. 'But this is better Robert?' He nudges the leader.

'This is Benoit, and this is Gilbert,' he points to the other resisters. 'My code name *is* Cesar,' he reminds them, and then to me, 'But these men and I have known each other a long time, and they still call me Robert, that is spelled Row-bearrr,' he explains in a low voice.

'Now I know I'm in France,' I say, trying to keep my voice low too, but only Robert hears me and smiles again reassuringly. He seems like a calm person – what I would call unflappable. He wasn't what I expected as the circuit's leader. I expected someone who's not as understanding or empathetic. I feel I have luck on my side, but I still feel a bit out of my depth. Being mostly younger than the men I come highly trained, but I don't tell them that, it doesn't seem like the right time. I had practised the parachute drop during training for SOE, but that was the part I was dreading. I feel relieved to have landed without breaking anything. Now I must act the part of a confident agent come to help them.

I shake my hair free of the helmet. I feel battered and bruised by the fall, but I won't show that I hurt myself. Robert shows some sympathy.

'Are you sure you are all right?'

I'm glad they can't see me blush in the darkness; I'm not used to such kindness from men. During SOE training if you hurt yourself you were expected to get back up and not complain. So I don't.

'Yes fine, thank you for your concern.'

Benoit helps Pierre gather in the parachute from the tree and they eye me up and down.

'I wonder if she is any good?' says Benoit.

'I can speak French you know, and I can understand you,' I tell him indignantly. 'That's why I'm here. I'm the replacement wireless operator.'

He looks at me for a few seconds as if he doesn't believe me.

'We need to get out of here,' Robert tells the others. 'I'll take Emily to Maria's. Benoit, do you have the torches?'

One of the men nods, still looking at me.

'Where's your case?' He asks.

'I'm not sure. My bag was ripped from me when I got caught in the trees. It has one hundred and twenty-five thousand francs, my radio and clothes.'

'Scout the area,' Robert tells them.

I take off my flying suit and give it to the man called Gaston, who takes it away with the parachute. Then I realise how cold it is. Robert looks at me in my town clothes.

'You'll feel the cold a bit now you've taken the flying suit off. We must drive then walk for a while. It's dangerous to hang about here. Someone may have heard the aircraft or seen a light. And there could be informers around.'

Benoit returns with my bag. The bag is the reason I'm here. It's my lifeline, my radio is in it. Plus, the several thousand francs for the *réseau* which will help the circuit in its efforts to sabotage and fight against the Nazis.

'Mon Dieu! This is a big bag,' he says.

'It contains my radio transmitter in a case.' I hold it up to show them. 'This is my raison d'etre.' Robert relieves me of the case. 'And the rest are my clothes. Oh, and the money. Here you are.' I extract one hundred and twenty-five thousand francs from its interior in a leather wallet. I open it up and show Robert. He takes the wallet.

'Thank you. This makes the difference on whether we operate or not.'

'Any arms or ammunition?' asks Benoit.

'Not this time,' says Robert. 'But now we have our radio operator, we can ask for a lot more.'

'London will be waiting for me to give them instructions as soon as possible,' I tell them.

'Very well. Saint Just is poor after years of occupation,' Robert explains. 'The Boche bleed us dry. They take our food and take our young men for slave labour in Germany. You will need to blend in and keep your head down. Perhaps even covered up with a head scarf, your blonde hair will stand out. The Boche like blonde women. We'll need to keep you away from the Gestapo and the *Milice*, they're both just as bad as each other.'

'I say the *Milice* are worst!' Gaston swears something and his friend spits into the earth at their mention.

'I know who they are,' I tell them.

'Let's go.' Robert picks up the bag and the radio case. We walk until we reach a small Citroen baker's van hidden from sight, and some bicycles.

'This is my van. We must move carefully and quietly from now on. Hopefully, we don't meet a German patrol. They're not usually around at this time of night.'

The others wave goodbye to us as they cycle home quietly in the dark.

'Bonne nuit,' whispers Pierre to me as he joins the others. Robert leads me to his baker's van and settle in as he drives off slowly. It's a lot warmer inside, and I start to thaw out.

'No lights,' he says to me by way of explanation. 'The Boche have stepped up patrols since someone shot a German soldier last month. There's a curfew after 8 PM now. No cinema, no theatre. No bars open late. It's been very difficult for everyone.' His voice is low, though he sounds angry.

I nod. I know the importance of not being caught out after curfew. If the enemy catch us, we will be instantly arrested, not counting the fact we have an illegal radio on us. Robert drives cautiously, the moonlight glitters on the frost settling on the grass on the sides of the road. The moon shows the way when it emerges from behind a cloud, the wind is picking up, and the trees on the road in front wave their bare branches in a mad fashion.

'It's about twelve kilometres to Maria's where you'll be staying. But if we do get stopped, I'll tell them I am taking you to your great aunt from your village near Rennes. The fact that it's after curfew, maybe a problem, so I'll say I needed to get some black-market petrol. Dealing with the black market is not uncommon. I am a baker, I need the fuel for my van, which is difficult to get. But it is better than being shot as a spy.'

I look at the sideview of his face, he seems attractive and enigmatic in a quiet sort of way. I can't quite see him clearly and I haven't quite worked him out yet, and I am generally good at assessing someone's character within minutes of meeting them. So, I sit and stare at him while he drives.

'Another agent was supposed to accompany me and take over as your new instructor,' I tell him. 'But he didn't. I don't know why.'

'I see,' he says eventually. 'I don't know why London is giving us another organiser, but we like to choose our own leader.'

I feel like I have been admonished, so I defend SOE.

'We were sent because we found out from the Scientist circuit that you haven't had a wireless operator or organiser for a long time. We hadn't heard from you, so we contacted Scientist because we thought they might know you. Fortunately, someone did know you.'

'We don't talk to other cells,' Robert continues quietly, completely unperturbed with my defence. 'It's safer not to know about each other. We used another radio operator from another *résistance* circuit forty kilometres away in Bordeaux to get in touch with London last year, because one of us has a cousin there. We begged for guns and ammo. But heard nothing from London.'

We turn down a lane, the bocage is so high it cuts out the moonlight. It's so dark Robert drives slowly, I don't know how he can see with no lights, but he seems to know his way.

'We're underfunded, we need people. We're hungry. We need ammo and supplies. We need boots. London is clueless what we need.' He sighs as if he's tired of it all. I can't see his face, and can't tell if he's angry or not, he sounds like he's tired. I feel sad and somewhat guilty that this man and his *reseau* have been passed over until now, and he has had no communication with London and no support.

'Well things will happen now I am here with the radio. I'll be able to arrange for ammunition,' I say brightly. He glances at me and concentrates on keeping to the road. I look sideways at him and feel embarrassed. He sighs again with that resigned look on his face. I say no more. But I can tell occasionally he glances at me as if assessing me. Then he pulls the van in under some high hedges. The overhanging branches hide the van from any moonlight., and their dense foliage drips with the cold. The moon is behind clouds, and I can't see the outline of his face and work out what he's thinking. It's deathly quiet under the high hedges.

'This hedge is called Bocage. These are old cattle trails, built so that the cattle can go unheeded to the pastures - before the roads were made for cars,' he says by way of explanation.

'Handy for us,' I say.

'We have to get out here. We'll carry the bags up the last bit to Maria's house where you will stay, that is so the car doesn't wake up the dairy farmers. They get up early to milk the cows, but nobody should be around at this time of night.'

We get out and our breaths turn to condensation as we start to climb up a hill towards some buildings. In front of us the cloud's part, and a full moon shines down on us. It lights up the countryside. It's cold, clear, and there's frost in the air. The grass crunches underneath our feet and I shiver.

We get to the top of the hill, the track forks to the left towards a house surrounded by a high wall. A dairy farm is to the right of us. I hear some distant sounds, perhaps cows, coming from the shed, but there are no lights on. A cobbled road meets us outside the dairy farm gates and continues down a road towards the town in the distance - remnants of an ancient road, but still used. Robert leads me quickly to the left where a large house looms in shadow surrounded by trees. It looks ghostly, its outline accentuated with the full moon behind it.

'The cobbled road on our right leads to the town.' He lowers his voice and points in an easterly direction. 'It's about six kilometres to the walled embattlements and the outskirts.' I follow behind him to some bushes leading to what was once a front garden and is now patches of dead plants. I trip and hold onto his jacket. I feel him physically jolt. I apologize. He's carrying my bag. I am carrying the radio case and I drop it in a pile of dead, frozen grasses. I stumble, and he picks it up for me. I rub my hands together.

Robert continues in his unshakable way. His voice in a whisper.

'If you hear anything, it'll be the dairy farmers,' he whispers and nods towards the farm. 'They may be *collaborateurs*.'

A thought occurs to me. 'Did they find the last wireless operator's radio?'

'Yes, his girlfriend escaped with it and hid it.'

Chapter 3

I walk round the wall to find it has crumbled with age. From what I can see the front garden is overgrown, and the house is smaller than I thought. It's the grounds that are large.

'The radio's hidden but has broken crystals. I hope you have some spares. There were no following arrests. We assume Jean-Pierre didn't tell them anything. As far as we know, he was taken for slave labour in Germany for the STO. This is something the Vichy French have introduced in the last few months – it stands for *Service du Travail Obligatoire*.'

My heart sinks as we walk up the front path, it is totally in darkness, I thought I might get a bit of a welcome from the owner of the house, but I understand she is elderly so she may be asleep in bed. The moonlight doesn't reach to the front garden, and it's so overgrown I stumble and try and keep myself from slipping by holding onto Robert's arm.

'Yes, I've heard of the STO.'

'You must whisper too as the sound carries.'

As we get closer to the front door, I see how run down the house is. There are creepers and brambles growing over the front of the house, and the windows have shutters hanging off their hinges. As the moon shines on the house, I see there is ivy which has grown from the front door and has wound its way around and over the side gate.

'The house needs some work. I don't have much time for maintenance. My mother and I try to help with the vegetable patch to grow some food for Maria, but she can't do much. Maria had a fall last year and she seems to have lost interest. She's been here for years but can't maintain the house and we don't have much time to help her - since the Nazis invaded, but we do our best.'

I try not to look surprised; this man is more intuitive than I realise and seems to understand what I'm thinking. He sets my bag down at the front door. An animal screeches in the shrubbery nearby, which makes me jump.

'Watch out for the rickety stepping-stones hidden amongst the weeds. There's only one good thing that comes out of having a dilapidated house and that's the Boche tend to ignore it, it's not worth their time.'

'I haven't had time lately to help Maria. It's good now you are here to help. I work at the local bakery. I am the only baker in the town, and the local German garrison takes most of the bread, so I am kept busy all day,' Robert says. 'The cows will be due for milking soon, so we don't want to attract attention with lights..'

As we go inside, the door creaks and he has to lift it on its hinges to shut it again. I ask him about the dairy farmers.

'What makes you think they're *collaborateurs?*'

'The dairy farmer and his wife don't seem to be feeling the pinch like the rest of us. Don't tell them anything. In fact, don't tell anyone anything. Some people you can trust are Eve, my second in command, and her son Pierre, whom you just met, and Eric, his mentor and colleague. They both work for the railways, they are Les Cheminots, and the heart of our *résistance*.'

The front door sticks and creaks, as if it's just managing to keep upright. I wonder if the old lady is awake. It's the middle of the night, and pitch-black inside.

'Pierre's eighteen. He and Eric are our eyes and ears on the local railway. The railway workers are imperative to our cause.' He catches me under my elbow as I stumble up the steps. I feel embarrassed, I'm acting like a toddler tripping up.

I shiver again. Robert finds an old candelabra with wicks where the candles have burned down and he lights the remains. The hall opens out to show the parlour on the left and on the right, the stairs leading to the first floor.

I follow Robert into the front room parlour. I think the room is empty until I see a dusty old armchair with an old woman sunk down into its saggy depths. She looks ancient. Her thin, wispy white hair contrasts against her black widows' weeds.

'Wait out of sight for a moment while she wakes up,' he says, pointing into the hall. 'She often falls asleep in the chair and stays here all night.'

A large candle flutters from the draught by the door, its waxy balls at its base. It looks like candles are Maria's only source of light. There doesn't seem to be any electricity here. I step back into the hall. It has doors leading off giving it the appearance it was once a large family house; now almost empty. There are a few hanging pictures which are faded and dusty. Downstairs there is what looks to be a kitchen and scullery. Maria's chair is positioned in front of the fireplace; the fire has long since died. Her armchair faces the door. Robert is trying to wake her. She slowly wakes up from her sleep, her eyes blinking and trying to adjust to the light.

I walk in to stand at the room entrance. There are heavy velvet curtains at the big windows, now tattered and torn, they are relics of a once affluent age.

The woman is wrinkled, dishevelled. I feel guilty that Robert is waking her up because I'm here. She looks unhappy about being woken up, and grumbles at him, I catch some choice French phrases as she struggles to pull herself up in the armchair. She reminds me of a character from Charles Dickens, Miss Havisham from Great Expectations. I remember it's a long time since I read a book out of choice, the past few months have been training and reading manuals.

'Just wait out there a moment,' says Robert as he shuts the door. I feel as if I've been pushed out. But then waking up to see a stranger in the middle of the night would be a bit of a fright for her. I can hear him talking in low tones; it sounds like he's cajoling her as she wakes up, and I can hear her murmuring. After a few minutes, he calls me in. The candelabra are lighting up the parlour. Maria is sitting up and straightening her mop cap, her skin shrunk on her bony hands.

She turns and looks at me for the first time, she has a wizened old face with piercing blue eyes. She is dressed in thin black clothes, and her shoes have seen better days. I feel guilty again. I wonder if this was such a good idea staying with this old lady after all. She looks me up and down.

'Madame, this is Emily. She is your great-niece from Rennes. Do you remember we talked about it the other day?' says Robert. 'Your niece sent her to look after you.'

'I have no niece.'

He ignores her and helps her to stand, coaxing all the time like she's a child to take more steps towards the kitchen. He reminds me of my brother the way he talked to his children. This was before he left for the war.

Maria pushes him away as she stands up taller, trying to retain her dignity. Robert shows her the way with the candelabra.

'Perhaps we should go into the kitchen?' I suggest. 'We could light the stove.'

'Madame,' he tries again. 'Don't you remember what we talked about yesterday? This is your great-niece, Emily. She has come to look after you.'

'I don't need looking after.' The old woman grizzles, grabs her walking stick and drags her feet, shuffling past me towards the kitchen, where the embers of a fire are keeping the cold at bay. I see a big fireplace and a window which looks out into the back garden. It's still dark outside so I can't see anything. Robert takes a lump of wood from the fireplace and stokes up the old range.

It's the first time I've seen Robert in the proper light. He is probably nearer forty, attractive, his black hair suffused with grey at the sides and combed off his brow. He helps her to sit in the armchair. He takes his jacket off and the muscles on his arm contrast against her frail body as he bends on one leg to put socks on her feet. It looks like she hasn't eaten properly for days. Although a big man, he moves gently with her. Her thin, pale skin wrinkles over protruding bones. One bony hand adjusts the grimy felt cap on her head while the other hand tugs the edges together of a shawl.

The embers of the kitchen fire keep the room in a warm glow. I place the candelabra in the middle of a long wooden table and view the scene. He is fussing around Maria as she lets herself down into a solid wooden chair which looks as old as she is. The kitchen is sparse apart from the stove, there's an old white sink, and bucket. An ancient wooden table is almost white with years of being scrubbed clean.

'I'll make some tea,' he says, as he searches through a sparse cupboard. He finds none and looks embarrassed.

'I have some tea.' I pull some English tea out of my bag. It's not in its original package because I wouldn't want the Nazis to find it. It has travelled in a plain, small box. Tea is a commodity which is also a luxury here. But I think it's safe to bring it out into the open. Maria doesn't turn her nose up at fresh tea. She's now paying attention, watching us boil the water on the stove while I look for cups, and her smile slowly spreads lighting up her face.

'Do you have any milk, Maria?' I ask her, which is probably a silly question, milk is hard to come by these days in France. She stares at me in a daze and before long she is dozing off again in the armchair.

'You may have to get some from next door tomorrow.'

'We were told in training not to ask for milk because it is taken by the Germans.' I tell Robert.

'They will accept money next door, just show a coin though, do not take any notes, that will make them suspicious. Maria doesn't bother to eat much.' Robert carefully places a large log on the kitchen fire. The fire picks up and small flames lick around it. 'I stock her up with wood when I go into the forest. It should keep the house warm until morning if we leave the doors open.'

'It looks like she has hardly any food at all.'

'I usually bring her bread and my mother brings what she can. I'll bring you some tomorrow.'

He turns to Maria. 'I am going to show Emily to her room, Maria.'

He turns to me. 'I hope Pierre has prepared the fires, as I asked him to.'

Robert indicates his hand towards the door and takes my bag and the candelabra.

'And I suggest you go to bed too, Maria. You'll wear yourself out in the chair all night,' he says. And he leaves a candle for her on the kitchen table and the door open to warm the rest of the house.

'Maria's had a hard life, take no notice, she'll get used to you. Especially now that you're here to help her.'

'Was she born in the house?' I look up the stairs and wonder how old it is, there are portraits that line the stairs.

'Are these her relatives?' I ask as we pass each portrait on the stairs.

Robert shrugs his shoulders. 'Yes, I believe so.'

'What time do you get up for the boulangerie?'

'About four.'

'So you have been awake for nearly twenty-four hours.'

He takes me into one of four rooms leading off the landing, mostly bare without any furniture. My room is next door to Maria's above the parlour, looking out onto the overgrown front garden. The curtains are thin and don't stop much light.

There's a bed with a grubby mattress. A fire, which isn't lit. A wash basin and jug. *Le toilette* is in the back garden. The bedroom over the kitchen looks over the dairy farm, a thin, holey blanket acts as a blackout, that has seen better days too.

I pull the blanket aside carefully, putting my candle on the floor. I look out into the moonlit night overlooking the fields beyond. I can see the milking shed and the end of the dairy farm. There are no lights on there.

'I grew up on a farm in Normandy. It had cows, and goats.' I turn to Robert. 'You should go, someone will be about soon in the dairy.'

'I was hoping Pierre had prepared a fire for you.'

We both look at the empty grate. I shiver with the cold and the musty smell of dampness pervades the air.

'I can light my own fire. I'm not completely helpless.' I am a bit disappointed with my safe house. I must admit I thought there might be electricity and a warm fire. I start to feel homesick for my mother's house in Norfolk. At least I had a reception committee to meet me, many of my SOE friends didn't even have that. They had to find their own way to a safe house. I have to remind myself that I'm here to fight the Nazis and not be looked after. But there is no food, and no bedding. Only an old mattress and a blanket which smells of dog. I turn my face away and look up at the walls, I shrivel up my nose in distaste. Robert bustles about laying the bag and case on the floor on a small table.

'You have somewhere to hang your clothes,' he says, he points towards a tiny wardrobe, trying to sound positive. 'And I'll get you some food tomorrow. I didn't realise the larder was empty.'

'Do you have any bedding?' I look disappointedly at the bed.

He looks embarrassed, and says, 'I'll try and find you another mattress.'

'Don't worry, you have enough to do, I'll find something in Maria's cupboards, no doubt.' Trying to sound more cheerful than I felt. I try to sound grateful. Only now tiredness hits me, and I really need to sleep. I sit on the bed and close my eyes, I might have dosed for a minute or two, as Robert has brought some wood from downstairs.

'The citizens of this land have been demoralised,' he says as he scrunches up a piece of old newspaper and lights it. He watches as the fire catches hold, then puts the pieces of wood on top.

'Food has been taken from the citizens of this town to give to the Germans. They eat the best food and drink while we go hungry. The young men are sent to camps in Germany to work down German mines. They've really lost all sense of pride and independence. No French citizen has enough to eat, unless it's bought from the black market. And you really have to run nefarious activities in order *not* to go hungry.'

No wonder everyone seems so thin. 'That's all right. I had to learn to live off the land in Scotland. Scotland is a darn sight colder than Normandy.' I move on the bed and the springs creak, and it wobbles unevenly on its legs.

'I can make it more comfortable tomorrow. Why don't you go now?' I can see he is tired too. 'You go home, you have a family and work?'

'I am due to start baking in two hours.'

'Then go. I can handle myself here. Thanks for your help so far.'

'I will see you later today, Emily. Oh, and may I suggest you change your hair colour. It may save your life.'

And with that comment he was gone. My watch says two thirty am. I sit on my bed with dirty mattress and contemplate my hair colour. Vera had tried to persuade me to die my hair, but I had resisted, thinking it would be more of an asset. The Germans might be more lenient with a blond Aryan-looking woman perhaps? But now I'm beginning to think I should have done as she said. If Robert comments on my hair and he is an experienced leader he would know how a blonde woman would stand out. Suddenly I lose any confidence I had. As I study the fraying curtains, I begin to feel differently, the bravado I had when I landed has changed to a feeling of insecurity. I begin to think perhaps I had better have stayed in England. The house feels full of gloom and doom. And because I'm tired, I become despondent. I sigh and lay down fully clothed and fall asleep straight away on the smelly mattress.

Chapter 4

The insides of the windows are frosted over when I wake up with a start and I think I'm back in my bedroom in Norfolk.

My chilblains itch from months of wet and cold, training in the highlands of Scotland as a secret agent. My mother's not here to bring me a cup of tea. The last time I saw her was when I stayed with her a few days ago, before I left for RAF Tangmere to fly here. I couldn't tell her where I was going, just that it was abroad. I had signed the Official Secrets Act, and anyway, she wouldn't believe that I was flying over enemy territory and parachuting into Normandy. As a wireless operator I have an estimated six-week life span once I'm 'dropped,' and the threat of torture and a horrible death if I'm discovered. As far as the British public are concerned, women work in the posts that men have left when they went to war. A lot of it dangerous such as working in munitions factories, working out the calculations on an anti-aircraft gun and perhaps being the target for German bombers, but certainly not as a trained killer and saboteur behind enemy lines.

I can see the weak winter morning light coming through the gap. Then I remember Robert, and the *résistants* who are trying to hold body and soul together, and Maria.

I need to send a message to London that I'm in the safe house, although any confidence I had twenty-four hours ago has evaporated when I think of the enormous task ahead of me.

I had declined the use of a pistol on leaving England. If the Gestapo stop-searched me and found it on me, I would be sent to Germany as a terrorist, regardless of not having done any sabotage. No guns, no ammo, and only me and my radio to contact London and our rescuers. And that's if I don't get caught.

I stretch and change my clothes. The clothes bag Robert carried for me up the hill and the radio are so heavy I can hardly lift it. Obviously being a baker keeps him fit.

I have the town map of Saint Just but keep it hidden in one of the spare bedrooms under a loose floorboard. If a map is found on anyone in occupied France, they could be arrested as a spy. Maps and independently travelling around Normandy isn't a phrase used together during this occupation. Too much independence equals subversion in Nazi language.

It's been a particularly cold winter in Europe. I hadn't expected such a cold first night here in Normandy. But this winter has been bad for all sorts of reasons. The coldest winter on record and my brother recorded missing, presumed dead. Which means he's been killed but they can't identify his body. This happened while I was in secret training in Scotland with SOE. My mother didn't know how to get hold of me, so when I went to see her for the last time before 'I was shipped abroad, on a secret mission,' I felt all the guilt due to a lone daughter leaving her mother on her own.

Mother was lonely. Papa died a year after my marriage to Luke. Papa was the kindest man. We hadn't heard about my brother's company in the desert then, at last we got the news that Montgomery had beaten the Germans at El Alamein, and we were all so excited that the tide of war was at last turning.

Then we received the telegram which sent my mother into floods of tears. Sam was killed at El Alamein. The two men in her life gone. And me trying to fill the emotional gap. Only that I'm not – I'm going to France to help my cousins fight back against the Boche.

Of course, I couldn't tell her that. Women didn't go to fight in war according to my mother, and when I joined the Women's Auxiliary Air Force, she cried for two days until I left for Portsmouth. Two years later I told her I was going abroad to work for the government. She was confused and begged me not to go, thinking I was going to Egypt or another 'strange' country. I worked with women who had joined The First Aid Nursing Yeomanry, or FANYS, which are a cover for some of the women operating as spies in German-occupied Europe. If she discovered that I was being parachuted into occupied France to support the French, she would probably have written to Churchill himself.

In the WAAF's working at 53a - Grendon Hall, Grendon Underwood, Buckinghamshire, a radio listening and transmission station where I worked as a wireless operator it was hard work and long hours. I enjoyed the camaraderie between the women and the men as we worked side by side decoding agents' secret messages reporting on enemy troops and events in occupied Europe. I realised the impact for the agents living behind enemy lines was taking a toll on them, they were constantly living in fear and hiding from the Nazis. And they weren't just men - we had female agents too. I got to know their particular style and wording, even their touch on the keys. Suddenly they would stop transmitting and when it restarted the words would change. We knew then that the agent had been taken and the Germans had taken over her or his transmission. It dawned on me how much these women and men were giving their lives for their countries. Bit by bit the agents were going silent behind enemy lines in different parts of occupied Europe and disappearing. I could only guess the worst for these poor souls – they had been captured and probably tortured to get as much information out of them before they were shot as a spy in front of a firing squad.

I was approached in the summer of 1943 by a senior official, in civilian clothes, so I knew it was 'hush hush.' Because I spoke French, he suggested I work for them in a new department called the 'Inter-Service Research Bureau.' It became known to me as 'Churchill's Secret Army' or as we also called it 'The Baker Street

Irregulars.' Vera Atkins, Maurice Buckmaster's second-in-command, promised to send a postcard to the agents' families once a month to say all was well with their son or daughter. Considering a radio operator's standard lifespan is six weeks, I would expect my mother would receive a maximum of two postcards.

Although the window is misted up, from my bedroom window I see a vista showing a winding valley and rolling landscapes to the fields and the bocage beyond. Maria's bedroom door is open. She is asleep in bed. In her room the only extra furnishings are a set of drawers, a washstand, and a chair with clothes on.

As I walk around the house, I look out of the windows. The house is on higher ground and gives a good all-round view of the area and the road leading to the house. This is ideal if I want to see who is coming down the road.

From the bedrooms at the back, I look out onto the dairy fields. As the pale sun tries to stretch its rays across the sky, the flowers that grew last summer are dried and twisted and now folded down with frost crystals. The cows in the fields are flicking their tails and their coats are steaming in the morning sun.

There are tall Cypress trees at the boundary of Maria's house that have grown over the years and reach the roof providing a certain privacy, and I still have a clear view of the skyline. I can almost see the sea on the horizon but it's just that bit too far. The house looks even more decrepit in the cool light of day. I slip outside to the toilet, the sun's warmth on my face reminds me that spring is just around the corner.

My negative thoughts last night regarding Maria's hostility towards me are not as effective now I've had some sleep. The poor lady has been told to get used to having a stranger around the house. Her reaction is understandable.

I have a look around. The parlour furniture is old and sparse and smells of damp. The windows are draughty with the curtains drawn. I pull them back so that it is possible to see if any visitors walk up the front path, whether they are welcome or not. There are burned out candles around the house. How different this is to the busy city I have just left where I had taken electricity for granted.

The kitchen is still warm from last night's fire, and there is wood by the stove. As I put the kettle over the stove, I hear creaks on the stairs. I wonder if the old lady has woken up, she takes a long time to move. Eventually, she comes into the kitchen and looks at me as if seeing me for the first time. Her brows knit together.

'I've just put the kettle on for some coffee, Aunt Maria. Would you like some?'

'No milk,' she says abruptly. 'And I am not your aunt.'

'Well, for the *résistance's* sake you are.' I look her in the eyes, I can feel my temper rising. 'We are supposed to be on the same side, after all. Do they sell milk over there in the farm?'

'I know you are English,' Maria mutters. 'Fight your own bloody war, don't bring it to my doorstep.'

'We're in this war together, Aunt Maria. It's the Nazis who started this war, not the English. And anyway, I was born in Rennes, and so was my father. We moved to England because my mother was homesick.'

I move about the kitchen becoming familiar with where food and utensils are kept. She's trying to rile me, and she nearly succeeded. Plain clothes men spent weeks in our training trying to get us to divulge secrets, but it's easier to resist when you know they are secretly on your side. I think Maria is trying to get rid of me by being hurtful. But I can be as stubborn as she can.

Maria sniffs and wipes her cold nose with her sleeve. The old woman's eyes are as bright as a squirrels, and she is not giving an inch to be friendlier. She sits down at the long kitchen table and stares out of the kitchen window. I go to the larder, there is not much in there, just dried bread, which I give to her.

I head outside to the back garden to look at the vegetables. What is left has been frozen to the ground. Some dead and frozen onions. Some shrivelled plants with frost. It looks like there has been lots of activity here in the last growing season, in this large back garden. Someone has planted, cared for, watered, and harvested rows and rows of vegetables. I imagine the people in Maria's life got too busy doing this for her but tried to come and help when they could.

There's a small shed to the right of the toilet. It's out of sight of the kitchen window, but about three metres long. As I step in there, I am delighted to see rows of garlic and onions, and boxes along the length of shed. I find potatoes, swede, carrots, and turnips, even apples, as I lift the sackcloth which protects them from the freezing cold.

I don't think Maria has even used them. She is so thin and there's no evidence of her doing any cooking. It would be Robert and some of his friends who have helped this lonely old lady. It probably helped feed their families too. The vegetables would keep them fed through the freezing winter months. My spirits perk up. The locals and friends obviously think a lot of Maria to support her like this.

I look over the dry-stone wall at the dairy farm beyond, and wonder if the farmers are really *collaborateurs*. They still have their dairy herd, which looks healthy from a distance. The place is quiet and there are cows in the fields beyond. The morning is bright and the layer of frost we had in the night is melting in the sun as its rays spread its arms across the white buildings.

My breath blows clouds into the cold morning. I pick some vegetables from the shed to make a *cassoulet*. The old woman keeps an eye on me the entire time from the kitchen window. I ignore her mutterings as I go inside.

'It's very cold out there.' I say loudly.

'I am old, not deaf,' and she swears away to herself or at me. But I ignore her as she walks about the house stiffly looking for somewhere to settle and watch me like a hoverfly on a flower. I try to remain calm and not let her rankle me. Shouldn't she be just a little bit grateful because I am now making sure she's fed? I probably have underestimated her need to retain her independence. I feed the fire with logs at the side.

This time I go further down the garden. There is a small gap in the hedgerow next to the shed, like a well-worn pathway of a small mammal, a fox perhaps. It will make a good emergency exit if I must leave the house quickly. There's one most important thing I learned in SOE training - ensure you have another exit, wherever you are.

I can't see the kitchen window from here and I am hidden from the dairy farm, even better. Maria's not looking out of the back door, so I pull some brambles away. I need to attempt to make it wider if I want to bring my radio with me. I go back inside and retrieve my gloves from my room. Maria is dozing by the fire in the kitchen.

I am happy with the hole by the time I've made it wider but still not obvious. I pop my head up and look over the dry-stone wall and I see a middle-aged woman walking the cows to the milking shed.

I drop my gloves in the shed and make my way to the dairy farm. We need milk and the smells of the farmyard entice me with the promise of it. I dodge the cow pats and mud which are steaming in the sun. I stand looking dreamily at the pale sunlight reflecting on the cow shed and there's a cough behind me.

I nearly jump out of my skin. A sharp intake of breath. Behind me stands a sour-looking man with a huge grey beard, a round belly, and dirty overalls. He looks like a very grumpy Santa Claus.

'I came to buy milk.' I try and smile at him, but my smile freezes. He grins but it's not a nice grin, he doesn't smile, because two top teeth are missing like he lost them in a fight and his hair sticks out from under his cap. He practically snatches the French coins which I hold out in my hand, which I brought with me from England. The door of the outhouse is open, and I follow him into a small office with a table covered in papers. He deposits the money in his pocket and pours milk from a churn into an old milk jug.

'I want the jug back.' He glowers at me, shoving it into my hand so hard that I must take a step back.

Suddenly, the farmer's wife appears behind me. She has thin grey hair either side of her rosy cheeks which shows she's been exposed to the sun for most of her outdoor life. She's much cheerier than he is.

'Don't mind him, my dear,' she says. 'He's a bit rough in his ways.' She scowls at him; he scowls back. He doesn't hang around; he's already walking off towards his cow shed.

'I am Bella Chevrolet, that man's my husband. So, you're new next door – come to care for Maria, have you?'

I wonder when she'd first noticed me; she must have been watching us all morning.

'Yes, I am her great niece, Emily. My mother sent me to look after her.'

'And about time too.' She smiles at me. 'I am sorry to say this, but poor Maria has struggled to keep herself fed and clean. She's been on her own and going downhill for years.'

I jump to Maria's defence. 'Well, she is ninety-three. And I am here now so everything will be all right.'

'I have tried to help her in the past, but she hasn't wanted my help. Well, you know what she's like.'

I nod. Yes, in my short time of knowing Maria, I've discovered she is ungrateful to people who want to help her. Yes, I *did* know what she was like.

Bella talks non-stop about the herd, telling me their names, and asking me questions about where I'm from. I dodge most questions and answer some honestly. I let her know that I come from Rennes.

I look from the dairy's back door to Maria's back garden and wonder if you can see into the kitchen when the light is on. I realise they can't see the hedge with the hole in it if I need to escape out the back. As I am observing the hedgerows and our

43

house beyond and wondering how much they can see at night, I miss the last bit of what she is telling me.

'Oh yes,' I say, oblivious to her. She rattles on, asking questions, was I married? Time to go.

'I'd have thought you would be married by now at your age. I am surprised you're allowed to leave your hometown to care for Maria.' She smiles and jokes, expecting an answer as I back out of the yard, all the while I'm avoiding her questions and thinking that I'd rather go without than be tied to someone like her husband. Smiling back and as a parting shot, I say to her, 'I'll bring the jug back tomorrow.'

Monsieur Chevrolet will not meet my eyes when I speak to him, and Madame asks too many questions. I feel they are not to be trusted.

As I reach Maria's house, Robert pulls up beside me in his van and pulls out two long loaves. 'For you and Maria.' He gets out of his van. He seems to be more cheerful this morning, although it's gone midday.

'Oh, thank you. I'm so hungry.' We walk back to Maria's house. 'Have you been to the boulangerie this morning?'

'Yes, my mother is finishing off for me.'

'Oh?'

'We have important things to do Emily.' He says more business like. 'I'll need your radio case. I have a place to hide it. If the *Milice* or Gestapo turn up unexpectedly, and I am sure they will, we need to make sure it's not in the house.'

That makes perfect sense, so I hurry and retrieve it from its temporary location under the bed. He looks behind him in the direction of the dairy farm and quickly puts in the back of his van, covering it with a sack.

'I'll need to use it to report back tonight or tomorrow at the latest,' I tell him.

'I'll take you tonight. What time is your schedule? Do you have enough food?'

'Midnight. And there isn't much bread left in the larder, and I bought some milk for Maria this morning. I am surprised she eats so little. Does anyone else look out for her?'

'Maria used to be part of the *résistance* during the Great War thirty years ago. She did a lot for people; she sheltered and fed those who were desperate, and people don't forget.' It seems strange to me that Maria was an active *résistance* member, but she's shown a fighting spirit and it doesn't appear to have left her. I feel guilty of my first evaluation of her.

I lead him outside where the sun is shining and open the outhouse to the logs of wood and boxes full of vegetables.

'Have you done all this for Maria?' I ask him.

'My mother, Stephanie and a few of us in the group help Maria out when we can. But mostly it is my mother. Maria's sister died at the beginning of the occupation, she used to live down the lane at the end house with her husband, but they passed away. One of the *Milice* moved in as soon as she'd passed on.'

'Did they buy the house?'

'If they did, the money didn't go to Maria. We're still trying to find out what happened to it.'

He takes some of the vegetables from under the sack cloths.

'I thought it was the men who did the gardening for Maria. I should have realised. My father did everything for my mother, so it hit her hard when he passed away.'

'Pierre and Laurent, me and Benoit. We share the produce between our families. The enemy don't know it's here. It's not only growing the food which is important but hiding the food as we store it, because if the *Milice* find out what's here they'll come and get it for themselves. They don't think to look in a dilapidated old shed. We all share in the *reseau*. But don't take anyone at face value. Some of the townsfolk are scared, so they'd sell their soul to the devil. Many are selling information to the police. I grew up with the chief constable; he's not as bigoted as the *Milice*. They are ruthless and in the pay of the Gestapo.'

I shut the outhouse door, and I see Madame and Monsieur Chevrolet talking to each other in the distance by the milking outhouse. No doubt they would have been watching us. I tell Robert I think they are definitely *collaborateurs*.

'They know me as the local baker. They've seen me here helping Maria out in the garden. They now know who you are. You could get a visit from the local *Milice* soon, so be warned.'

'Thank you. I'll be ready. They must have about twenty cows in there. They do very well, don't they?'

'I've seen cars go in there from the police. The milk they sell goes mostly to the garrison, *Milice* and Gendarmerie. Very few citizens can afford to buy milk.

'She asked a lot of questions about me. No doubt to tell her friends in the *Milice*.'

'Then keep away from there and don't buy milk. She may wonder why you have so much money to buy it when the locals don't.'

'I've fixed Maria's front door as well as I can. Make sure it's bolted, then go out the back on your bike. It looks like the side gate doesn't open from the front with all the ivy and brambles stuck on. But you can squeeze in and out, and no one will think to come around the back through a side gate covered in brambles. I'll try and explain this to Maria. Although she tends to ignore the front door if strangers come. It didn't happen before. But it may do now.'

'All right.'

'I want to talk with you about the set-up here.'

'It's not safe to talk outside,' I remind him. 'We should stay inside the shed.'

The shed is warm and cosy with the two of us in there. Robert's frame fills nearly one side of it. His black jacket smells of damp wood he has collected from the forest. He opens it, and the smell of flour and soap drifts out from his shirt.

My eyes flicker with the sensation of him. I try to remember what I had to talk to him about. His chin has two days beard growth, and he has a small scar on his cheek which moves with his jaw in a fascinating way.

'How did you scar your cheek?'

'A childhood accident,' he says, embarrassed.

'I beg your pardon. Normally I'm quite a shy person, but now I'm in France…'

'Your training will have changed you too,' he says as he picks up a sack. He picks some vegetables from different boxes, uncovering the sacks, taking out some carrots, potatoes and turnips and putting the covers back.

'I heard about it from another agent we housed.'

I wonder what he knows about SOE, it may be best to be not so familiar, so I change the conversation. 'Tell me about the *Milice* and what's been happening with the *résistance*.'

'Gisard Mauvais for instance is a schoolmaster, but a part-time *Milician*, and someone you should keep away from. He knows the students and parents, and therefore he knows nearly everyone in this town. He was two years above Eve and me in school, and he was a pain in the arse. No one liked him, he was a bully then and is a bully now. That's why they employ him to be a *Milice* officer. He knows the locals and the area. Nothing gets by him. He has his spies everywhere and he reports back to the Gestapo."

'I've heard about the *Milice*, isn't it their job to arrest undesirables?'

'Yes, including the Jews and any locals they don't like the look of. Eve, my friend, who you will meet soon, was attacked by Gisard Mauvais on her way home from school when she was thirteen. He is now in the pay of the Gestapo as the leader of the *Milice*.' He watches my face change.

'Oh, my goodness. What happened?'

'Nothing. His parents spread it around that it was a lie, and Mauvais got away with it. Now, he thinks he can come and go as he pleases to her house. So, she must hide when he comes. He waits until Pierre her son, isn't there of course.'

'I don't plan to let you meet the rest of the *résistance*. We've had some new people join recently especially now the allies are winning, and we're feeling more confident. Some will be curious about you. It's best to keep you isolated from everyone, what they don't know, they cannot tell the Gestapo. They know you're here, some of the *réseau*, but not everyone knows where. So, we keep it that way; anonymity works best in a town of this size.' He sits on the edge of a box so he can face me. 'Why are you here, Emily?'

I catch my breath. 'You know why. I am here to help you set up a fighting *résistants* group.'

49

'We have a fighting group. How do you think we managed before you came? I mean, why are you *really* here.'

I go pink in the face. I suddenly feel embarrassed. I suppose I had sounded condescending, but I hadn't expected questions from the leader whom I had considered an ally right from the start.

'Well, to free France of course. And to help the *résistance* on the Le jour de la liberation. It's what I've been trained for.'

'But you're an English girl.'

'Born in France and didn't leave France until I went to a school in Zurich when I was thirteen. So, I was still speaking French when I went to live in Norfolk. By which time my papa had given up trying to get back here. I thought I'd do it for him.'

'Well, we're glad to have you. Are you any good as a *pianist?*'

'I've had plenty of experience. First in the WAAF's, then in The Special Operations Executive.'

He nods. 'Well, my job is to find someone to take you to different venues to transmit our messages. At the end of the day, it'll probably be me.'

'But you have enough to do. I can cycle, but I don't have a bicycle.'

'You may have to go it alone sometimes, but I'll do my best to take you to other places. And I can get a bicycle for you. It's inner tubes we're short of. My biggest concern is disappearing before they grab me for German slave labour.'

'Will someone give you the nod?'

'I hope so.'

'We had someone like you who came to help us about two years ago. He ended up getting shot. He was followed back to our hideout and three of my friends were shot as they tried to escape. He wasn't careful enough. He treated it like a game.'

'I'm sorry. But that's not me.'

'There are secrets you won't find in London. They don't know a lot of what's been happening.'

I look outside the gap in the door, there's no one outside. I feel the need to tell this man everything, to get things off my chest. I feel a lump in my throat, and I'm not sure why. This man has empathy, he's one of those people who listens to you rather than talks at you. I'd had enough of the latter to last a lifetime, particularly in the military.

'What is it, Emily?' he says softly. For a moment, I think he is going to put his arms around my shoulders and comfort me.

'The only reason I was approached to join SOE was because I speak fluent French. But I wouldn't have been allowed to join the WAAF's if my husband had had his way. It sounds terrible and you will think me shocking to admit that I'm glad he's gone, and I can live my life now how I want. Not how he wanted.'

'I am glad that you are here. I did not mean to criticize.' Robert looks at me, takes my hand and holds it for a moment, genuinely concerned. I don't mind him holding my hand.

'What happened to you?'

'Luke was going to sea imminently and so we decided to get married. His ship didn't survive the first trip across the Atlantic, he was on convoys, so it was a bit of a shock when I got the telegram: Lost at sea. Sorry…you are easy to talk to.'

His hand feels warm, and he smiles encouragingly. I swallow. England and Baker Street feel a long way away.

'I feel as if I have known you for ages.' I tell him.

'People often tell me that,' he says and squeezes my hand and doesn't seem a bit perturbed when I move away from him, now I feel embarrassed.

'Perhaps Maria is wondering where we are.'

'Well, she won't be. But if the Chevrolets are watching us, they'll be extremely interested in what we're doing in the shed,' he smiles.

I lead the way into the kitchen. Robert brings in wood and puts it next to the kitchen fireplace.

'I've brought some wood for you both. I don't think it's the right time to be collecting wood for the fire now. It's still frosty at night.'

'Thank you, Robert,' Maria smiles at him. It's the first time I've seen her smile. As he kneels by the fire piling up the logs, she looks fondly at him. She doesn't look at me.

Robert walks over to the kitchen windows and washes his hands. Maria goes out of the kitchen towards the parlour, her favourite room. I wait until she's out of earshot.

'I'd better do my schedule tonight, and let London know I am here safe here.'

'We'll be meeting up with two of the *résistants* as soon as I can organise it. You'll need to meet Eve. It's also a safe house you can go to if you need to. I'll take you in my van. We'll go when I've finished work one day. For tonight - if we meet before nightfall, we should be safer than meeting after curfew when it's dark.'

'What about the *Milice*?'

'Do you have your travel permit with you?'

'All my papers are correct and were organised for me by the best forger in France, who is now in England. Thank you.'

Robert stays a little while longer while I break up the bread and make some chocolate with the milk for us all. I follow him out to his van. I tell him I have a map, as I follow him out. He's stayed longer than I had anticipated. Maria stares at me and smiles at Robert. I walk with him to the front door, and he shows me how to lock it after he's gone. Not that that will keep the Gestapo out, but I feel more secure at night now he has fixed the door. He waves as he drives off back down the lane, past the dairy farm a light goes off in the farmhouse as he drives past.

Chapter 5

Gisard Mauvais sits at the front of his class, on an elevated platform, watching his students scribe onto their boards.

His self-belief is great, born out of being the only teacher in the town who is in Saint Just. He did not join the French army. This left him the only one left alive to become the headmaster of the town, because his peers are now prisoners of Germany or have been killed.

Mauvais gives his young students grief on a daily basis. He is forty-three years of age and unmarried. He lives at home with his mother.

Mauvais had been taunted as a schoolboy, by people who were now in positions of significance in this town, and he hasn't forgotten it. He thought they'd been mean to him because he was shorter, and his mother tended to feed him more than he needed. But really, it was because he was a bully.

His mother dotes on her only child: he can do no wrong. She did not allow him to go to fight in the first war, which had killed his father. Mauvais is really a coward. He's been given a pistol by the Gestapo whom he works for, as a part-time *Milicien* and he does all their dirty work for them. Like arresting Jews and clearing them out of their houses, putting them on the trains to Germany, then making sure he gets anything of value from their house. This makes him over-confident and encourages him to threaten vulnerable people of the town, and his students who dare not challenge him, so that he can get his own way. Everyone in the town hates him, they look the other way or cross the street when they see him coming.

With his new pistol he can now threaten and bribe the local citizens and get the things he's always wanted, which is to threaten them and humiliate them. Particularly those people who have denied him in the past. He is looking forward to visiting Eve Velliat, his schoolboy crush, especially as her husband has been sent to Germany via the *Services Travail Obligatoire*. He has made sure of that. He will have to be careful as she has many friends, like Robert Dusacq, who's fought in the French army, and has returned home to become the local baker, with an exemption certificate for the STO. Dusacq had been younger than him at school, but Dusacq had also beaten him in a playground fight over Eve. He hasn't forgotten that. Mauvais can get his own back on Robert Dusacq, and his friends, because he has power now he is in the *Milice,* and he has a German pistol.

'Claude, come out to the front.'

Mauvais combs some hair strands from the side of his head over to the other side to cover the bald patch on top. He also puts grease in his hair, which he thinks is a fashionable thing to do, but this just accentuates the odd look of the patch of hair on top of his head. His students laugh at him behind his back, if he catches them, he beats them.

Claude, wearing holey trousers that are too small, and shoes which are falling apart, drags his feet to stand in front of the school master's desk. He hasn't done anything wrong; he wonders why he's been called out. It's probably to hit him across the head with a ruler again. Mauvais always picks on him in class. Claude knows that he's the poorest boy there; he doesn't know when his mother will feed him next. She works hard all day at the laundry, and he often has to wait for her in their home until it gets dark, when she will walk wearily up the hill towards their home. Their home is one of the tiny shacks leaning against the remains of the old castle ramparts of Saint Just. He has never known his father, and he doesn't ask. It's best not to when you're only ten years old.

Saint Just is a small-sized market town. It grew up around the medieval ramparts of an old castle that flourished as a textile town with the river Vire flowing parallel to it. The ramparts are still evident on the north side of town where the poorer folk live in shacks which lean against the wall, and they run the length of the ramparts. In the winter, the folks are sheltered as they're not affected by rain run-off. But in the summer, they bake at the side of the hill. Some misshapen and broken gargoyles are all that's left of the parapet on the West side of the castle wall. The wall on the

East side has no parapet or gargoyles left. The two walls are being eroded gradually each winter by the weather. The walls North and South were knocked down long ago to make entrances into the ever-expanding town.

Mauvais picks on Claude incessantly in class, so the other children do the same in the playground. The school master does it, so the children think it's all right to do the same.

'Claude. What is your mother's name?'

There was something up here, asking him about his mother. Why not ask where his father was? He had never seen his papa since he left when he was a baby.

'Jeannette.'

'Very well. You may sit down.'

Claude was worried now. Picking on him is the norm. But now the school master is after his mother.

Mauvais has a reputation for being a sleazebag. He has often been seen hanging out with prostitutes in a bar the German soldiers frequent.

Just because Mauvais flaunts his new pistol on his hip, he thinks that he is God's gift to women. He was a *collaborateur* with the enemy, the Nazis. And Claude knows what a *collaborateur* is. It is someone who kills Frenchmen on the Nazis behalf. People spit on the floor behind Mauvais' back, making sure he doesn't see them. If he knew they did that, he could make it difficult for them to continue living in Saint Just. Claude hates Mauvais with a vengeance.

Sure enough, that evening, when Claude's mother is finishing her laundry job for the day, in the early evening darkness and walking home to Claude with some food in her bag, Mauvais came out of the school gate as if he has been waiting for her. He follows her up the hill towards one of the shacks leaning against the walls of the ramparts in the poorest quarter of the town.

Chapter 6

After lighting the fire in the kitchen and parlour, I sit down with Maria and try to make conversation with her. She is trying to concentrate on some sewing in her lap. Then she suddenly pipes up,

'What are you up to?'

'Pardon?' I'm taken aback.

'You.' She points her arthritic finger at me.

'I don't know what you mean.'

'He's like a son to me. Don't think you can steal him from me!'

'What are you getting at Maria?' I turn away from her and get up, I'm feeling extremely uncomfortable. I try to regain my composure. I know what she's getting at, and I suddenly feel guilty.

'I have done nothing wrong.' I get up to go, tired of this surprising show of jealousy.

'I saw you fluttering your eyelashes at him. He's not a fool. He has no time for anyone but his daughter.'

'I have no designs on him, or anyone, I'm surprised you think such a thing,' I say indignantly. But I'm unsettled and go into the kitchen out of her way, leaving her alone in the parlour.

While she dozes in her chair, I make a vegetable cassoulet. At midday, Robert turns up in his baker's van with a better mattress. He knocks at the front door and as I struggle to pull it open, he pushes the mattress through, then drags it behind him upstairs to the bedroom. I watch him open-mouthed.

'That was quick!'

'We don't need it.' He lifts it up the stairs as if it's a bag of peas and puts it in my room. 'I have something else for you.' He says as he trots back down the stairs. I follow him to the van, and he hands me some bedsheets. Then, he lifts out a bicycle. I am delighted. It looks a bit old and rusty, but the seat has been renewed. It looks like someone has cleaned it up and oiled it.

'It has new tyres, something I managed to obtain recently from a friend who owed me. All above board, of course.' He smiles, pleased with himself.

'I've never owned a bicycle.'

'You'll need it to get around in case I can't take you to do your skeds. My mother has taken pity on you trying to sleep in this old house it's over one hundred years old. And I didn't realise there was so little upstairs to keep you warm and comfortable. I apologise. So, here are some of her sheets that she doesn't use anymore.' He hands me a pile of sheets that smell wonderful, and instantly cheer me up. It makes me happier than anything in the past two days.

'Thank you and thank your mother for me. It's much appreciated. I don't want you to think I'm a princess. I've been used to sleeping down air raid shelters until recently where sleep is impossible. We'd huddle scared to death with Hitler's Luftwaffe dumping bombs on us night after night.'

'I expect we have more bombs to come when the allies invade on *le jour de la libération*. I'll take you over to meet my mother and daughter soon. You can thank her yourself.' He stands back, showing me the bicycle. 'It's a few years old, I fixed it up for my mother, but she doesn't use it. So I'll adjust the seat for you if you sit on it now.'

He takes it out to the roadI try to balance on the bike, but I'm wobbling all over the place, and I laugh as he tries to hold the back of the bike and steady me. I hold onto him with grim determination. He tries to prise my taught hands off him.

'I haven't been on a bicycle for a long time,' I explain.

'No need to hold so tight. Everyone has a bicycle here, it's the only way to get around.'

I release my hold on him put my hands on the handlebars and try to cycle in a circle, in front of the dairy farm. He is holding me on the bicycle like a child, but I end up wobbling and then grip onto his shoulder while the other hand is trying to steer. The lines at the corners of his eyes crinkle up as we both end up laughing at my antics. He grabs me round the waist as I fall sideways and the bike slips from under me. I relax as I fall into his arms. We both laugh at my ineptitude.

'I am surprised that they didn't teach you to cycle.' He lifts me back on the bicycle as if I'm a doll, and clasps my hands on the handlebars, and then holds the back of the bicycle as he pushes me along. I turn the pedals slower and this time I manage to balance and stay on. He stands back, hands on hips watching me cycle back and forth in front of the dairy farm.

'Better. But come back, the saddle's far too high. Stop. I need to adjust it. Get off please.' He lifts me off not waiting for me to descend, I feel rather like a child again. I feel self-conscious and a bit breathless. He doesn't seem to notice. He's someone used to doing things himself and to people listening to him. He adjusts my saddle and stands back while I get myself back on the bicycle. I struggle a bit until I get my confidence, then I start to cycle along the bumpy road on my own. I feel very pleased with myself. For some reason we both think this is funny, as I bump up and down, and we spend the next few minutes in a jovial mood while I develop my confidence on the bicycle.

My mother would be horrified that I am becoming familiar with a man I only just met. How very English of me to wonder what mama would say. I move away from him a bit awkwardly, conscious of being so close, but he doesn't seem to notice. The French in me thinks differently, of course. This is fun, especially falling into him to make him catch me. My mother called it the 'exiting French side' as my father, Sam and I would jump the waves on the sandy beaches of Norfolk, fully clothed and getting them soaked. She would scold us, tutting with irritation. I like to think I had more of my father's personality, which was a love of life. My mother was often cold towards us, and I often wondered what she and father had in common.

'This is incredibly good of you, thank you Robert.' I'm trying to get my breath back. He gives me a beaming smile; he is glad that he's accomplished what he set out to do. I push it to the road and cycle up and down, then come back.

'Wonderful. It's great to be back on a bicycle again.' I gain more confidence as I try a turn in the road and it's successful. I don't fall off. Then I turn down the hill opposite the dairy farm, try to pull the brakes up too quickly and end up face down on the road. Fortunately, I manage to put my hands up to protect myself and I only have grazes, and I'm still feeling optimistic.

Robert hurries to help me up, his face full of concern. 'Are you all right?'

'Of course.' I look at my grazed knees. 'Next time I cycle I wear my trousers.' He helps me up and we push the bicycle back to Maria's. The day feels warm now and I point out to him a Robin flitting back and forth in Maria's garden, it makes me feel at home.

'*Rouge-gorge*, it is called,' he reminds me.

'I wonder if the farmers are watching our antics?' I say looking back at the dairy farm.

'They will be interested in why I brought you the bicycle. But trying to find a bicycle that works these days is challenging. This is how everyone gets around, apart from some tradespeople like me where transport is a necessity. Petrol is still hard to get hold of - the Nazis have priority for fuel.'

'Thank you for the bicycle. I shall be able to get around and do my skeds from different places, without having to rely on others.'

I notice the basket at the front.

'The basket is to put the radio in,' he says and fixes it more securely on the front of the bike.

'Of course. I'm grateful, and I have a question to ask.'

He leans the bicycle against the wall next to the front door. Picks up the bread and hurries straight through to the kitchen. 'Go ahead.'

I hurry after him through the house.

'Let me help you in the bakery. You've helped me so much and seem to rarely get enough sleep with the résistance work keeping you so busy. Let me help you for a change. I can knead and prepare baguettes and loaves; I helped my family when I grew up on a farm near Rennes.'

'How old were you then?'

'Twelve.'

He looks doubtful. 'It's too dangerous. It would bring attention to yourself. But thanks for the offer.'

'I could help out say from four until you open – might it help?'

'I will think about it.'

'I don't have much to do with Maria sleeping all day.'

'Lie low Emily. Without a wireless operator or *piano* we're stuck, we don't function efficiently. I found that out when Jean-Pierre was arrested. And then look how long it took before they sent you. We're seriously underfunded, and we need people. We desperately need supplies and ammo. London is clueless.' He says with feeling. It's the most emotion I've heard from him. He sounds angry. 'We need more radio sets and more pianists!"

He goes out the back door to the shed. I follow, curious that he shows emotion. Besides, it's the only person I get to talk to during the day. Inside the shed, he helps himself to onions and garlic hanging from the roof. For several minutes he's busy. I think of all the questions I want to ask him, but don't ask any of them. I just watch him while I'm getting my breath back. He suddenly asks me a question.

'Tell me Emily, what age did you leave France?'

'Thirteen.'

'How did you get to England?'

'My mother was very homesick, so we visited my grandparents in Norfolk and ended up staying there. My parents met in Switzerland while on holiday after the war. Aren't we supposed to ask each other questions about our background? In case we tell all under torture?'

'That's for Paris and London. We do things differently in the French countryside. We're made differently here.' And he grins at his own comments. It's hard not to smile too, and then I find myself saying something that is completely out of character.

'You know, your face lights up when you smile.' This takes him aback.

'I haven't had…we haven't had much to smile about during the occupation,' he says seriously, but I detect his cheeks have more colour in them.

'Have you lost many friends?'

'Too many.'

'It must be sad to lose so many friends.'

'It just makes me want to work harder in the *résistance* and to kill every Nazi we can,' he says with feeling. Then he changes the subject and picks up some gloves hanging in the shed and hands them to me.

'That's to keep your hands from freezing while we sort out the vegetables.' Head down, he's rummaging through a box of vegetables when he adds; 'It's really not worth getting involved with people. They only end up being taken away or shot.'

Is that what happened to his friends? Or is that a warning for me? For some reason I feel sad, although I have no intention of getting involved with a Frenchman. This is the English side of me talking but I know I must listen to this, after all I've been taught and the skills I've learned in SOE, I have a mission to accomplish, and that comes first.

'That sounds so sad. Wartime is when we do need friends,' I tell him with feeling. The longer I stay here the more French I become. There is a love of the country that I feel from the locals. Nowhere is this stronger than in Robert, his love of his country and his countrymen show in his leadership and the way he respects everyone. SOE protocol dictates I shouldn't encourage anything between us, but I'd like to get to know him better.

We start to clear the brambles from the side gate which is stuck from years of growth and tangled vines. Robert uses a knife, I use a trowel.

'I'll clear the brambles from this side, you clear them from the other,' he says. 'You need to be able to get the bicycle through the gate without other people seeing it and getting through themselves.

We work silently apart from some grunts here and there, and sighs from me as I get tired, and the sun gets too hot to continue. After a while we've cleared most of the brambles, front and behind the side gate. At last, I can open the gate and slip through with the bicycle.

'Come and see my emergency exit out the back,' I show him the gap I have widened in the hedge behind the shed.

'It is one of the most important things I learned in training. Always make sure you have an emergency exit for a quick escape.'

I pull the hedge apart wide enough so that a thin person can get through.

'Can you get your bike through as well?' Robert gets down on his hands and knees to see and I copy him. I giggle suddenly thinking what a curious situation to be in and stand up. He looks up at me.

'I will make the hole bigger,' I say trying to be serious. 'I hadn't thought of that.'

He stands up as well, serious now. 'All right.' We seem to have lost our light hearted rapport .

'I have to go. I'll take you later to be reunited with your radio, and to where you can send your first transmission tonight.' Then I see his bloody hands, that are cut all over because he didn't protect them.

'Oh Robert,' I take his hands in mine instinctively, 'Your hands will be no good tomorrow when you're kneading bread!'

'It is nothing,' he pulls his hands away embarrassed.

'Let me clean them. I have some salve that is good.'

'I will tend to them when I get home.' He pulls his hands away.

'Thank you - for the bicycle.'

'De rien,' he says, no problem. I follow him back into the kitchen.

'There aren't many people who have transport like I do. We must have special permission to get the petrol coupons. Even then we can't drive far there are often roadblocks stopping us. Tomorrow, I'll take you to meet Eve. She is my second-in-command. And we need to organise a drop of arms and ammunition, as soon as possible,' he says, in a business-like way.

He's stayed longer than I expected, so I'm pleased, but feel guilty too and I'm not sure why. I watch his van drive off causing a dust cloud behind him.

Chapter 7

It's about forty kilometres from Saint Just to the Normandy beaches and one of the major transport routes for the German army between Saint Lo and Cherbourg. It's also a railway centre, with regular trains coming from Germany. The trains carry supplies and German soldiers to Normandy, and Frenchmen back to Germany for their *Service du Travail Obligatoire*. The trains also send Jews to concentration camps, most of the Jewish families have been extricated from Saint Just, there aren't many that remain unless they are hidden by Jewish sympathisers.

Gisard Mauvais loves rooting out those who help Jews and *résistance* members or as he calls them, terrorists. He's made it his mission in life to find *collaborateurs* and terrorists, those of his countrymen who won't bow down to the German rules that govern his land. He would sell his own soul for his German bosses, especially if they give him guns and power over people.

The gothic steeple of the Catholic Church of Saint Marie towers over the town square. It was a growing town with young people before the outbreak of war, these days there aren't many young people walking the streets. There are mostly women cycling or walking to market, the young men have been taken to work on the Normandy coastal wall or sent to Germany for forced labour. The market stalls spread from the town square down the various passageways of the town radiating to the outskirts, with the forest on one side and the bocage on the other. Spring is on its way and some market stalls run down two of the narrow roads running off the square. Women in headscarves sell flowers and vegetables and argue over the price of potatoes.

Since the Gestapo have entered the town the price of food has gone sky high, and the availability even less as the German garrison takes most of the good stuff leaving the dregs for the citizens. The town hall is on one side of the town square with the Church of Saint Marie's facing it. A tricolour hangs limply from its flagpole.

The Geheime Staatspolizei, or Gestapo, is the official secret police of Nazi Germany and German-occupied Europe. They have a central office in the towns of Saint Just and nearby Saint Lo.

A black Citroen, a Traction Avant, the car of choice for the Gestapo, drives up outside the prefecture of police. Citizens passing by cross to the other side of the street. There aren't many young men left in the town, most had been sent off to Germany to fill the hard-labour jobs the German soldiers had left. Sometimes the Gestapo round up any men in the town square and take them off to the train to Germany straight away. Sometimes they turn up in the middle of the night and take people away.

SS-Sturmbannfuhrer Major Hans Weber gets out of the car and eyes a woman in the street as she hurries by. The Gestapo are often promoted by reason of loyalty to Hitler and enthusiasm for fascism rather than because of their brains or ability. Major Hans Weber is one of those people. Hans Weber is bad news. A German soldier had been shot in January, the new SS in the town had rounded up those whom they thought were résistance leaders, and who were in fact innocent bystanders, and he had them shot in the town square. Weber arrived twelve months ago in the town and felt the Abwehr, the German intelligence service, weren't doing enough to control the bursts of opposition and dissent amongst the local population. So now he makes it his mission in life to root out the opposition in the town.

In December 1943, the Gestapo moved from the town to a chateau not far away in Plessis after turning out the family who had lived there for generations.

The SS, Abwehr and the *Milice* now arrest as many young men in the town as they can lay their hands on. Swiftly and without much résistance locally, Weber orders ten men to be shot and the rest of the men put in gaol. Since then, families have tried to get their men out and appeal to the Chief Prefecture of Police. But the Gestapo with the support of the Feldgendarmerie, the German military police, rule this area and they do exactly as they like. Occasionally they have been halted by some efforts of sabotage by the local *résistance* group. In November they derailed a

German train by setting charges along the line, but some of them didn't go off. Now soldiers patrol the train lines and stations. Orders from them on any attack on German soldiers leads to taking Frenchmen off the streets and shooting them.

The *Milice* have been created by the Vichy regime with German aid, to help fight against the French Résistance. They help to round up Jews and Résistants for deportation. Mauvais and Weber seem to be of one accord. Weber's reputation has soon spread. People have learned to hate him. He doesn't care about the citizens of Saint Just. He knows that by taking the young men from town, he is adding young blood to work for the German Reich. Just as he thinks there are no young men left to cause trouble, some fires are set off in the railway yard. Just kids, he thinks, otherwise how could they have evaded the security? German soldiers check around the clock during the night, and the railway yard which now has a barbed wire fence around it, is kept locked at night.

Weber stretches his legs as he gets out of the car. He knows he is a picture of German ideology, a picture of fair-haired Aryan manhood. His uniform is pristine, with the two SS (Schutzstaffel) flashes on his collar. He belongs to the Waffen SS, Hitler's protection squads. He is loyal to the Fuhrer without question.

Weber is proud of his Aryan looks. He is single, twenty-nine-years old, and an experienced SS man. Starting off as a fanatical Hitler youth, he was one of the youngest officers to take part during the Blitzkrieg of France. He is a favourite of Hitler and feels it's his responsibility for finding an Aryan looking female, so he can continue the Aryan bloodline. It is his dearest wish, to please his Fuhrer. But his reputation as a cold brute goes before him. And surprisingly in the French town of Saint Just he has no takers or admirers. His reign of torturing local citizens keeps him busy and motivated.

The citizens of the town liken him to Klaus Barbie, Hitler's Gestapo chief. Everyone has heard of how he likes to instil pain and torture on his victims. The parents of the young men shot in the square in January had seen evidence of their sons having been tortured before they were shot. Their faces swollen and bruised, their bodies bloodied and broken.

The light is fading fast even though it's five o'clock on a spring evening. Weber feels he might go out with the patrols tonight. He is bound to catch someone where they shouldn't be.

Last year, they caught an enemy agent, part of the local *résistance* group. Well, the *Milice* had caught him for STO but, as it happened, they released him to the Gestapo and Weber had tortured the living daylights out of the young man. He hadn't given anything away until the very end, when they found the hole under the floorboards with remnants of burnt paper and groups of codes on it. Weber guesses it has been used with an illegal radio. Unfortunately, the girlfriend has managed to escape; they are still looking for her and the radio. A major mistake that Weber has blamed on the incompetence of the local police, who have allegedly lost track of her.

The house was in Jean-Pierre's parent's names. They had been arrested the year before on suspicion of being Jewish and sent to a German concentration camp. Weber wants the names of the *résistance* and its leader. Unfortunately for Weber, Jean-Pierre had died because of the torture and before he could tell them the name of their leader. He was most upset, for the terrorist had bled to death because his manic assistant, a great beast of a man, whom he calls *Gorilla,* had gone too far and broken both his arms and legs.

But Weber is happy. He knows that a new radio operator will be dropped in from London soon to replace Jean-Pierre. And he is waiting for signs that this has happened, he hasn't heard anything for months, the British are taking their time. They will soon trace his transmissions through their direction-finding van dressed as an ambulance. It is full of electrical equipment and two Gestapo radio operators who sit in there patiently night after night listening through their earphones, trying to find the spies who parachuted in to help the French Résistance. It won't be long before they have him.

The calm exterior of SS Standartenfuhrer Kurt Riesel walking up and down in his first-floor luxurious office belied his underlying anger towards Major Hans Weber, whom he considers his inferior. His tailored uniform shows the SS epaulettes and infantry assault medals among his ribbon campaigns. Although too old to take part in military assaults he is now in charge of administration.

'You may have caught the radio operator, Weber, but you didn't get his radio or his *résistance* connections, did you?'

Weber stands with his hands behind his back, his great coat dangling just above his hand-sewn leather boots.

Weber irritates SS Standartenfuhrer Riesel. He had come up through the ranks because of his close association with the Fuhrer, not because he had fought in a campaign like Riesel, who had gone up through the ranks due to his age and experience.

'Next time you kill a member of the Résistance, I want you to notify me what you have planned. We can't afford to kill valuable people like that. If I'd known you had arrested him, I would have interrogated him myself.'

'You weren't here, Sir. You were on vacation if you remember. I did what I had to do.'

'Well, you did wrong, Hans. Your inexperience showed through. Next time, whether I am on vacation or not. You are to follow the chain of command. Do you understand?'

Hans was outwardly calm but underneath he was angry. Reisel didn't need much of an excuse to get rid of him. He had made things very awkward for him. And he now had to find excuses for Hans as to why they'd killed the radio operator and the only link with the whole of the local *résistance*.

Reisel starts to raise his voice. His secretary, Lieutenant Schiller, listens to the voices raised, he can't hear the words, but he's surprised his boss sounds angry. He has never heard him angry in the three years working for him. He hears the Major's protest. But then Hans Weber is an upstart, he thinks, with family connections to the Fuhrer and plenty of money. He ignores the underlings like the administrators, who keep the wheels turning in this prefecture. Weber makes it obvious that soldiers like Schiller are beneath him, and he treats Schiller with contempt, like he does the French.

'Any more rebellious acts like this acting without my permission, Hans, will bring serious consequences. Now go and find these *résistance* you keep telling me are present in this town. Go!'

Weber comes storming out of his boss's office, red in the face and angry. Schiller hopes his boss won't live to regret crossing a friend of the Fuhrer.

Chapter 8

It's already dark as Robert knocks the front door, but I'm waiting for him. He says he has left his van under the bocage further down the road, so as not to alert the neighbours aware he's around after curfew. He's wearing a black leather jacket, ideal for a cold night and camouflage. I am ready and waiting for him also in jacket and warm trousers they have a Parisian label in but were made by an English seamstress. To all intents and purposes, they are French if I'm searched, and they look authentic. Maria has fallen asleep in the parlour where I lit the fire for her and have drawn the old velvet curtains which hang ominously as if they're ready to fall down any moment. We go out into a crisp cold night and walk down the hill and he shows me where the van is hidden under a huge bocage hedgerow.

'We can cut across fields here,' he says, helping me over a style. An owl hoots in the distance, low cloud hides the stars that I saw last night.

'I'll follow you, Robert. I can't see a thing.'

'My torch can go on now we are away from houses.' He stops and takes my arm. 'Here.' We walk side by side following the torch with me holding his arm.

'We'll have to pretend we're old friends if we're seen by anyone, so a cover story is essential,' Robert says. He seems to be back to his usual positive self, so I feel quite cheerful.

'That's good. Yes, we knew each other before. But where?' Our talking causes condensation clouds in front of our mouths.

'Well, you could have visited the area with your mother to see Maria a few years ago, and we met when I was helping her one day. I've been visiting Maria since I was a child. So that would work.'

'Yes, I like the idea. I memorized the local maps before I left. So I should remember places.'

'It hasn't changed much over the years.'

'How old would I have been then?'

'Well, ten years ago when I came home from the army before I was married, I would have been twenty-five. How old would you have been, fifteen? That might work. Where were you at fifteen?'

'At a school in Switzerland. I would have visited Normandy on holiday with my parents.'

'So, you visited in nineteen thirty-four. It could work.'

'It's cold tonight. I'm glad I put warm clothes on.' The icy air catches my throat. We walk in single file when we come to a narrow sheep path.

'There's going to be a frost.' I say keeping my voice low in case anyone is around. But there are no other sounds except our breathing. The vapour from my breath disappears into Robert's back as I keep in step behind him.

'I've moved the radio case to a derelict farmhouse within walking distance,' he says. 'It won't take us too long to get there if we keep moving. It should be safer there. You can keep the radio in this place for now, no one comes here. It'll be safer than at Maria's.'

We step over a broken-down old fence. 'It won't be dark until about seven next month. It's closer to home for you. You can just cycle down the hill, and apart from the dairy farm, there's no one else on this side of the town. Just be careful of the Chevrolets, they could be watching you from their house.' We stop to squeeze between two columns of wood which had once been a gate.

'I would still rather bring the radio to Maria's. And use the bedroom. I'll just keep a lookout from the back on the lane.'

I could tell he didn't like the idea. He was quiet and thoughtful.

'You may be able to escape quickly. But what about Maria? She won't be able to get away. And it would probably kill her.' I realise he's right. Most of the local citizens take many more risks than we do.

We continue in silence for a while and arrive at some woods on our left. Robert takes my arm, and we stand for a moment under a high hedgerow so we can't be seen from the road. I look out at the land before us, it's undulating here, and I can see the outlines of bocage hedgerows to the right and left of me. Good hiding places.

'Now follow me along here. Mind you don't slip.' He points his torch down a slope to a ditch. I fall forward heavily onto his back as my right foot slips from under me. I move away suddenly with the warm contact of him, slightly embarrassed, but he continues as if nothing happened. 'This place is so secret that not many people know of its existence.'

The undergrowth is longer here, it slows us down. As we walk along the side of the field, we take a left through a gate and enter the edge of a wood.

'I am taking you to the old farmhouse. It is surrounded by trees and shrubs. It is remote and ideal for your sked. It's a pity we can't use it twice,' he says. 'I thought it would be quiet.'

'It's perfect. You're with me, so why would I be worried?'

His shoulders relax, and he stops in front of me and turns around so I can hear. 'I have thought about it. This place would be good for you later if you're stuck for somewhere to transmit and I am not around. You have several exits for escape.'

'You've thought of everything.'

'I don't want to lose myself another *piano*.' He says with his soft voice but then he turns his head and I see him smile and my spirit's lift. I follow him as we continue avoiding the clumps of turf and mud as we get deeper to the place where people haven't been for years.

'Why would you not be around?'

'In case they take me away for German slave labour, you know, the STO?'

'Oh, yes, but you have an exemption certificate because you're the only baker in town.'

'It doesn't mean I'm safe. Especially with the *Milice* around, Mauvais will do anything to get me out of here. He doesn't know that I'm the local *résistance* leader. Eve relies on me, so does Maria and the *réseau*. He's not been clever enough to work out how to trap me yet. Especially as I have friends in high places.'

We are quiet for a while as I follow him along an overgrown track. Another track meets us from our left and widens out as we come to an old wooden gate which is falling off its hinges. It's only the dead wood and weeds entwining through it that has secured it from falling.

The track takes us to our right then bends to our left in a few metres, and before us are the remains of a farmhouse with dilapidated cattle shed nearby, half of its roof is missing. It looks like it has all been abandoned long ago. I hold my torch up towards the top of the house.

'Careful, don't raise your torch too high. Someone in an aeroplane might see you,' he points upwards. 'Even a torch light travels a long way in the dark countryside.'

The house is overgrown with shrubs and the trees which surround us are encroaching on the house, their top branches bending over to the centre in an attempt to fill the only space above us. There's another level with small windows, perhaps they're bedrooms. The windows are empty of glass, I'm already thinking how I can hang my sixty-foot radio aerial out of the top window. The ground slopes upwards behind, making the trees growing up the hill seem taller and imposing. It smells of damp earth and wet and cold shrubbery. What a good place to hide and transmit from. It's a pity I can only use this place once. We look in the hard mud around our feet. As Robert shines the light down on the ground, our muddy footprints are everywhere as we walk around the house.

'The light doesn't get down this far, so it doesn't get to dry out. And we can't go all the way around, there is too much overgrown,' he says.

The windows are empty, there's the damp sour smell of rotten wood. The front door has fallen and it's hanging off its hinges and the planks of wood underfoot are soft and rotten in places.

I stick my head through the door, 'It looks dangerous to go inside.'

'That's why it makes an ideal place to transmit from. Anyway, they say it's haunted.'

'What? You didn't tell me that.' I jump back from the door.

'Don't be ridiculous. Ghosts can't hurt you, only people can.'

'I'll remember that for future reference when I'm here on my own.'

'I will show you where to tread. But I want to show you the old cattle shed first where you can hide the radio.'

'Where did you put my radio?'

'Follow me. Careful underfoot, follow my trail. I've been here in the daylight, so I know where I'm going.'

I follow his receding figure. The wind has started to pick up, the wind blows against an empty window and something rattles. I reach out and grab his arm, trying to stop myself from being scared. No one said SOE agents didn't get scared. The contact is reassuring. I lean on him as he leads the way, feeling a bit like a child. My boots by now are covered in mud.

'No one ever comes here. It's an empty old farmhouse, and too remote from other farms to be used by anyone.'

'It's perfect Robert, no one would dream of coming here!'

I can see his face beaming with pleasure.

'How did you find it? You can't see it from the road.'

'We used to play here when we were children. It was empty then. We'll go to the shed first.' Robert points to an entrance.

I hold onto his sleeve as we get to the shed a few metres away, the grass grows all around it, it's on the edge of the wood. As I shine the torch on the inside, I can see it has a roof. Robert pushes aside a hay bale blocking the door.

'There is no door, but the hay bale protects the inside from the elements and other creatures trying to get in,' he says.

We shine our torches around the inside. There's an old wooden step ladder to a mezzanine on a higher level. On ground level there has been an attempt to clear the undergrowth inside the shed.

'I had a go at cutting some of the grass inside the shed. But it's difficult in winter, the rain gets in in that missing panel up there,' Robert points to a gap higher up, where I can see the stars through a hole in the roof.'

It's easy to get to the ladder which leads to the mezzanine now. Robert has put some hay down, so it's drier underfoot. As he shines the torch ahead of us, we climb a ladder and tread carefully across the floorboards towards a pile of hay. Robert pulls out my radio case and I breathe a sigh of relief. Even though there's a panel missing above us it appears dry.

'It's a great hiding place, Robert.'

'We don't have any ammo until the first parachute drop, we need to request it as urgent.'

I look out of a hole in the wall and hear the faint calls of owls from somewhere in the wood. I can see the Vire river reflecting under the stars in the distance. It's a beautiful spot, but lonely, I wouldn't want to be here without Robert. I never liked the dark as a child, my father would sooth me until I went to sleep; I feared the monsters lurking under my bed.

'It's a good hiding place for the radio. Due to the protection of the trees around us no one can see a shed is here. But let's try the house for transmission, it's higher than the shed and yes, I would be able to see in both directions if someone's coming.'

Robert retrieves the suitcase from under the hay including a torch. It's an unassuming small suitcase. Nowadays only nine pounds in weight, whereas not so long ago a radio operator's case weighed thirty pounds. How many agents were captured because it was a heavy suitcase and aroused suspicions? Radio operators try to keep themselves hidden and out of harm's way, moving from safe house to safe house they are constantly trying to stay one step ahead of the Gestapo. It's a lonely life and usually the radio operator has no contact with the rest of the réseau, I feel blessed that I have been able to meet most of the circuit.

'It's a pretty safe place don't you think? he asks, I can see he's eager to please me.

'Yes, it's a good place, as long as I transmit under fifteen minutes.' I say with irony. I put the torch under my chin and make a funny face trying to get him to smile. He looks at me with a stony expression. I sigh, it's a serious business. No time for messing around.

'I can still only transmit for fifteen minutes or less. Jerry will soon track me down if I transmit from here twice.'

'You could transmit from the house and hide the radio here under the straw,' he says more cheerfully. If you know where to step and remember where the boards are broken, you'll be all right. I'll go with you next time and act as your lookout.'

He highlights our way to the derelict house a few metres away by torch, keeping it pointing towards the ground.

'Watch the well!' he warns me as I kick the edge of it. I don't see the broken boards criss-crossing a wide hole. It unnerves me because some stones I have inadvertently kicked, shoot down the well. I hold my breath, it's several seconds before I hear distant plops at the bottom. My heart starts to race. Being out here with Robert is ok, but on my own in the dark? I try to act braver than I feel, I'm supposed to be a trained agent, yet still fearful of the unknown.

I keep close to Robert as he pushes the broken door of the house wide, it scrapes on the floor. With an extraordinary effort he lifts it and plonks it down as the top hinges break away from the door frame. It's top heavy like a drunk leaning backwards, only the bottom hinges are keeping it from toppling over. Robert leans it against the wall. I gingerly follow his footsteps and I keep close because I can hardly see a thing. He shines his torch ahead of us going slowly, our eyes become accustomed to the dark after a while. We tread carefully. I can feel cobwebs tickling my cheek as I pass under them.

I jump back, 'Oh!'

'What's the matter?'

I imagine lots of creepy crawlies hanging from the rafters trying to drop into my hair as I walk underneath. I was never particularly good at ignoring creepy crawlies.

'I remember one of the girls, Edith, I trained with at Beaulieu, our 'finishing school' for spies. She was an expert safe cracker but when it came to spiders she would scream and run away as fast as she could. We laughed at her, and I would pick up the spider and pretend it was chasing her.' I sniggered thinking about it.

Robert turns to look at me, I shrug my shoulders. Thinking about her now I know how she felt.

'She was terrified. We became good friends all the same. She disappeared a few days later. I assumed she was sent abroad but no one told us what country she was sent to. She didn't even have time to say goodbye.'

The wooden floor is broken and there are gaps here and there before our feet.

'Just shine the torch on the ground, avoid the holes and find your way to the stairs behind me.' I shake my torch and it comes back on, aiming it at the bottom of some stairs, we point our torches downwards because there are some holes in the roof, so it won't be detected from outside. As we look around Robert leads me up five stairs into a small room. It seems firm underfoot, so I walk over carefully testing floorboards as I go and crouch There are the remains of a broken rusty bed frame right next to an open window, ivy is creeping in through the window and fixing itself on the wooden frame which is rotting. Outside is a place to hang my aerial. It's an ideal place. There are windows facing the East towards the River Vire through a gap in the trees I see the stars.

To my right is the path we came along by the side of the fields. If someone followed us without a torch they would sink in the ditch. We would see the enemy coming.

'I think I'll do my sked from here. It looks more comfortable.' I lean the radio on the bed frame.

'What's in here?'

At the other side of the room there are another five stairs down to a small landing and a closed door. The door is broken, but intact and stiff. It hasn't been opened for years. I go and have a look to see if I can use it as an exit.

'Robert, can you open this door please? It'll be good for a quick escape if need be.'

Robert puts his weight against the door. But next minute the floorboards in front of the door gave way and his foot goes through about six inches of rotten floorboards.

'Are you all right?' I hang onto the banister to stop myself from laughing. He looks sheepish as I laugh and point at him.

'Sorry, that's too funny.' I try to stifle a laugh, as he looks too ridiculous. He tries to keep such a serious face that it makes it all the more comical.

'Do you always laugh at people?' His face breaks into a smile. He can't help but laugh now, as I sit down on the top step and the wood breaks underneath me. Which sends me into a paroxysm of laughter. I try to stop myself laughing, choking back a giggle.

'Are you all right?'

'Yes, no harm done.' He steps out of the floorboards with difficulty and bits of rotten wood fall around his feet. I am doubled up with laughter as he tries to get out of his predicament, he looks even more comical as he tries to shake off bits of wood stuck to his foot. His face ends up in a grin. Eventually we're both laughing. Then he gives the door a huge tug and with a heave pulls open the door. The ivy growing around the door falls off, the door grates as it opens just a few centimetres.

'This isn't safe,' he says.

'But just enough for me to squeeze through in an emergency if I need to get out quick and across those fields if the RDF catches up with me.'

Robert shakes his head, flicking dead bits of wood from his feet and leaves it open ever so slightly. We retrace our steps carefully back to the iron bed frame; my torch is fading fast. I give it a tap, and I follow behind him smiling. Back to the seriousness of transmitting clandestinely. The torches send dancing shadows across the walls. He stands motionless looking out of the window. There is some scurrying in the tops of the trees, it is birds squabbling amongst themselves.

'I am glad you're here with me Robert, it would be scary and lonely without you.'

I look outside at my surroundings, in the moonlight I can see the tall trees, and look up into the canopy. This wood must be hundreds of years old. The trees are all hemmed in and doing their best to reach up to the sun. I don't like the idea of hiding amongst the creepy crawlies much. And I'm not sure what I might come across in the dark unexpectedly. But it is better escaping into the dark than being discovered by the enemy and shot.

'I'd probably run towards those fields if I see the Gestapo turn up. What's beyond the fields?'

'Well, more fields. There's nothing until you get to the river. If you walk along the side of the Vire river and follow it to the town you should come out beyond the station. But I haven't followed the footpath since I was a boy. It's probably overgrown. If you had to walk along by the river it would take you a few hours and tiring if you're carrying a radio set as well.'

'Fifteen minutes is all I'll have before the Germans radio direction finding allocates the area I'm in. My life as a radio operator is supposed to be six weeks. I better give myself twelve minutes.'

'I hate to think of you trying to escape the Gestapo. We haven't seen an RDF van recently, but they span the area occasionally. No one comes here. We could use it as a possible place for an emergency.'

'It might be better to transmit during the day.'

'I'll come with you where I can. It's my job after all,' he says. Robert highlights a noise near us; I hear the flitting of bat wings amongst the tree canopies.

91

'Don't forget to bring your pistol with you when you come to these places alone.'

'I suppose I should. They tried to give me a pistol, but I can't think when I'd have it on me. I mean, if they search me and find it, they'll know I'm an agent!'

'I would feel happier Emily if you did hide a gun or pistol about you. You never know when you may need it.'

'All right, I will start taking my knife with me, just in case. I was good at silent killing anyway.' Robert's eyes open wide. 'In training,' I add. 'That means I was jolly good attacking a dummy from behind.' I add jovially. He frowns at me, I'm obviously not taking this seriously.

'I wonder what happened to Jean-Pierre,' I say quickly, changing the subject. 'He obviously didn't talk because the *réseau* is still intact.'

I show my watch to Robert, it's almost midnight, time for my sked. I look down with my torch, seeing the old well and the remains of a path that leads out of the wood to the river beyond. I peer out into the darkness. I can hear bat wings, and a fox cries out somewhere. Apart from us there seems to be no human life out there. Robert gives me a piece of paper with a message on it, we discuss the message. No one is around, time to do my sked. He goes down the stairs and watches and listens outside the front door; he is my lookout.

I open the suitcase and prop the lid against the wall. I put on the headphones and immediately pull the one-time pads out of a compartment in my case. I note the time as I glance at my watch. I take square printed with a complex table, it's a series of transposition keys already worked out and printed on silk. To encode my message I copy out the keys. The keys are random groups and are different for every agent in the field. They contain keys sufficient for 200 messages – one hundred from the agent to London, one hundred from them to me. Next to the pairs of keys are five letter indicator-groups to tell London which pair of keys I've used to encode my message. But I never use these indicator groups exactly as they are printed, for security reasons I have prearranged with London always to add 3 to the first letter and 2 to the fourth. All evidence is destroyed and if the Gestapo torture me there is no way they could ever tell I was lying.

It's a failsafe one-time encryption system, unable to be decoded unless you have the original, which I burn at the end. When I've encrypted the message, I tune the dial to the broadcasting position. Robert watches for a few minutes then goes downstairs walking quietly up and down outside leaving me on my own so I can concentrate.

I begin with my call sign – waiting for Grendon Hall to acknowledge me. At last, a faint reply comes back whispering through the airwaves. Somewhere in Southern England a radio operator will be listening for one of their agents within Europe, to call. I hear the faint call sign of Station 53, Grendon Hall, Buckinghamshire, in my ears. It's ironic I know who most of the girls are, having worked beside them. I can see some of their faces and remember their names. Who will be intercepting my Morse code today? I try to relax my fingers cautiously touching the keys. I send out my call sign again. Adrenalin and the cold are making my fingers shake, but then the practice of the past few months takes over and I am transmitting with confidence. Even so, for my first sked behind enemy lines I am nervous, and my heart is beating fast. Will it work? So much to remember. I continue until I've finished my message. I start slowly then rush to finish it. I look at my watch, it's nearly twelve minutes and I'm anxious to bring it to a close.

The Silks or worked out keys is a bit of ingenuity invented by Leo Marks our *chef de codage* at Baker Street. I can carry it hidden unobtrusively amongst my clothes and if I'm searched and frisked by the enemy, they would be none the wiser. The codes, like me, would be safe.

Contact made with group Baker repeat Baker new chef de réseau codename Cesar request ammo guns and boots to be dropped next full moon 24th confirm with message personnel Yvette aime les grosses carrottes repeat Yvette aime les grosses carrottes.

Listening, with receiver on, I stretch my legs out. My muscles are tight. Robert's head pops up to see how I am getting on. I scribble down the dots and dashes. The message is repeated. They acknowledge my first message. I turn on the transmitter and wait for the valves to warm up. A few taps of the Morse key, a moment's acknowledgement, and '*Toodloo*.' An agreed personal comment to identify that I am me. Not some Gestapo who has captured a British agent and is using his radio to send false information. I turn the power off and wait for it to cool, and reel in the aerial from the window. Thirteen minutes and ten seconds, the radio detection vans will have nothing to seek.

The moon shines through a gap in the treetops highlighting Robert standing on the edge of the well and looking down. I stand watching him for a while. And realise I've only known him a few days and realise that if he were captured, I would be devastated. I don't know what I would do without him. Now he's making his way back sideways through the overgrown shrubs in his path. I meet him at the back door of the house.

'Do you have a cigarette?' I ask him.

'I didn't know you smoked.'

'I need one. It's the war.'

He lights one for me and I hang up my cut away silk and set it alight with the cigarette, it burns. We watch it disintegrate; it has literally gone up in a puff of smoke.

'Jean-Pierre used a poem code. I used to act as watch out for him sometimes.'

'We've come a long way since then. The silks are safer. Quicker.' I tell him, then I remember a message. 'By the way, we need to step up our sabotage of the telephone exchange.'

'Why is that?' His brow furrows, he holds eye contact. 'Where does this come from?'

'London.'

'Why?'

'I can't tell you.'

'If you don't trust me, how can I trust you?'

If the *résistance* continues to cut telephone lines it forces the Germans to communicate by radio. It gives Bletchley Park, the principal Allied code breaking centre in England the advantage in decoding German traffic, in particular the U boat communications, which could shorten the course of the war. But I can't tell him this, it is Top Secret. I give him the brief version.

'If we prioritise cutting telephone lines it forces the Germans to communicate by radio. Then we have an opportunity to break their codes and find out what they're doing.'

His eyebrows shoot up, 'Is that possible?'

'We try our best.'

'Mon Dieu, that could shorten the war, non?'

'It is possible, but of course the Germans won't realise that.'

We stand companionably smoking together.

'Seriously though, I will need to recharge the radio battery after about two more transmissions. Unless I have a house with electricity, because I only have six amps for a transmission, depending on how long the transmission is of course.'

'I will charge the battery next time. But tonight we'll go back to storing the radio in the shed.'

'The Germans could still track me down by the amount of electricity I use in someone's house.'

We retreat to the shed, and he climbs the ladder. 'I will put your radio under the hay where we found it. I'll draw you a map with the empty barns and outhouses of the area, so you'll find somewhere to transmit next time.'

My heart deflates. 'I hope you're able to take me. But I understand if you can't. The good news is now after this first sked, I can transmit any time of the day or night.'

'That makes it easier,' he says. 'Jean-Pierre used to have to stick to one time slot. It was very inconvenient at times, for him and me.'

'That's why they changed the rules.'

He jumps down from the edge of the mezzanine in a much more cheerful frame of mind.

'Some of my best childhood days are playing around here with my friends. They have all gone now.'

'Where?'

'Killed at Dunkirk, or somewhere else.' He shrugs his shoulders. 'Forced to move out to Germany for their *Service du*

Travail Obligatoire.' He relights his cigarette. Moonlight shows his face for a moment..

'I'm glad you told me of that news, about German communications, it gives me hope that we can one day beat them. They're not as infallible as they think they are. And rest assured I will tell no one.'

I hand him back his cigarette.

'I must go to work soon. We need to protect our *piano*,' he says quietly, and he puts his hand in my hair and softly pulls it away from my face. A sliver of delicious pins and needles go down my arms and across my chest. We are close enough to kiss. I feel compelled to lean towards him and, before I know where I am, I am kissing him in the middle of the road. My heart is pounding suddenly, and I feel a little dizzy as I pull away.

'Robert!' I touch my top lip where it is moist, and I am short of breath. He just smiles.

'You left France too soon. You're still very English. If you were French, that wouldn't have bothered you.' And he chuckles to himself as he holds my hand, and we make our way back to the van.

'Time to go home.'

'Do you think I can do it?'

'What, keep incognito? Of course.'

'I mean,' I falter, embarrassed that I am talking about me. 'I am basically a shy person.'

'We need to change your hair colour to something less attractive; it makes you stand out.' I look alarmed, as he continues, 'Some of the *résistants* are upset at losing Jean Pierre,' he hesitates. 'But London wouldn't have sent you here if they didn't think you had the balls. And I don't believe you are shy, or you won't be by the time you've been here a few days.'

I am secretly pleased that he thinks I am attractive and that I have the 'balls' to do the job. Nothing moves except us as we walk silently back to Maria's, creeping along like wraiths in the night.

Chapter 9

I wake up to a lovely sunny spring day. I leave Maria in bed as I pull on my clothes and cycle down the lane as the sun is rising. It only takes me a few minutes, as it's early and there's no one around, it is the ideal time to talk to Robert.

Trees are bursting out into buds making everything fresh and green. I delight seeing and smelling the blossom of fruit trees as I cycle by the orchards. Daffodils are emerging between new growth in Maria's garden. The little blue wood violets, *Violette des bois*, the cowslips and primroses and forget me nots are turning their faces to the sun as the ground warms up. I cycle past fields of wildflowers towards the town of Saint Just and continue under the Medieval archway which leads to the town centre. I search my memory for the map details and arrive at Robert's boulangerie and cycle right into a woman looking like a German housewife. She is a middle-aged woman in an expensive coat, most of the local women cannot afford such a luxury she is probably the one married to a government official.

The woman jumps back out of my way and yelps, 'Mon Dieu!'

***

Meanwhile, Robert contemplates his last 24 hours. He is tired. Dog tired. He's had little sleep in the past forty-eight hours. He spent most of the early hours driving to an area for a parachute drop some twenty kilometres away, he had organised *the parachutage*, and the men ready to carry containers full of ammunition, guns and boots, but the drop didn't happen. The aeroplane did not appear. Everyone was disappointed. What had happened? Bad weather? Perhaps it was shot down over the Normandy coast. Robert thinks that is more likely. They had to drive back empty handed and disconsolate. He's hardly spent any time with his daughter or mother. He's wondering how he's going to build up his *réseau* when he doesn't have the time to work and organise the group. There are people wanting to join their *réseau*. They ask at Henri's bar how they can join the local *résistance*. Henri says he will pass the word around, so someone will get in touch with them soon. They don't know that Robert is the *résistance* leader, but it won't be long before the truth is exposed. He feels he's lived here on borrowed time as it is. The Germans don't need any excuse to arrest a fit, healthy man and ship him off to Germany for slave labour. He knows he has to stop his work in the boulangerie and escape to the forests to join the Maquis while he has a chance to escape. The trouble is the *Milice* will arrest his mother as she will know where he is. He can't let that happen, so he has to organise a safe place for them too.

Perhaps this new agent from London will be his saving grace. She has plenty of energy and appears self-reliant, that's something he's grateful for. He's had lots of young men escaping from the *Milice* who want to send them to Germany. The problem is feeding the ever-increasing groups of men in the local woods and forests who have evaded the Germans and become *résistant* fighters. Numbers are growing daily. They need training and organising. Sanitation isn't the best.

Robert is kneading dough thinking of these problems and the smell of baking bread fills the air. Then he sees Emily come into view and cycling towards the shop. Madame Fisolee is just leaving his shop. Damnit, he thinks to himself. Madame Fisolee will extract as much information from her as she can, he hopes Emily holds her own against her, and she's listened to what he's said about her being a *collaborateur*. He watches the older woman intercept Emily with his hands in mid-air covered in flour. He sees them collide and to his surprise the older woman jumps back but then recovers and starts conversing with Emily. He can't hear what they're saying because of the glass in between, it's just muffled noises. He is all ears but can't catch what they are saying. Madame Fisolee has been known to ask question people for hours in the street. Emily is smiling and nodding. Robert can't stand it any longer he wipes his hands on a cloth and goes outside. Emily greets two locals in a friendly way as they cross the street. Madame Fisolee is still talking to her. He interrupts them.

'Put your bike around the back Emily,' he tells her, agitated. 'I've been waiting for you. Quick, I need help to get the order out to the garrison.'

Fisolee looks at the two of us. 'Oh, how long have you known this young lady?'

We ignore her, although Emily is torn between answering her and moving in through the door.

'Now hurry, Emily, I need your help this morning. *Au revoir* Madame.'

Fisolee follows Emily like a predator around to the back of the shop. He says *bonjour* to the two women who are watching, and they are smile and laugh as they watch Fisolee do her best to forestall them. Robert races through to the back door of the shop. As Emily leans her bike against the wall, he promptly pulls her in roughly and shuts the door in Fisolee's face.

* * *

'Phew, thanks. I see what you mean. She is a real busybody. And did you mean you'd been waiting for me?' I say a bit shaken up.

'No. It was to get you away from her. You would have been there all day. She doesn't give up questioning people until she gets what she wants. Then goes back to her husband, a *Milicien*, to tell all.'

Madame Fisolee knows that Emily's French accent is not from around here. But that doesn't matter, the Germans around here aren't likely to notice. But the *Milice* would.

'You don't have to be too friendly with people. I know it's in your nature. But in this situation in France, right now, you can't afford to be friendly. Keep to yourself. Even then be reticent. Madame Fisolee is constantly after information; however it's come by, and she'll take it back.'

'I can't be rude to her, though, can I?' I put the apron on he passed me. 'Am I to help you after all?'

'Yes, now you're here. But just for an hour, then you must return to Maria.'

'I came to see how things went last night.'

'Fine. Now no more talk about that. It's not the time or place.'

'Of course not.' I had missed him and just wanted an excuse to see him today.

'Now wash your hands and get your apron on.' He shows me where things are, and we start off in silence until the next customer comes in.

I watch him kneading dough. His dark hair is framed by a baker's cap a faint sprinkling of flour over his cheek which makes him seem vulnerable. His forearms are strong and muscular, he kneads the dough with experienced hands. After five minutes of kneading, I am breaking into a sweat. He laughs and throws me a small towel.

'Ha – you need a baker's hat like mine.' There is no sweat on his forehead.

'I wouldn't have told Fisolee anything, you know,' I say quietly.

'I know. Still, it doesn't hurt to remind you. And don't say too much when Oberleutenant Sachs comes in, he likes to come in and talk. He'll ask you questions about yourself. Just pretend you're a bit simple.'

I stop and look at him aghast; he's surely joking. Then I see his face crack into a smile.

'Oh, is this appropriate?' I make a funny face so that it makes him laugh.

'Yes. It's easier that way.' He continues kneading the dough and he continues to laugh until some customers come in, even then he's smiling all morning, and looking at me as if we share a private joke.

There are rows and rows of baguettes, simple *pains* and *batards*. A gingham red-check cloth covers a table with the loaves piled up ready for the locals to buy. Robert nods and smiles as I talk to customers, and we serve them between us. As he brings more loaves out of the oven with the paddle, the aroma of freshly cooked bread teases my nostrils, and the sight of the delicious-looking loaves and baguettes stacked up makes my mouth salivate. I realise I am hungry. The shop smells bring back so many memories of my young life in a country town in the Vendee, and I tell him about this. He observes my repartee with the locals. I can tell he is seeing how I will fare with others and how I will fit in. It makes me rather nervous.

Chapter 10

As I am up to my elbows in flour, I suddenly see a tall man in German Lieutenant's uniform looking at me through the window, the sight of the dark grey uniform makes me start.

'What's the matter?'

'That German. He's watching me through the window.'

My heart starts thumping as he opens the *boulangerie* door and removes his cap to get inside. Robert looks at me as my face goes pink, as if I'm here to be arrested. I feel guilty already, although I have done nothing.

Robert mutters under his breath, 'Do you always blush at strange men?'

'No, only when I am nervous.'

'Oberleutnant Sachs,' says Robert pleasantly. 'How are you today?'

The officer stands comfortably, drinking in the effect his sudden presence has made on me. He is about Robert's age, he is immaculately groomed with his iron cross at his neck, and a row of medals along his breast. Although his face is smiling, it doesn't reach his eyes when he looks at me. However, his eyes light up when he looks at Robert, and I have an inkling he is here to see him.

'Someone new,' he comments, looking me up and down and particularly at my clothes. Can he tell they're not French, I wonder?

I shrink behind the floured table, trying to make myself less obvious, which is hard to do with blonde hair. I don't know why I didn't take Vera's advice and dye my hair brown; I'm beginning to realise it makes me more prominent.

'Now who is this?' he says to Robert, who continues with his kneading without looking up. I see some customers standing outside when they see a German uniform in the boulangerie. It's best to stay out of harm's way, especially considering recent events with the Gestapo taking hostages.

Oberleutnant Sachs is imposing. He's very tall. He speaks particularly good French with no German accent, and he looks at me as if I am a mouse waiting to run away from a cat.

'Ask the mademoiselle,' Robert answers him.

I look unsure from one to the other. There's some kind of game they're playing between them, with me in the middle. I say proudly in the best local French accent I can muster:

'I am Emily Boucher. I've come to care for my aunt.'

'He's a bit melodramatic,' Robert says in my ear. 'Don't let him shake you.' Sachs hears this and smiles. The smiles are only for Robert.

'Your usual, Oberluetnant Sachs?'

'Yes, two baguettes *s'il vous plait* Monsieur Boulanger. You bake excellent bread. I have to come and get it fresh from the baker himself.' He says as if it needs explaining.

'And you're also helping our friend Robert? Well, I am glad, because he works too hard. He needs an assistant.' He smiles at Robert. Then turns to me and asks where I am from.

'Rennes,' I answer quickly.

'Ah Rennes, I particularly like the bandstand in the park.' He speaks looking at me as he says it. Robert turns and goes to the oven and withdraws a batch of bread out of the oven and inserts the next batch. Robert has a well-rehearsed routine. The bread is baked perfectly, and it smells wonderful. Sachs stands and watches Robert, that's when I know acting the innocent is a waste of time, he isn't looking at me, even so, I know enough not to be tricked.

'You're mistaken, there is no bandstand in the park monsieur.' And he looks at me. I surprise myself blushing. He continues as if I haven't spoken.

'I am afraid we won't be buying your bread from you for much longer Monsieur Boulanger. You may not be as busy in the future. The garrison is getting its own bakers.'

Robert digests this and looks at him.

'When will that be?'

'Soon, my friend, soon, I will let you know.' An almost imperceptible no, an unspoken agreement between them. I am staring at the German as he picks up the baguettes Robert has put on the counter for him. He straightens his uniform and puts on his cap and calmly walks out of the door. I don't see any money change hands. And with a backward glance to me he makes the door clang as he goes out the door. Two women come into the shop after he's gone down the street.

'He didn't pay.'

'No, it's a kind of reciprocal agreement. He keeps me informed, and I give him free bread.'

'I think he likes more than your bread.'

'As long as it's not in front of customers. I am safe.'

'Robert? Does he have the hots for you, I wonder?'

'Waste of time if he does. I am a one-woman man.'

I look up at him curiously.

'Mila, my daughter.' He smiles.

We serve the last few customers then he puts his closed sign in the window.

'Sacre Bleu, how much bread does one town eat?' I say looking at the piles of bread on the table.

Robert looks up from piling up the bread, 'Don't think that's for the townsfolk – this is going to the German garrison.' As if summoned, a truck pulls up and two German soldiers jump out and carry piles of baguettes in baskets back to the truck.

'How have you managed to keep it going on your own?' I am aghast at the huge number of loaves and baguettes being piled into the truck. Finally, the last basket is boarded, and they drive off. The bakery now seems empty.

Robert locks the door and closes the pretty checked curtains cutting out the sun.

'If they get new bakers for example, they won't need me. So, I could have the *Milice* banging on my door in the middle of the night to take me for *Service du Travail Obligatoire*. It won't be long. I shall have to disappear soon.'

He takes off his apron and adds it to some others. 'Mother will wash these. Time to shut up early.' Then he goes through to the oven, and I follow him. I am relieved when he shuts up the boulangerie and we leave the shop by the back door.

'A word of warning Emily. You need to be aware of the *Milice*. They are vicious, dedicated to ferreting out members of the *Résistance* and slaughtering them. They are arrogant, savagely cruel, treacherous, and sadistic. They are hated intently in this town even more than the Gestapo. And the man to worry about is a little Hitler, Gisard Mauvais. The school master, he's the older, uglier one. He was two years above me at school. He's a nasty piece of work. The Gestapo have given Mauvais a gun and he goes around town acting like a monster. He's power crazy, and a dangerous individual.'

'What about the *gendarmes*?'

'The chief of police is more sympathetic to our cause. But don't give anything away. Henri, my friend who is the bar owner

111

over there.' He points to the edge of the town square where a café is full of locals. 'He knows the chief inspector. So that can be useful.' He locks the back door of the shop and points me towards his van. 'Let's hope we don't need to use him. Now, it's time to go and meet the others.'

Madame Fisolee watches them from outside the shop. They don't see her as she's out of their sight, but she is watching the two of them talking together. She raises an eyebrow and asks her neighbour.

'So where did this young woman come from, I wonder?' Her friend shakes her head. 'I wonder if she has a work permit. Where did she say she was from?' She walks purposefully down the street towards the police station.

Chapter 11

Robert has brought some food in a basket and lifts my bike into the back of his van which is parked behind the boulangerie.

'I have prepared a little picnic for us.'

'I am hungry.'

Within a few minutes Robert's driving us out into the Normandy countryside via one of the back roads to avoid meeting German patrols, who would probably stop and search us if they came across us. It's unusual to see a family out in a car, but Robert's baker's van is sanctioned for his business. The sun is warm, but the grass is damp, and it smells fresh and warm. It reminds me of a happy childhood growing up on a French farm. The van pulls up a hill and we stop at the top; we look out over the escarpment that leads our eyes to the shimmering sea on the horizon.

'*Nous déjeunerons.*' He sets a tablecloth out on the grass and invites me to sit, share a bottle of wine with some bread and cheese.

'Not many people come this way. We should be all right for a while having lunch.' The warm spring sunshine and peaceful scene below us belies the fact there is a war on our doorstep. That around the corner are a group of men in uniform who will shoot you in cold blood if you are a *résistant*.

We look out over the hill on which Saint Just precariously sits. The shacks and houses below the ramparts shimmer in the early spring heat in the distance, while the tall spire of the Church of Saint Marie stands majestically behind. From the top of our hill, I can see across the valley. The forest rises up an escarpment in the distance, and the river Vire meanders its way along the valley floor. In the winter it flows faster. I haven't been in this area before, but it seems familiar especially as I grew up not far from here in Rennes. I realise I should treasure this moment in time, as I'm sitting next to someone whom I admire, because next month things may be vastly different. Neither of us could be here. Once the allies land, we will be fighting tooth and nail to sabotage everything the Germans rely on.

'What a view.' I look out over the river and watch a bunch of spring flowers dying in the warm breeze on its banks, their once perky heads bending with the wind. The cherry blossom trees are bursting with colour in the fields below it makes me happy I'm here, it's so pretty and it gladdens my heart.

I feel a catch in my throat for some reason. Robert is observing my facial expression.

'What is it Emily, homesickness?'

'Just a bit. The bluebells will be out at home now. I just thought of my mother today and wondered how she is. It's the first time I've let myself think of her. She has no idea I'm in France. There's no one to look after her if anything happens to me.'

'What happened to your father?'

'He had a heart attack last year and died. My mother was devastated. We all were.' I dig my heel to extinguish the cigarette with gritted teeth like it's something to be hated.

'SOE send relatives a card occasionally to let parents know we're okay. My mother has no idea I'm an agent. Although she knows I am working for the government.'

Robert grinds his cigarette into the ground. 'I didn't realise you left a widowed mother. Were you left any recompense when your husband was killed?'

'Luke? Good Lord no. he left us with nothing.'

Robert mutters a word under his breath which I don't hear clearly.

'Luke was a bully. I didn't find out until I married him. He had my parents in his pocket. I knew they wouldn't believe me if I told them how he wasn't the gentleman they thought he was. I looked forward to him going to sea. And I was glad when he didn't come back.'

'So, what's the problem?' he asks.

'I feel guilty,' I tell him. 'It comes over me like a cloud.'

'For what? It wasn't your fault; you didn't know what he was really like.'

'My brother, Sam, told me not to marry him. We haven't heard from Sam in a long time. His last letter was from somewhere in the Middle East. Now he's gone too. Sam knew Luke's true worth. The house my parents contributed money to, was put in *his* family's name. His brother and family now live in it. My father passed away, and I had to go and live with my mother. She had very little money after my father died so I joined the WAAF's to get paid regular employment. That was in 1941.'

We sit companionably in the sunshine looking out over the scene below us.

'I sent my pay to my mother, so she could survive. Luke's brother tried to get that off me too. Do you know in England a woman under thirty can't have her own bank account? It has to be in her husband's name.'

Robert stares at me as if working that out. I move and sit next to him, our backs against the van.

'It took me a long time to sort that out. Then I was called in by my father's friend to join SOE.'

'Your parents believed in him. It's not your fault.'

'I am angry with myself for believing Luke's lies. Sam tried to warn me, but I wouldn't listen. By the time I'd married him it was too late. Only Sam knew what he was really like. And now I don't know if Sam is even alive.'

I start to feel dizzy it's probably the wine.

'He was a liar. You were duped into marrying him. And he took over your life and money. People like that are power crazy, rather like Hitler. They usually have something wrong with them. Some weakness.'

He moves over and puts his arm around my shoulder, and I feel comforted. I swallow hard.

'Pardon, it is not like me to tell a stranger about my personal life.'

'I hope I'm not a stranger anymore.'

'No. but it's amazing the effect you have on me,' I tell him. 'I always end up telling you my secrets. That's not like me at all.'

'I'm not a stranger, and I can keep a secret. The Gestapo won't get anything from me.' And he squeezes my shoulders, which makes me feel a lot better. I could stay like this. Robert pulls me closer to him and I rest my head on his shoulder. I can feel his warmth through my jacket, his mouth on the top of my head as he kisses it. A delicious thrill runs through the length of my body.

'Men like that have an inferiority complex,' he says. I feel quite comfortable in his arms, and don't move.

'They need to bully women to make themselves feel superior. They weren't breast fed by their mothers.' We both laugh. He gets out a scarf from his pocket and wipes the damp from my face with it.

'And then you joined SOE? And they trained you into a killing machine.' He smiles as I move away from him reluctantly. 'It seems strange that you could kill someone. But I, on the other hand, have killed and will continue to, until we have our country back in our hands.'

I sit up, suddenly filled with the need to tell all.

'I had to toughen up in training. It did me good. Now I know how to defend myself. And I learned to live off the land, to set primers and booby traps, dismantle Bren and Sten guns, handle commando knives including German weapons.

'*Sacre bleu,* you are a dangerous woman to know!'

'I enjoyed it. It's not every day you learn to pick a safe or get taught how to handle explosives. I hope I get to use half the skills I learned. But I'm supposed to keep low and out of sight. I am glad things are warming up though.'

'In more ways than one,' he says.

We eat the bread and cheese in companiable silence. But I'm worried.

'Will you disappear before they come to get you?'

'I have to. Anyway, if they take me, there's no one to take over as organiser.'

'There's loads of people to take over. Plus, there's Eve.'

'Maybe.' He sighs and stretches out his legs leaning against the van.

'I suppose there are a few – Gaston, Eve, You.'

'Not me. I'm not confident enough.'

'I think you are.'

I shrug my shoulders.

'Anyway, there are no young men left in this town,' he continues. 'Any fit enough to serve have been taken to the German mines or camps. A new Panzer division has just moved into the town, and I am only here because I'm the only baker in town, and they need their bread. But it won't be long before they get a baker, and I am taken away.'

'Who looks after your daughter?'

'Mila? My mother. My father was killed in the last war.'

'What happened to your wife?' I ask him. Then I wish I hadn't asked; he is suddenly quiet and looks far away into the distance.

'She died when I was away in the army. I came home to look after Mila and my mother. My compatriots who escaped imprisonment joined the Maquis in the forest when the Germans started to take men for slave labour. I came back to live with them and a friend who was an *administrateur* managed to procure the letter excusing me from the STO. But now the garrison has expanded they'll be baking their own bread. That means my usefulness will have ceased. And Mauvais will be banging down the door in the middle of the night to haul me off to the German mines.'

'Oh no.' My heart sank.

'I hear some men from here are building up the Atlantic Wall's defences. At least that's not too far away.' He tells me cheerfully.

I don't feel cheerful. 'Then you should disappear now. Tomorrow at least. We can't do without you as our leader.'

'Can't you?' He's leaning against the back of the van with a conspiratorial smile he watches me and raises an eyebrow. He has a charming smile; I notice the scar on his chin and watch it move up and down as he talks. I sip my drink and blush and pretend that his closeness hasn't affected me. He takes my free hand and kisses it gently.

'Merci Emily, it's nice to be wanted.'

'I can see they listen to you and do as you tell them. To act like that means you have earned their respect. You are a well-loved general.'

'A general? I don't think I will ever be one of those. Most of us have grown up together. Have served in the army together.' He sighs and looks away towards the plateau in the distance. 'Then the Germans came and desecrated our town. Taking over the town and killing people. The Gestapo came next and took over the policing and STO came after that. And then they started herding groups of young men in the town square dragging them off to their camps and forced labour to keep the German machine working. That's what they do. Half the town has been sent to camps in Germany. But I will tell you before I disappear. We will still meet up to organise the *réseau*. Also, I want you to get to know Eve, it's her farm where we're going. She's my second in command, if you like. We've known each other from school. Her

120

husband was taken for STO last year. Everyone looks up to her, her family has lived in the valley for generations. Her son, Pierre, is a railway worker, a *Cheminot*. He and Eric have been draining engine oil from some of the locomotives that pass through their terminus, including some petrol.

I listen intently, I can see a train in the distance as it goes under a tunnel in the escarpment of the plateau.

'If anything happens to me, I want you and Eve to work together to organise our sabotage for *le jour de la liberation*.' He smiles again at the look on my face.

'You look worried, *ma cherie*. You don't need to. I know what I am doing.'

'That's what Jean-Pierre said to you, I'm betting.'

We smile at each other. He's trying to guess what I'm thinking, and I watch his scar move up and down.

'I've just met you and now you're going. How annoying of you. You know just how to make me blush,' I tell him. He smiles and pushes the hair the wind has blown into my face.

'Could it be me you are worried about?'

'No. Course not.' I shake his hand off. 'I'd just got myself a job and now I'll be losing it.'

Robert laughs at me. 'You give yourself away too easily. You're so English. We'll make a Frenchwoman of you yet.'

I shrug and then my face blushes again. 'You have the canny gift of making me blush at the most inopportune time.'

'I thought I had said something perhaps that was too informal. Forgive me,' he says.

'It's a long time since I've spoken French to Frenchmen, and I may say something inappropriate,' I tell him.

Robert leans forward his eyes bright.

'No, it is my inappropriateness. You have done nothing wrong.' And he takes my hand and kisses it again on the back of it. His touch warms my heart.

'Promise me you will be honest Robert, at all times. I would rather you be that than worry about being inappropriate. The Nazis are inappropriate, not us, so you won't offend me.'

'Yesterday on the bicycle was the most fun I'd had in a long time.' I say, and he smiles. 'Me too.' And reluctantly packs the remnants of the picnic away in the basket. I look out at the quiet countryside. I am thinking of the calm before the storm. We are high up on the hill and apart from a few cows and the birds, the countryside is serenely quiet. This world of farms, fields and forests seems unblemished, it seems hard to believe the enemy is just around the corner ready trying to defeat us.

'Ah I wish it were always like this,' he sighs. 'Spring shows us warmth and colour, after an exceptionally cold winter.' He looks at the landscape about him with the blues, whites and yellows of the wildflowers stretching down the hill as far as the eye can see. The sun is shining down on us, and I remove my jacket. Nothing about except a bird of prey gliding over the escarpment down to the river, its finger-like wing tips spreading to catch the warm air currents.

We reluctantly get back into the van. I take one last look at the view, at the glistening river winding away towards the escarpment and beyond. The yellow and pink flowers. The air smells wonderful it's full of spring promise. It's hard to think at peaceful times like this that we're in the middle of an occupation. And spending some time alone with Robert, I finally feel more relaxed than I've ever felt in anyone's company.

Chapter 12

Driving down the hill towards Eve's farm, Robert is going slowly to avoid the bumps in the road. Two years ago a bomb was dropped from an RAF Vickers Wellington by mistake, a huge crater about two feet deep is still evident and appears in front of us. Robert carefully negotiates his way around the crater and stops half-way down the slope, to show us a beautiful view of a small old brick farmhouse nestling at the bottom of a valley with the river flowing alongside.

'The crater has been filled in by some of us, it was several metres deep originally. But the filling sinks down more and more each year. There's one good thing that's come out of it - it puts the Boche off coming down the track, and especially at night,' he says wryly.

He points to a big tree in front of us. We are level with the canopy of an oak, it looks incredibly old.

'The huge tree that hangs over Eve's farmhouse as if protecting it, was planted by Eve's grandparents in the last century when they built the farmhouse. You can see the old cow shed the other side of the yard.' He points to a corrugated building. 'Eve no longer keeps cattle, but that was built by Eve's father.' As we drive closer,

I see a large shed that's falling to bits with some chicken pecking around it.

'It keeps us in eggs, which we keep quiet about,' he smiles. 'We don't want the Boche to find out.'

The river winds slowly at the bottom of the valley. The fields are fallow, they follow the bend of the river and out of site around the corner towards the next farm which has been empty for two years, he explains.

'There used to be a family living there. The children were the same age as Eve's son, but they got taken away three years ago. The Nazis have rounded up most of the Jewish families in the area and sent them to camps in Germany.'

We drive on down to the farm as Robert negotiates more bumps and hollows down the driveway to the farm.

'The forest over there looks a perfect place to hide.' I point to the other side of the river where there is dense woodland. The trees stretch towards the East as far as the eye can see.

'That's where the Maquis live, that's where I'll be going if I can outwit the Nazis.'

We arrive at the bottom of the valley in front of the farm. It's Eve who comes out to meet us. She has a bubbly and cheerful personality. Her hand out ready to greet me as I get out of the car. I like her already.

'Bonjour Emily, welcome to France. Thank you for coming to help us.'

She greets me like an old friend. Her smile lights up the day. She embraces Robert. She wears a short bob in the fashionable Parisian style, her hair is almost black with no hint of grey. Her muddy dungarees show she works on her farm. She takes both our hands, and we face the river below.

'I love it here. My family have lived here for generations. Although I don't grow much in the fields, I can't manage them on my own. Why grow food for the Boche? I just grow what I need to feed us behind the house.' She takes us to the back garden. The river bend meets her farm boundary and then picks up speed and disappears into the distance. Some water birds take flight in front of us and follow the river towards the East. It's flowing quite fast because the recent spring rain is still draining from the hills.

'When we have storms in winter it's dangerous to try and cross even in a boat. I lost my boat about a year ago when it was picked up by a flood and taken downstream, it was bashed against the rocks.' She points into the distance, and I follow her finger. 'The river widens and deepens there before curving out of sight. Anyway, come in, we have work to do before the others arrive.' She leads me through a vegetable garden at the back of the house I brush past a pile of mint and coriander, the smells remind me of home.

There is a pot bubbling in the kitchen, and she tells Robert to stir it. Then she takes my hand and leads me up a narrow little staircase to a small landing with three doors leading off it.

Opening one, which is the *salle de bains* she sits me down on a chair and shuts the door.

'Now then. Robert says your hair is to be disguised.' She says sitting me next to a basin and preparing things behind me. 'It's criminal to change your lovely hair colour Emily. But it must be done. It will keep the enemy from the door. Don't worry it will only last a few weeks and it will grow. Then we may have to colour it again.' She sees my face fall. 'I know it seems drastic, but we have to do it, Robert is right, you could be recognised by the Gestapo. You will attract too much attention to your blonde hair. Let's get to it. Our visitors will arrive shortly.'

'What visitors?'

I hadn't realised I was having my hair dyed, and I'm a bit put out that they have decided to change my hair colour. Eve is gentle and coaxing and she talks non- stop to distract me, while she mixes dyes together and plonks cold water on my hair. There is no mirror. I swallow, I'm nervous, I have never had my hair dyed. But with Eve's coaxing I start to relax and surrender to her deft hands. At the same time she tells me about her husband whom she hopes is still alive and hopes to hear from him soon.

'Do you think they will let him receive letters?' I ask her.

'Well, they let prisoners of war receive parcels, don't they?'

I don't think the Vichy government who organised this with the Nazis care what happens to our countrymen. But I don't tell her this. She needs to hang onto any thread of optimism she has.

127

'I'm sure you're right Eve.'

She smiles at me I can see she has hope in her heart. I tell her a bit about my family. At the end of an hour, we are talking as if we have been friends forever, and she swills my hair through with a jug of clean water and dries my hair with a towel. Then she cuts the length to my shoulders, and I watch with dismay.

'No need to look worried. I was a hairdresser in another life.'

I feel guilty that I have already said too much about my life. But I feel as if I have known Eve for a long time, she is so friendly and easy to talk to, and I tell her so, which makes her beam again, as piles of my hair are spread across the bathroom floor like a cat shedding its fur.

As I descend the stairs with light brown hair, I see some men helping themselves to food from the pot over the stove. There is a group of people milling around the kitchen. Robert looks up and stares at me.

'You look different,' he says coming towards me and sticking a *coup de rouge* in my hand.

'Well not as noticeable now, am I?' I say.

He smiles and quickly goes to talk to someone else.

Eve introduces me to Giselle who is sitting at the table, she has long blonde hair and an attractive face, but Giselle doesn't smile, she doesn't say anything when I greet her with my hand held out to shake hers. She just stares at me. I feel a bit awkward and put my hand down at my side. I feel her animosity towards me, and

I'm not sure why. Her pinched lips make her look impatient and frustrated. There's an embarrassed silence.

Yvette and Gaston Sainson, introduce themselves, they are husband and wife farmers from the next farm, three kilometres away to the South.

'*Bienvenue en France, Mam'selle,*' Yvette says, and kisses me on both cheeks, '*Je suis Yvette,* Laurent's *maman.*' I shake hands with Gaston who appears to look sombre but his face breaks into a smile when he sees me. He is much larger than his wife with a good head of bushy grey hair. Everyone seems thin apart from Gaston. His wife is petite and pale, and very friendly. Everyone is talking to each other. Compared to the quiet house at Maria's, it's noisy, but it's a lively atmosphere. It's so nice to finally meet people who I will be involved with for the next few weeks.

Laurent Sainson is a gangly, spotty-faced sixteen-year-old, he's a friend of Pierre and is leaning against the fireplace. How could a tiny woman like Yvette have a gangly teenager six feet tall? Next to him stands Pierre, who is the image of his mother, with thick black hair, he has the exuberance of youth and a cheerful countenance.

There are two older farm hands, Gilbert and Benoit, who work for the Sainsons. I recognise them from my parachute drop, Gilbert smiles at me but the other one looks at me suspiciously. They wear farm worker overalls, and their boots are old and have holes in them.

'These men are les Cheminots - Eric and Pierre.' Robert introduces me to an older man and young Pierre. They are railway workers; their dark overalls show years of oil and grease.

'They are our eyes and ears at the railway station,' he explains.

Eric smiles at me, he is a man of few words, but proffers his hand to shake. He has a weather-beaten face, he looks like he's seen a lot of life, his grey beard belies keen blue eyes that are alert; he is an observer.

'Pierre and I act as one team,' Eric tells me, 'Especially when it comes to freeing France from the Nazis.'

The young man who freed me from my parachute is waiting next to Eric to speak to me. It's Pierre, he blushes as he hops from one foot to another. We shake hands, he is eager to tell me about his clandestine work helping the *résistance*.

Robert lowers his voice so that no one else can hear. 'They obtain petrol for us from the railway yard. We have our own petrol dump, but only a few of us know where it is. We're building it up for our *jour de la victoire.*' He turns to Pierre as Laurent comes towards us from the other side of the room. 'Be careful Pierre, it's best not to say too much in a roomful of people.'

'But they're *all résistance,*' he says, crestfallen.

'Nevertheless...' Robert says gently and squeezes Pierre's shoulder. Robert is most definitely their leader, they all look up to him, they ask him questions, giving the occasional person a pat on the back. The women, he gives a smile, and a low word of encouragement. His voice is soft when he speaks, he leans his head to one side as he listens to what Pierre has to say. He speaks gently to Pierre who nods and goes and sits down. I can't hear what they are talking about, but the group listen to his every word when he speaks to them individually. I observe the people in the room and think to myself if I gain half of Robert's charisma and popularity, I will be happy. Even though London didn't know of his existence, he leads these people with conviction and motivation. He hasn't had SOE training, whatever he learned in the army has made him an excellent leader.

Robert asks everyone to sit at the long kitchen table. I sit on one side of Robert and Eve sits the other side of me. As I sit down Yvette tells me her older son has been taken by The *Service du travail Obligatoire,* to work for the Germans. They don't know where he is. They were once pig and cattle farmers who have none left now because the Nazis have taken them all for themselves.

'There's also Henri, my friend and a bar owner,' says Robert. 'He has to maintain his presence at his bar. He passes on information from the Maquis if the dead letter drop is not possible. The courier, usually Giselle, drops information at his bar and he passes it on to the rest of the *réseau* when they drop in for their *coup de rouge* after work.'

I nod, that makes sense. An enticing aroma wafts through the kitchen from the stove. It smells homely and Eve tells us the ragout is available for those who are hungry. Most of the men are eating already.

'This seems a bit risky all meeting like this.' I say to Robert and Eve quietly.

'If one of us is caught?'

'They wouldn't give the game away,' says Eve.

'How can you be so sure?'

'We don't normally meet altogether,' says Robert. 'It is dangerous to meet like this.' He looks at Eve and she blushes. He sees her discomfort and adds, 'If anyone here gets arrested, they'd pick the rest of us up too. The Gendarmes that know us – know that we've grown up together.'

'Eve wanted us to meet you,' Yvette says defending her friend. Eve blushes again.

'Well, if I get caught, I'll just take my suicide pill,' I smile at them all. Eve's face goes white. Giselle just glowers at me.

'I am joking Eve,' I say guiltily. 'They won't get me. Don't worry. I'll keep the radio direction vans busy and I won't get caught.' I smile at her with mental fingers crossed hoping that I don't.

'Even though my Jean-Pierre got caught,' comments Giselle from the end of the table.

'On that note,' Robert interrupts her, 'I need to organise a series of safe houses for you to transmit from and I haven't found anywhere yet. I am hoping the people here can help. If you can help everyone let me know later, the less anyone else knows the better.

'I can't risk you transmitting from our house,' Yvette pipes up. 'The Nazis have already taken one son from me. I need to keep Laurent at home, he is too young to leave me.' She looks anxiously at her son who comes to sit next to her.

'If the Gestapo suspects a fugitive is given shelter,' adds Benoit staring at me, his dirty hands stroking his beard, 'The whole family ends up in a German camp. We never hear from them again. No one is safe.'

I study the table, half listening to Robert talk to the group, it is well scrubbed and worn. I think of all the relatives that have come and gone in Eve's family. And of her husband who was taken a year ago, no longer here but a prisoner in Germany.

'Don't worry about me I'll find somewhere. I'll be all right with my bike.'

Robert and Eve sit like defenders, as Giselle watches me across the table.

'Well now you're all here I'll introduce you all to our new *piano*.'

'We know who she is,' says Giselle glaring at me across the table. There's an uncomfortable silence.

'We were fine before Jean-Pierre was taken,' adds Benoit.

'We had no way to work the radio after Jean-Pierre was taken, and with the crystals broken, and no way to communicate to

London for equipment, we haven't been able to work efficiently. We all agreed - we need a new radio operator,' says Robert.

'We managed before, using the one in Rennes,' Benoit points towards the west.

'We can't do that every time, it's too far. And anyway, the different *réseaux* are supposed to keep separate from each other, so if they arrest one group, they will not be able to give details on other groups. Now Emily is here we are better off, we have our radio operator, and we need to build up the *reseau's* ammunition store ready for the *le jour de la liberation.*'

'We need to plan the actual operations too,' adds Eric. 'With a view to doing the maximum harm to the Germans while getting a minimum of reprisals against our civilians.'

We nod in agreement. Giselle continues to complain.

'I thought she was going to be a man. What good is sending a woman?' And where's the ammo and guns we need? They should have dropped them off instead of her.' Giselle sits with arms crossed glaring across the table at me, challengingly.

'For someone who's the newest to the group, I hardly think you're in a position to complain Giselle.' Robert says.

'I would have thought you'd have realised by now,' I aim at Giselle, 'That women are far more able to move about undetected than a man. The Germans are less likely to stop a woman on the street.'

'This is why we don't usually all meet up in the group.' Robert says, his irritation starting to show. 'As long as you do your job and don't interfere with others Giselle, then that's fine. Leave us to organise the rest.' He looks at Eve and says,

'Now we need to discuss the *parachutage*.'

Giselle starts to say something, but Robert cuts her short.

'That's enough about people joining the group. I should tell you the *Maquis* will be joining us on a lot more missions as well.'

'Résistants de la derniere heure!' says Benoit sardonically. 'They decide to join us now it looks like the Allies are winning.'

'We need all the help we can get. Particularly as it is getting closer to our *jour de la victoire*.'

'When is the invasion going to happen? How long do we have to wait?' They all ask at once as if on cue. The continued questions are irritating. I wonder how Robert can remain so calm. Giselle blows cigarette smoke into the air in a defiant gesture.

'Any time soon. We will be told as soon as they decide.' I tell them.

'London doesn't know what we're going through!' Giselle declares.

'That's not true. We do know. That's why I'm here. I was born French, I remember the good days, before the occupation.'

'If you can't fight, you're no good to us,' she continues. 'A man is more able to take care of himself.'

Benoit agrees. 'Unless you're born around here, you don't understand, and you don't stand a chance.'

'I've been trained…' I start to say, but they interrupt.

'You're young, inexperienced, and you look as if you wouldn't be able to kill a fly. That's not going to be helpful to us.'

'Don't be childish Giselle,' says Eve. 'Emily's here to help us. She comes highly trained.'

'I'm trained in warfare and sabotage. And I am here to train all of you in guns and explosives.'

There are comments around the table, there were obviously two camps of thought, those who trusted me and those who didn't. Robert hadn't expected half of his *réseau* to turn up at Eve's invitation, and we hadn't expected animosity from some of the group. I felt for Eve, who looked frustrated that the meeting wasn't going how she'd hoped. I could see she wanted us all to become friends. But Giselle and some of the other workers had their own agenda.

'What good is she going to be to us?' Giselle insists.

'You seem to be emphasising too much on the job I am going to be doing. Why is that Giselle?'

Giselle goes pale and glares at me, about to say something, but Robert cuts her short again.

'That's enough. Giselle go home now, if you don't agree with how I am organising things then you can leave. This isn't achieving anything. If we can't have a civil meeting between us God help us against the Boche!'

'What about the mission you were going to talk to me and Eric about?' asks Pierre.

'That'll be done on a need-to-know basis. So if anyone gets caught, they won't be able to tell the Germans any secrets. I want to speak to Gaston, Benoit, and Gilbert now, and Eric and Pierre. The rest of you can go.'

'Why can't I listen to your plans?' Yvette complains. 'I am his wife, his mother.' She points at Gaston and Pierre. 'I've a right to know what's going on.'

'Listen to the boss Yvette! Can't you understand?' Gaston raises his voice. 'If any of us get caught our planned missions and any information on the rest of the *résistance* could be tortured out of us. The least you know the better!'

Yvette huffs as she stomps out of the room, with Eve and Giselle following.

'Emily, I want you to listen to what we are organising, it will help with getting the messages correct on your transmissions.'

I sit uncomfortably round the table with the men. After the recent exhibition from Yvette and Giselle, I'm not feeling particularly welcome. But I have a job to do, and Robert is in charge. So I listen intently, and Eve re-joins us. Later, when everyone's gone, he thanks Eve for providing the food.

'But' he says, 'We can't meet like that Eve. Please don't invite everyone again.' Robert says gently, as her cheeks go pink.

'I was hoping to just introduce Emily to you, Eve, not to the rest of them. If someone gets arrested, the Gestapo will get the information from one of us. And if Mauvais turns up like he has done before here, we'd be finished. From now on we use Henri's bar for sharing information and the dead letter drop will be activated for passing on information to those in the area. Confidentiality is the key from now on.'

'The trouble with my wife is, Emily,' says Gaston gently, 'We've all grown up together and know each other so well. Now there are new people joining all the time, she feels left out.'

I nod. But I'm still upset by the hostile reactions.

'My eldest son was taken last year for the *Service du Travail Obligatoire*, he was only just twenty. We haven't heard from him since.'

'Has Robert warned you about the *Milicien*, Gisard Mauvais?' Eric asks me. 'Beware of him, he is evil.'

'He fancies his chances here, and sometimes comes looking for trouble,' says Eve. 'I believe he organised for my husband to be sent to the *Service du Travail Obligatoire*. There's usually somebody here, Pierre or Eric. Be careful, make sure you're not on your own with him. He makes my skin crawl. He was a creep when we were in school, and he's still a creep now,' she says and shudders.

'I'll kill him if he tries it on again, *Maman*,' says Pierre. Eve smiles at her son. 'Keep away from him my dear. He's a snake.'

'Right. We need to get down to business and order guns, ammo and boots, Emily.'

'Where will the parachute drop be?' I ask him, 'Pardon, *parachutage*.'

'I've looked as far as Coutances. It's further away than we are used to travelling, which is risky in the middle of the night. But there doesn't seem to be any anti-aircraft guns there. There's also a group of Maquis this side of the forest, they'll be helping us out to store the new equipment.'

'Wouldn't it be better to have an ammo store nearer to home. Rather than leave it to a group of unruly rascals?' I ask, and everyone looks at me with surprise on their faces.

'The *Maquis* will join us as part of our group,' Robert answers with a sideways look at me. Obviously, everyone has sympathy for the *Maquis*, who are a group of civilians and old soldiers who have evaded capture from the *Service du Travail Obligatoire* by hiding out in the forests. I had heard about them in my training and how *résistance* groups are formed from them.

'Someone's coming,' Eric says, keeping lookout at the front door. A black car stops at the top of the drive leading down the hill to the farm. It's nearly two kilometres away, he can't make out whose car it is and says so. Then it slowly drives off to a sigh of relief from all of us. The Gestapo have black cars.

'We'd better leave. We'll use the dead letter drop on the Vire Road like we did before. I'll show you where it is Emily. Any questions?'

I wait by the van as Robert speaks quietly to Eve and she comes out to see us off. Eve hugs me. 'Let me know if you need anything Emily.' I hug her back and thank her.

'Don't let Giselle put you off, you're very welcome. Her boyfriend, Jean-Pierre was our wireless operator, we've all been worried about him since he got taken for German forced labour.'

'Any news of your husband?' Robert asks. She shakes her head.

'Even so, let me know if you need anything or you're worried about anything,' she says

'Only about your group accepting me I think,' I say ruefully.

Robert says he's going to collect some eggs from Eve's barn for his mother. While we wait, the day's events obviously play on Eve's mind.

'I don't know if my husband will survive. It's been over a year; I just fear for his very survival.' Tears fill her eyes.

'Let's hope he does,' I say and squeeze her hand.

'Anyone who rebels or says anything against the Third Reich gets tortured and beaten. Antoine was never silent about the Nazis, it got him into trouble before. I hope he manages to keep silent.' I put my arm around her, and she wipes the tears away with the back of her hand. 'I don't normally cry, I have to keep a brave face for Pierre, but it's been easy to talk to you Emily.' She holds my hand until Robert comes back from the shed.

As Robert drives, he says, 'Eve should not have organised that meeting. I only wanted you to meet her and Pierre. The less the *réseau* know about you the better. We'll visit some places outside the area, where the Gestapo are less likely to be. I have some ideas where you can go to transmit that involve the countryside and not people's houses. If you're discovered the whole family, including children, will be arrested just for harbouring a *résistant*.'

It was a sobering thought, something I'd heard about before, and I know how fear can affect how a person reacts.

'Nowadays so many innocent citizens have been deported that the citizens remaining just don't want the risk,' he says. 'I know somewhere that would be good for a couple of skeds and not near the town. It is within cycling distance of Eve's house, and you'll be able to hide the radio. If it comes to it, I may have to hide you in Eve's barn.'

'That sounds good. Although I have made it more comfortable at Maria's house and I am looking forward to having a clean sheet on my bed, and to get a better night's sleep.'

That night I put a blanket over the bedroom window blocking out any light and put clean blankets on our beds. I look out through the edge of the curtain and see out into the road towards Saint Just. It's not dark until 7pm now, so it's not as easy to get out and remain hidden after curfew. Tonight, I will send a message to London to request guns, ammo, boots and cigarettes. In a more positive mood, I light the fires in our bedrooms, and I fall asleep on my clean sheets and blanket. I feel much warmer than the night before, and thankful that another day has passed without meeting any Gestapo.

Chapter 13

Spring is around the corner as Robert gets out of bed. It's not as cold as it usually is at four in the morning. His breath can usually blow a cloud of condensation even in the bedroom, and some winters his windows have frozen on the inside. It's been a freezing cold winter, but not today, because his fingers aren't frozen for a change by the time he gets to his *boulangerie*. His hands soon warm up when he is kneading bread, two lots of bread are cooked and out of the oven already. It's 6am and a few people are making the most of this warm sunrise by being out and about. But no one comes into his shop just yet.

Robert breathes a sigh of relief; he needs to get things underway before the queue starts forming outside. Suddenly he sees the woman who has parachuted in from the sky and changed his life. He has liked her straight away and the way she makes him smile. God knows there isn't much to smile about these days. He sees her bouncing in the morning sunshine; she is so full of energy.

He has told her to lie low, but she comes bursting into the *boulangerie*, ignoring his request to stay with Maria. Why did she come in today? She will blow her cover if she's not careful.

'I thought I told you to stay at home with Maria. *Lie low*, I said.'

'I know. Good morning to you too. But I thought if I came out early enough, I might miss the Boche, and be able to help you a bit. I am getting a bit bored at home.'

He scratches his head in frustration.

'*Mon Dieu,* what part of *lie low* do you not understand? You'll raise questions by those who see you. The Oberleutnant often takes an early walk this way to pick up his bread. If he comes in, we'll just have to say that you are visiting Maria if somebody asks who you are.'

She pulls a forlorn look on her face. He tries to hide his frustration.

'I'd like to attend the parachutage too.'

'Absolutely not.'

'But Robert, I'm not doing anything…'

'You're doing plenty, and if you're caught our *réseau* has had it!'

I start to protest again, but he cuts me off. 'No. And that's my final word. Now go and open the door if you want to help.'

I let the few in who are waiting outside, but pleased he's decided to let me help him.

'You can carry on kneading while I serve these people.'

Later on he admits, 'I am glad you popped by,' he says quickly and smiles. He feels a lot more optimistic now, he decides not to mention the parachute drop again. Robert feels guilty he admonished her. But he may acquiesce another time. She has

144

worked well this morning better than he had thought she would. She had fended off questions from curious customers, acting like she has worked in the boulangerie for years. He likes the way just seeing her brightens up his day. It's a long time since he felt like that.

A little while later, she asks 'What can I do to help?'

'Just carry on kneading this bread while I take baguettes out of the oven.'

'Don't worry Robert, I am able to act out the part of great-niece. SOE has covered my tracks well.'

'The trouble is,' Robert tells her, 'The more you're seen out and about the more likely questions will be asked, and then you might get a visit from the *Milice* or Gestapo.'

Chapter 14

As I cycle home and walk the last few metres to Maria's, I get a bad feeling as I turn into the driveway I inwardly groan. It's a police car, so it's the dreaded *Milice*. I hurry inside to see what's happening.

It happens to be both Gestapo and *Milice*. I hurry into the parlour where a man with thinning hair and brown uniform is waving his gun at Maria, it is, I assume, the notorious Gisard Mauvais of the *Milice*. He stands over her threateningly as she sits up her back straight and looks at him with an expression of anger and defiance. I can see she's angry. But out the corner of my eye is a Gestapo officer, leaning against the wall. His uniform is resplendent with its shining insignia of the SS. He is standing back and letting Mauvais have his way with a smirk on his lips. He looks me up and down as I enter. His Luger hanging from his hips. He is obviously used to getting his own way. I want to knock that smirk off his face.

'You were no good at school as a snotty nosed little twerp and you're no better now,' Maria says to Mauvais with contempt. He is trying to bait her, so he can respond with violence. I step in between them; I am getting a bit too close for comfort to this despicable man.

'Leave my aunt alone. What kind of man threatens an old lady?'

He waves his pistol under my nose. His power crazed eyes level with mine. I stand defiantly in front of Maria. His face is puce and his breath stinks of garlic and bad teeth.

The officer watches this exchange with some amusement.

'*Mademoiselle*, charmed, I am sure.' He stands and bows forward, but I step back into Maria.

'What's the meaning of this intrusion? I am sure my aunt didn't ask you inside.'

Mauvais stands up tall to try to exert his power over me. I stand tall in front of him and pull my shoulders back, our eyes are on a level. The Gestapo officer leans forward.

'Madam was asleep, so we walked in, we were looking for you. The officer did struggle with the front door,' he says, 'but he soon managed to fix that.'

'I assume you're the superior officer?' I say, glaring at the SS Major. 'Why are you letting this low life threaten my aunt?'

'Constable to you,' bristles Mauvais, already incensed with Maria's insults and points his gun at me threateningly. I am afraid for her life and mine. Maria pulls herself up to stand behind me.

'You're the newcomer, Emily Boucher.'

'*Mademoiselle* Boucher to you.' I answer back. Pulling my height up a bit so I can stand taller. I am determined to stand up to this man. The officer puts his pistol in his holster. He smooths his white-blonde hair from his big forehead. He obviously fancies his chances by the way he looks at me up and down.

'Travel permit,' Mauvais demands, holding out his hand, his yellow fingers stained from nicotine. 'Quickly. We haven't all day. The Major is a busy man.'

He tries to move closer, this time smelling strongly of nicotine and body odour. My hackles rise like a dog sniffing out a bad man.

'I've heard all about you. You don't frighten me.'

'Give me your papers!' Mauvais shouts into my face. The Gestapo officer remains calm watching this *contretemps* between us with some amusement.

'Fraulein, fraulein, calm yourself. Mauvais gets a bit excited when he has to question a pretty woman.' He smiles as I continue to stare at Mauvais. The Gestapo's French is rather good.

'Your French isn't from around here, is it?' He moves closer to me and looks me up and down like a prize cow, his hand resting on his Luger. I try to calm my anxiety; was I a bit over-zealous in defending Maria?

'Your papers, *Madamemoiselle?*' He looks at me with his wide, annoying smile and holds his hand out.

I hand the officer my papers. He nods and takes them over to the windows where the light is better. I try to calm my racing heart; he comes back and hands them to Mauvais. He looks at me keenly particularly the clothes I have on. I needn't worry about them. SOE has sewn authentic looking labels into my clothes. Even clothes are checked on suspect spies in France these days. He nods and smiles as if liking what he sees.

'Your clothes remind me of Paris my dear, you don't look like a local.'

'In Paris, there is more variety, even though there's no food.'

'When did you go to Paris?' he asks. I realise I'm going to come unstuck if I don't get my facts right.

'About twelve weeks ago to visit relatives. When I arrived home, my mother asked me to look after Aunt Maria, so I came straight here to care for my aunt.' I hope inventing another story is not going to drop me into trouble.

'Your Great Aunt.'

'Yes, my Great Aunt.' I swallow, he sees that I am nervous, perspiration breaks out on my forehead.

To my relief, he seems to accept this for now and doesn't ask me anymore questions. Mauvais looks me up and down which is unsettling but then I'm used to men doing that. It's an insult to me, but some men think it's a compliment.

I stand in front of Maria. She pushes me to the side, she's not afraid of Mauvais. He looks at my papers and I try not to let him rile me. His smell makes me want to vomit but I keep calm, and edge away from him to Maria's side, aware of the Major's eyes watching me. Mauvais looks at my papers for what seems like an age. I swallow again. While the papers would escape brief interest, on closer scrutiny they might not hold up to authenticity. He hands them back to me. Our forger has outdone himself.

'Where are you from, *Mamselle*?' The Major asks.

'Rennes.'

My heart is beating in my ears. I am so nervous, but at least he doesn't smell like Mauvais.

'Mauvais, you know what you're looking for in this instance. Being a local, Mauvais is much more competent in finding out who is false and who is genuine.' He shows his brilliant white teeth in a smile.

Mauvais leans closer I nearly pass out with the smell of him.

'What is your name?' He isn't going to be nice.

'It says so there.'

'What is your name?' he demands angrily. 'If you continue in this way, I will arrest you!'

I repeat my name.

'What is your address?'

I tell him Maria's.

'Not hers. Yours.'

I try to slow my breath and be calm. He's trying to antagonise me. I am making it easier for him. I try to calm myself, what was I thinking? I tell him the address in Rennes that SOE has given me.

'Why are you here?'

'To look after my aunt.'

'So I heard.'

'Who told you that? I've only been here a few days.'

'Nothing to do with you. I have my sources.'

'Oh, Madame Fisolee.' As realisation set in, I say with disgust. 'I've heard all about her as well; she's a *collaborateur*, a traitor to France.'

'What do you mean by that?' His brows knit together. I shrug it off. I am really dicing with death here. I am making an enemy of him. But after what Eve told me about him, I am not going to be walked over.

'Everyone knows she's an informer. I've met her. She's a busy body,' I say, trying to remain calm. I can feel Maria tense next to me. He starts waving the pistol in my face again. I step back. He knows I will not do anything while he has a gun in his hand. He's blown up by his own self-importance. I grit my teeth. I hate him with an intensity I hadn't thought possible.

'You sound like you're the enemy. You better be careful who you're talking about.' Mauvais is getting angrier. I try to keep calm but just his attitude sets my hackles rising.

'What work did you do before?'

'*Administrateur.*'

'Where?'

'*Counseil municipal* Rennes.'

'I will check.'

You do that, I think to myself.

'Now, where's your travel permit?'

'Here.' I offer the travel permit, the one SOE also forged.

I am crossing my fingers behind my back.

'You answer a bit too quick, for my liking.'

I stare at him, eye to eye, he is a slightly smaller than I. The fact that I am taller than him and he has his cap on gives me a feeling of bravado, but it's soon knocked out of me as he says with a grin, 'We didn't find anything this time, but you can be assured we will next time. Oh yes,' he says gloating even more, 'We have checked your room.' I balk as I think of them going through my things. Even though I have been careful to hide the map. I'm thankful that Robert insisted we hide my radio away from Maria's house.

The SS Major is tiring of Mauvais' tactics. 'Come now Mauvais, let's leave these ladies. It's time to go.' He steps forward towards me and bows to my surprise, then leaves. I am glad my papers stand up to scrutiny. I can only stand and stare at him. There's something about this Gestapo officer that's unnerving.

Behind that wide smile is another emotion. Irritation? Frustration? He seems not wholly convinced. I take my papers back from Mauvais and take a step back. I have his measure, but I will watch my back.

'I'll be back,' Mauvais says, 'I won't be as friendly next time.'

I go pale because I believe him. Like when he found Eve on her own. My response makes him smile. This only encourages him. He turns eventually and follows the officer out, taking his smelly breath with him. He tries to slam the front door, but it's broken and heavy and it doesn't shut properly, leaving his exit an anti-climax. I immediately run upstairs and the few things I have in my bag have been emptied out, my underwear flung over the floor, the sheets on the mattress pulled off and the mattress standing on its end. I run downstairs angry now, that my personal items have had Mauvais' grubby hands on them. I find Maria who is sitting in her chair, shivering. I breathe a sigh of relief.

'You shouldn't let the fire go out, Maria.' It's a relief they have gone. We're both shaken up.

'Come into the kitchen. I'll make it warmer for you.' I help her up, and bring her book and her cap, which has fallen. She walks slowly, pushing her bent body into the kitchen. She sits by the stove, looking out the window at the bare trees.

'It's been a long, cold winter,' she says. Maria is not one for small talk, so I look up at her in surprise as I put her slippers on her feet. She stares into the fire. My heart softens what a life she must have led before now. I can sense her heart pumping madly; I feel guilty I've brought the Gestapo down on her head with my presence here. She doesn't want to talk. So I add more wood to the fire.

'Let me know if it goes out.' I comment.

'It'll be spring soon,' she says as she pulls her shawl around her.

I acknowledge this and busy myself in the kitchen, it's still churning in my mind how I should've reacted towards Gisard. I've made an enemy there. He will want to get his own back. I wish the house weren't so darn cold. Gisard Mauvais has left a chill behind him, like icicles of death.

'I'll make you a hot chocolate, the way you like it. We have some milk left.' Any more episodes like that and I don't think her heart could stand it. I've had no caustic comments from her today. I can see her body is still stiff with shock. I keep myself busy making the drinks for us and as I sit next to her and keep her company, while I talk about nothing in particular. At the kitchen table we watch the evening sun slide down reflecting on the wall of the dairy farm. I shiver.

I've brought more attention to myself. It was impulsive of me and will add to my problems. I've done the opposite of what I was supposed to do. I have antagonised the *Milice*. The next day I cycle on a cool morning to the boulangerie at 4am to help Robert until he opens. He is quite pleased I help him but his face falls when I tell him about the Gestapo and *Milice* visit.

'Go home now,' he says. 'If you're found working here that could add more fuel to the fire.'

I didn't argue, I cycled home as the sun rising.

On the evening of the 23rd a few days later I lay awake at night listening for the sounds of aeroplane engines flying overhead. I'm not sure where the drop will be, Robert hasn't told me. I dream that the Gestapo suddenly jump out from behind the bushes and shoot all the *résistants* dead and I wake up with a start.

Chapter 15

I stumble on the cobbles. My breathing comes out fast as I start to panic, was that a German patrol I can hear? Perhaps it's just the wind making noises through the remains of the roof. I pull up my bike after cycling in the dark to this remote barn which Robert has told me about, which seems like it's in the middle of nowhere. It looks look an ideal place to send and receive secret messages. At least I have the option of escaping in different directions if a radio detection finding van comes looking for me.

It's damp, cold, and nearly midnight. The darkness descended five hours ago, but I can still see the clouds scudding across a forbidding sky; it may rain anytime soon. I tried to wait patiently at home, aiming for the midnight schedule, thinking no one will be out here at this time of night, and it's remote so I'm unlikely to come across a patrol. I'm not good at waiting. I paced up and down ensuring I had the right amount of words for my sked, until it was time to leave. At last I'm out here and I want to get this over and done with. Now I pull my warm hat down over my ears and keep my gloves on while I push my bike up this hill. I'm following an animal track which is probably from sheep and goats, it's too windswept for any other creature. In which case if the RDF's pinpoint my position, I'll be gone by the time they get here.

I should have rested before I came out this time and didn't. I look out over the vista to the west. I wished I'd not insisted Robert go to bed when he offered to bring me in his van. I could see he was tired, I am trying to keep out of sight, so it makes sense to do this sked on my own. At least he charged my radio battery for me. I reach the dilapidated shack used only by herdsmen during the Summer.

I start to panic as I imagine I hear the rumbling of a troop carrier below me on the main road to Coutances. But there are no lights and it's quiet again outside. My laboured breath is the only noise because I've been pushing my bike uphill. There's a roaring in my ears, which is probably the blood pumping around my body. The torch light is fading, which isn't good, I need to do this quickly before it fades altogether. Leaving my bicycle on the ground, I get out my radio and go inside the shack. The earth is damp but there are some wooden slats to sit on and they keep me dry. I balance my radio on a pile of stones, and I throw my aerial onto the roof through a gap in the side. I pull out a silk from the seat of my pants. As I tune into my frequency, I get a good signal. Try and relax. Concentrate. Below me is a thick wood which scrambles down to the main road. I can see any lights or automobile movement from my dilapidated old hut. I hold my breath and wait. I check my watch.

I am concentrating so hard I ignore the roaring in my ears and the owls hooting in the wood. I check my watch again. It's nearly midnight. I've encrypted my message. My fingers are balanced on the knob of the Morse key; I cautiously start sending out my call sign. The hesitant dots and dashes vanish into the night. Owls calling to each other have stopped. It's silent. I wait. Someone somewhere in enemy territory is hearing the new intruder and directional aerials with be shifting round the compass to find me. I have less than fifteen minutes to send this message before they get my bearings. They will know by now that I'm in the area.

I send my call sign again. I wait while a radio operator listens and works out my callsign. *Hurry up.* I tap my finger and wait, wait.

Twelve minutes until the RDF locate my position.

Then the call sign answers, and a rush of relief goes through me as I begin my transmission. Fingers shaking, the weather is clear but windy, the Morse code dots and dashes fly off into the night, as the airwaves buzz with the important message. I imagine the girl on the receiving end rush to decipher. I send my message.

Supplies required to be dropped 1.092 degrees West, 49.114 degrees North at 2am on 13th week of next full moon Required guns ammo plastic explosives and 6 dozen boots of various sizes message on BBC Start Michel is going in ten minutes End Repeat Michel is going in ten minutes.

Two minutes.

I end the transmission with *Toodloo*, and turn the set off. Then I use a match to light the bits of silk which I use for decoding, and they burn in mid-air and float to the ground. I will make sure any matches are buried before I escape into the night.

I sit and look out the open window as my eyes get used to the dark outside. It is pitch black in the wood below, and no one on the Coutances road. It's beautifully quiet, almost too quiet. It's as if the creatures in the night are holding their breath. I listen to the sounds of the night. I suddenly hear an exhalation of air and it makes my heart jump; I shine my torch into the face of a cow looking at me over a gap in the hedge. I turn the torch off as I rest it on the pile of stones, and my eyes strain in the dark as some bats nearby flit from tree to tree. I hear a noise outside. I automatically feel for the double-bladed Fairburn-Sykes knife tied to my leg just above my ankle. I can't risk the noise of a gun. But I know how to stick a knife in the shoulder clavicle to kill someone, and if I'm scared enough, I'll do it. I pop my head out of the door. No one there, there's the rustle of some small mammal outside scurrying along. There's a gap in the trees and the moon suddenly displays her beauty as she comes out from behind the clouds. I can see the craters on it even though it's a half moon.

With the receiver on and the transmitter disconnected, I listen with headphones on, cold seeping into my limbs, and my knees getting numb from sitting. I stretch my legs out. I listen for the sound of radio waves, when they come, they sound like the ocean. Suddenly I hear something, the dots and dashes respond to my message, it is repeated, it is received, a few taps and it's over. I turn the set off and wait for it to cool before I fold it into the case and close it.

Now I must hide the radio and find my way back home. And Robert needs to listen out over the next few days for the *message personnels* on the BBC. I pack up and get on my bicycle, I'm tired, it's nearly one in the morning. I check my watch, that was thirteen minutes, but they'll know I'm in the area. The radio detectors will scour the area every night, and if I don't move around every time, they'll find me. I'm convinced the Gestapo won't catch me, but I try to pull back my enthusiasm because I know being over-confident can lead me into trouble.

Behind the bocage hedgerows it's so quiet, the wind blows gently through the trees. I'm glad the nights are not as cold. There's a flutter in the tree canopy above which makes me skittish. It's just another bat or a bird settling in its nest. I need to get out of this area. The moon comes out from behind a cloud to guide me home. It only takes me twenty minutes to get home to Maria's, it's downhill most of the way. All lights are off in the dairy. I squeeze my bike through the side gate and scratch myself again on the brambles. I don't notice so much as I'm so tired, I hardly feel it. I put my bike against the wall and the radio in the shed under a load of turnips. I should have dropped the radio off at the derelict farmhouse as Robert instructed, it's safer there, but I'm too tired to do a detour. I feel a bit lonely when Robert's not here. I won't refuse his help next time.

The embers in the grate give off a small glow and keep the room warm. I hurry upstairs to bed. Maria is asleep on her bed, but she looks cold. I put another blanket over her that Robert's mother sent. I go to bed and am sound asleep by two am.

Chapter 16

In Robert's house it's 9pm. Mila is in bed. Robert and his mother listen to the radio with the sound turned low. His mother makes sure the door is locked and the curtains are closed. They sit quietly listening. She sits knitting, her thin, grey hair pulled back against her head. She's had a stressful life. First her husband was killed in the Great War, and now she is without her only daughter who died in childbirth. It's more than she can stand sometimes. But like any woman she must accept it and do the best she can caring for her granddaughter and son in law.

The set is in the parlour, a contraption in polished wood with Bakelite knobs and semicircular tuning dial. Robert tunes it carefully, the volume turned down low, his ear close to the speaker.

A voice announces; 'Ici Londres.' A voice from a world away, 'Les Francais parlent aux Francais.'

The correct news is always reported, good or bad. There wasn't much good news to report in the beginning of the War. The French listen to the BBC news from London because it's the truth. The French media, newspaper and radio are in German hands.

The news comes first about bombings in Germany. The tide of the war is turning, particularly after Stalingrad. Hitler spreads his armies too wide, and the Russians still survive in a decimated city amongst the rubble. It's illegal to listen to the BBC so the French do it under blankets and out of view of neighbours who may report them to the *Milice*, for their own personal benefit. At seven fifteen the messages begin:

'Before we begin, here are some personal messages.'

Then the absurd messages follow.

'*Grandmother has bought the artichokes. The clouds of autumn bring winter rains.*'

The message comes back loud and clear twice in the middle of a load of nonsense messages, each phrase means something to *résistance* groups far and wide - it means only something to their group and no one else.

'*Michel s'en va en dix minutes.*'

Michel is leaving in ten minutes.

'There, they've responded.' Robert smiles at his mother. 'I'll let Henri and the others know. The *parachutage* is on.'

On the night on which a drop is to take place the same message is repeated on the nine fifteen news bulletin to confirm that nothing untoward has happened since the earlier bulletin at seven fifteen to prevent the operation taking place, and that the drop is actually going ahead. Anything could have cropped up in between the two bulletins; weather conditions might have suddenly deteriorated, or HQ might have received news that the reception committee feared that they were under suspicion and that the drop would fall into enemy hands, or the members of the *réseau* expecting the drop had been arrested or were in hiding. Should the confirmation not be broadcast, the operation is automatically cancelled.

It takes time to organise these drops, especially since they are taking place every night during the moon period. The ten to twelve nights each month when the moon is bright enough for the pilots to navigate by to the numerous *réseaux* is busy, not only in France, but in every other German occupied country.

Before a drop can take place, the leader measures and prepares the landing zone. The *résistants* make ready on the ground before the aeroplane arrives to collect and dispose of the supplies dropped. If there is a problem with automobiles or petrol, the *réseau* will turn up in anything they could beg, steal, or borrow, and often it's a horse and cart.

It's repeated at nine fifteen. *'Michel s'en va en dix minutes.'*

Robert is talking to Henri in the early morning.

'At last our group can swing into action. We are all glad to be doing something finally. We'll be dropped desperately needed supplies. And everyone will be happy.'

The sun is starting to come up and light is spreading across the sky, and there is no one about.

'Who's doing it this time?' asks Henri.

163

'Me, the Maquis, Laurent and Gaston.

'Not Emily?'

'No. We have to keep our *piano* out of harm's way this time.'

'You're not making a good job of it. Here she is.' He points his cigarette behind Robert's shoulder. He turns around and sees Emily cycling up to the bakery and round the back of the boulangerie.

Robert sighs, and walks quickly to his bakery, as Henri smiles to himself.

* * *

Robert counters me as I enter the bakery from the back door.

'You've started without me.'

'Emily it's six am. What are you doing here? Remember we said, 'Keep out of sight?'

'You need help.' I remind him putting on my apron.

'But I need you to keep safe and not show yourself around the town, otherwise the Boche will keep coming here to see you and your cover will be blown. By the way, the drop is on.'

'Am I?'

'What?'

'Lovely.'

He shakes me by the shoulders, and I smile at his angry face. He appears angry, as angry as Robert can get, which isn't very angry.

'You're infuriating. What am I going to do with you?'

'Kiss me? Well, you might as well. There's no one here yet.' And so, I lean forward and kiss him. He starts to pull away, but I put my arms around his neck and pull him down. The doorbell rings and we look up to see Oberleutnant Sachs standing in the doorway.

'Well, it is springtime after all,' I say.

* * *

It is midday and warm for April. Giselle is cycling at a steady pace past the German soldiers who walk around the town square. She cycles past the police station quickly, but not too quickly in case she attracts too much attention. Just as she reaches the road that leads out of the town, she stops to let a German car go past.

'*Arrete! Mademoiselle Halte!*'

She daren't look round. But she does with irritation. She hadn't expected to be stopped and looks annoyed but her heart's beating fast.

'You have dropped your jacket from your basket.' A young German soldier speaks in French to her as he walks over to her and hands the cardigan to her from the ground.

'Oh, *merci, monsieur.*' A sigh of relief. She is grateful. Not too grateful. She takes it off him. That would give him a false idea that she is interested in him. He smiles that naïve smile of youth. He can't be more than eighteen. She's nineteen and feels like ninety. She's seen too many of her friends killed or taken away to camps. This one is innocent. But won't remain so. The German soldiers seem to be getting younger and younger. Only a Frenchman will do for her. But there are no young Frenchman left in the town, and her Jean-Pierre too has gone.

She holds her breath and continues to cycle on down the road, hoping she doesn't get stopped again. This time she makes sure her cardigan is pushed down into the basket. She reaches the dead letter drop. An ancient milestone set back a few metres from the road. It's at the junction of an old road that leads to the forest and the Maquis. To the South the road leads to a town called Lison a few kilometres away. She looks to see if anyone's around. She takes off the grip on her handlebar and slides out a piece of paper with the information. Looking around again, she gets off her bike and walks over to the milestone, and behind is a hole where she pushes the paper very carefully. The Maquis will check the dead letter drop at least once a day and find a message, which is from Robert, to say the *parachutage* is on tonight.

Giselle gets back on her bike and turns around and cycles the way back to town. She is going back to work. She works at the funeral parlour in Saint Just. It's a busy place and she does all the paperwork there. It's getting busier. She tries not to look at the open coffins when Albert, her boss, dresses the deceased. It used to be mostly old people who died, but since she's been working

166

there, there have been younger people in the coffins. Her parents were taken by the *Milice* as they were sympathisers with the Free French government. She has no idea where they are. Most likely in one of the German prison camps.

Albert is a kind man and in his sixties. He's sympathetic to the *Résistance* cause too. He offered her this job when her parents were taken. And he tries to shield her from the ravages of war. Most of the deceased have met violent or suspicious deaths, but Giselle knows better than to ask him questions.

She arrives on her bike back at the funeral home after her lunch break on her bike. She will take over the telephone and typewriter while Albert has a rest around this time. He waves to her as she comes in and lays her bike against the wall and next to an empty coffin. He's preparing it for the next person.

* * *

Henri is a middle-aged bar owner, he is part of the local résistance movement, and a friend of Robert. He tries to be a cheerful person, even though he sees some terrible things in his bar. For example when the *Milice* drag a poor unsuspecting man away for the *Service du Travail Obligatoire*, if he resists he is beaten up. The *résistants* use Henri's bar for passing messages. Since Stalingrad there have been more people who want to join the *résistance* movement, they have asked Henri if he knows of any *réseau* they can join, not realising he is actually one of the *résistants*. He wonders how long it will be before the Gestapo discovers he is one of them. For the time being he feels he is on borrowed time. When the German soldiers come into his bar the locals stop talking. On the way home from work the farmworkers and other labourers will stop off at Henri's bar for their coup de rouge. The message about them meeting at midnight tonight will be passed onto those who need to be at the drop.

One dirty looking man in raggedy clothes emerges from the forest whistling as he walks down a track towards the road. He stops at the ancient milestone. He plays the part of a vagrant. He must be careful that he doesn't get caught by the Boche. Looking both ways he sticks his hand in the dead letter drop, gets it out and pockets it. Satisfied there's no one around, he reads it. He's really a friend of Robert's, and although looks old, he isn't, he's thirty-years-old, and like Robert a veteran of the present war with the Germans. He's an experienced soldier escaping the *Milice* when they came to get him to take him to a German camp for slave labour. He has just made himself look like a vagrant; he was previously an accountant before the war. To save being sent to Germany for the *Service du Travail Obligatoire*, he hid himself in the forest with the rest of the Maquis. His parents don't know where he is and it's safer that way. One day he'll come out and tell them, after the le jour de la liberation. He goes back the way he came, a bit quicker now, to get out of the vicinity of the road, and people who might see him.

Back to his comrades, the *Maquis* in the local forest. He shows them the message he retrieved from the dead letter drop — it says to meet at a house on the edge of the forest where someone will take them in pre-arranged transport to the destination of the parachute drop.

Chapter 17

Behind us are the flat fields of the flood plain of the river Vire and the escarpments of the forests. We drive west where the sun has set, its blood red rays merging in with the darkness of the night. We arrive at a deserted old barn five kilometres outside Coutances on an old road. This is our meeting place where Robert will lead us, Maquis and *résistance*, to our next parachute drop.

We stop and pull up at the shed. Robert and I look from our vantage point in front of an old barn, empty but for the sake of some hay bales two old paraffin lamps and extinguished cigarettes. A prime example of a secret hideout for Maquis if ever there was one, I tell Robert we shouldn't leave the cigarette ends on the floor - it's a dead giveaway that it's a meeting place for *résistants*. I am a bit anxious about meeting the Maquis who live in the forests around here, I've heard stories of how tough they are and rather rough looking.

It's a mild night, the full moon is out and flitting behind clouds. Two vehicles draw up to the farm and off the road, a van and a truck. A crew of Maquis file out of the vehicles. There are about fifteen men in all.

The driver of the van is a bushy, black-bearded man who stands nearly seven feet tall. His size belies his agility because he jumps nimbly down from the cab.

'Ho, Robert, how come you always have a beautiful lady with you?' It's a very distinct French accent that I can hardly understand. This man is not from around here. Robert shakes his hand. Eight men from the Maquis in a variety of worn-out worker's clothes and cloth caps appear from the body of the truck. Some wear worn-out French uniforms. Some wear leather jackets like Robert, a vestige of the French army. Everyone is friendly, they all know each other. This is a better meeting than the last one I had with the *réseau*. I start to feel more positive.

'This is Bear,' Robert introduces me to him, and we shake hands, his hands are surprisingly gentle.

'We fought side by side at Dunkirk.' I can see they are all particularly good friends, as some of them come up to me to shake my hand too. I rub my hands surreptitiously on the backs of my trousers as some of their hands are greasy.

'Come into the barn,' Robert signals to them.

'I brought Bertrand's meat truck, but I've covered up the name. Just in case. We should have enough room to put everything in,' Bear tells him.

In the barn, I meet the other members of the group. The men look huge against the lanterns hanging from the beams. The unctuous smell of gasoline and cigarettes hangs around the barn.

They pass around a brown bottle and drink from it taking great swigs. Most have an old pistol or two which they have cocked in the waist of their trousers. They growl at each other and wink at me as Robert prepares his model of cups on an old wooden table in the middle. I'm the only woman present, and of our small *réseau* there is Robert and I, Laurent, Eric, and Pierre. They are in jovial mood, joking with the Maquis. Usually, the radio operator stays out of harms way on a *parachutage,* but Robert says I am to help this time to see how things work. I suddenly feel overwhelmed by the stale smell of sweat and cigarettes. I decline their offer of half a cigarette. I am a bit dubious where it came from.

On the table Robert places two cups to show the location of the farm building and the barn on the other side of the drop zone. Then he draws tracks in the sawdust with his finger to show the path of the aeroplane and the line that the men's torches must make. It is a large bomber, he doesn't know what make, but it will be heaving out ten large containers, with ammo, guns, and boots. No one is to move from his designated spot until they have all landed, it's too dangerous to be underneath the heavy containers.

Robert looks at his watch. 'Emily, you and I will go in the first car. It's a fifteen-minute drive to the drop, then we walk. Follow me. No talking from now.'

The men stamp their feet. Their boots are falling apart. No wonder there is such a heady smell. No wonder Robert has asked for boots on the drop.

The car engine strains against the slope, with three men in the back and two of us in the front, the Citroen van, its faint headlights, vaguely showing the ghostly hedges and the rough tarmac of a road which soon surrenders to gravel. We climb up the hill for a while, and then find ourselves looking over the sea on the horizon. We hide the van under a hedgerow and get out and walk the rest of the way. We follow Robert in single file down a narrow path beside a field in which six cows stand like stone statues. It's unusual to have that many cows still alive. There's no noise at all for some time, until some small animal comes out of the undergrowth to the side of me and makes me jump. Eventually we emerge on to the rim of a large clearing, which I can just see in the dark is surrounded by trees. When we arrive it's nearly one-thirty am. The moon tries to show itself through the clouds. The men stamp their feet and cough cigarette smoke.

'It may be a Whitley or a Halifax this time,' I say to the men near me, my eyes searching the skies. 'The pilots are young but have at least two hundred hours night flying time behind them so they can fly without lights, navigating only by the moon, following the course of rivers, church steeples, cathedral spires, chateaux.'

Robert nods, he's impatient to impart information, and for me to understand.

'The letter tonight is P. Only you and I and the pilot know this. If it's anything else, he'll fly off. He might think it's a trap or we've been compromised if you send the wrong letter.'

'It's okay Robert, I know morse for 'P'. I peer through the gloom trying to see his facial expression wondering why he is going into specifics. Then I realise he is actually nervous – his voice is shaky, and he doesn't look at me. 'Normally the *piano* wouldn't come but I need you to help organise things if I am not here.'

'What do you mean if you're not here?'

'If I get captured.' Then he changes the subject and tries to sound cheerful. 'It's important not to underestimate the value of a successful *parachutage*. It boosts everyone's spirits. Especially as we lost Jean-Pierre last year.'

Robert opens his case and takes out four torches, testing each one in turn and issuing instructions like a commander ordering his troops into action. Underfoot the grass is damp away from the trees.

'Emily, are you all right to send the code and count all the parachutes?'

'Of course.'

This is a side of Robert I hadn't seen before, he is obviously trying not to appear nervous in front of all of us.

Ghostly shadows move quietly across the dark countryside. The moon comes from behind a cloud suddenly lighting up the scene below. No one talks. My ears strain for sounds in the night. There's the sound of birds in the woods, an owl hooting, and birds fluttering, then silence.

On a damp, cold and dark night a Halifax leaves its base in the south of England, there are six men on board. And ten containers carrying valuable cargo for the French *Résistants* waiting for them across the Channel. They fly high over the flak then start to descend as they fly over Normandy. Leaflets fall out of the belly of the aeroplane, scattering propaganda to the French citizens below. Then onward to a pinpoint position to drop the valuable cargo.

We wait patiently. My eyes strain to make out a dark shape, and after a few seconds I hear it. Under the clouds is a four-engine bomber, the sounds rising and falling on the breeze, then settling louder to a steady growling noise. The men strain to see sit in the sky as the noise grows. I point my torch into the night sky. A flashing of the letter P – dit dah dit - and the answer comes back, a small star blinking in the blackness.

That's it!' says Robert. 'Let's go.'

He turns on the first torch, and the other men set off the other torches. It does a U-turn, and we face it as it turns towards us, hanging from its wings like an eagle stooping to its prey. Tilting in the flow of air, the shape grows larger and larger. The green light goes on as the correct sign is acknowledged and containers are pushed out of the hatch two at a time. Most of the parachutes open like dandelion seeds in the wind, but one doesn't and comes crashing down and splits, its cargo of guns spilling everywhere. The Maquis run out from their places towards the containers, and our valuable cargo. In our excitement, we forget to be quiet, Robert shushes us as we run like children picking up candy. One container lands in the next field, and two more, we all run like our lives depend on it.

'There's the tenth.' I call to Robert. He sees the last container fall at the end of our field, and we run to get them. We break open the containers. There are boxes full of guns, ammo, and plastic explosives. Hands break open the boxes, and hands grab the guns and ammunition and take the containers away to bury them out of sight. I grab some bright yellow bags that have plastic explosives inside. Other hands try to take it off me. I shout at them:

'Non! I am going to show you how to use the *plastique* properly. Otherwise, it could endanger lives.'

One of them turns to Robert:

'Englishmen are losers. And Englishwomen even more.'

'I am French,' I tell the accuser indignantly.

'In the wrong hands it's deadly,' he explains to them. Next minute Robert shoves a pistol in my hand, a .45 calibre Colt automatic pistol.

'For you, from one of the containers,' he says.

'But I refused one before I left.'

'Take it. Just in case. I'll sleep better.'

I tuck it into my trouser waistband like the rest of the Maquis. I run with glee amongst the containers, finding tins of beans and cigarettes, and taking what I can before they haul them off to the truck.

The containers are heavy, but the men seem to make light work. We shout with excitement as we continue to open the canisters. There is canned food, cigarettes, and boots. It's like Christmas. In the exhilaration of the moment, we clap hands and laugh and light cigarettes. Robert stuffs a bag in my hands. 'Hide this.' The sweat is standing out on his forehead, he looks stressed. I stuff it down my jacket.

'Hurry hide the parachutes over there! We don't have time to smoke. Get the stuff out of here!' He shouts at the men, waving his arms about, the parachutes must be hidden of course. With the speed of movement of the containers I can tell they've done this before in this same field. I put out my cigarette in the damp grass. Two of the Maquis help Robert roll them to hide two more containers in a hole in the corner of the field. One of them muttering under his breath he wants the silk for his girl. Robert won't let him have it. The man seems to give in, for now.

The guns, food and boots are dragged under the shadow of the trees, with men trying on boots, opening cans of beans, and consuming them out of the can, they sound so hungry with the slurps and noises penetrating the calm. By the time Robert has returned from the edge of the field, the boxes of ammo, food and cigarettes are on the truck. Bear talks to Robert they nod to each other. Robert gives the plastic explosives to Bear for safe keeping.

Then the trucks zoom off leaving no evidence there has been any drop at all.

'Is everything present and correct?' I ask him.

'You hid the cash I gave you?'

'Yes, here in my jacket. I also found the crystals for the spare radio. Although I haven't checked them out yet.'

'Good. Then everything's present. That's why I brought you along. So, you'll know what to do if I am not here.'

'If you're caught, we won't go through with the *parachutage*.'

'You have to. At least you have Eve and Gaston. If they're dropping more guns, you'll need to organise it. They dropped only one Sten Mark II. I want more of those.'

'But I thought I was to lie low.'

'You will from now on. I can only rely on you and Eve to organise things. Eve and Giselle will pass information to Henri, Gaston and the Maquis.'

'How long will it take them to trust me?'

'I trust you. So they'll trust you.'

On the return journey we split up, it only takes half an hour on the main road, but we use the back roads to Saint Just which takes an hour.

At 3am Laurent is dropped off at the corner of the main road on the junction to his parent's farm. As he walks down the road whistling in the bright moonlight, a black Citroen Traction Avant pulls up at the side of him.

Chapter 18

The evening sun is at our backs as a group of *résistance* fighters on the edge of the forest is having target practice.

'*S'il vous plait, votre attention!*'

I am waving at a group of men talking to each other; I am desperately trying to capture their attention. Eve puts two fingers in her mouth and does the shrillest whistle I've ever heard. Standing right next to me I go deaf for a moment. They all stop and stare at us. You can hear a pin drop now.

'Listen up!' Eve shouts at them, 'You might have time to waste, we don't. Emily's going to show you how to use plastique and the Sten gun.'

A voice pops up, 'I already know how to use them.'

'For those who don't,' she emphasises.

'Thanks Eve,' I launch into my talk, Sten gun in bits and at the ready to demonstrate.

'I thought Robert was going to show us. He's had more experience.' Girard pipes up. His comrades nod silently. They are secretly afraid of Eve, but she doesn't stand for any nonsense.

'He can't, and Emily's been trained by experts. Now listen to her. Especially you Girard!'

He glares at her but doesn't contradict.

'It's true. Most of us know how to shoot,' another says plaintively.

'Shut up and listen to her! Your life could depend on it!' She stares the incalcitrant down. It goes quiet. All eyes are on me.

'Right. One Sten gun – three pieces, barrel, body and butt.' Once I am into the flow it's quite easy and I pretend I am talking to children.

'But it's no good without the…magazine.' I click it in. 'Balance it on your wrists. As you can see it sticks out at right angles to the gun.

'It makes a good bag holder,' says Girard.

'Don't put your handbag on it Girard, it'll tip over.' I counter. A snigger goes around. I continue unhurried.

'It can be hidden very easily and put together easily.'

I put the Sten together so they can all see. I look up to see all faces now attentive.

'You hold it like so, if you don't hold it securely because of its light weight, then it's a waste of time. It tends to backfire, and you can lose two fingers. The ammunition magazine is fitted on the left-hand side. So, if you're left- handed you must get used to it. It can be fired in single or in bursts. Good for close quarter fighting. We'll be firing in bursts today. Single shots tend to get jammed. The magazine takes time to load, but keeping it loaded weakens the spring. Just bear that in mind. So, on the *le jour de la liberation*,

181

it's best to keep them loaded.' I show them how to aim it without a magazine

'We all need to practice putting each Sten together and taking it apart. Bear will take a group and practice on our straw dummy over there.' I point to a straw man dangling from a post.

'Just one round of ammo each, because we don't have enough of it to go around yet. Bear?'

Bear jumps up and starts organising them into two groups. He takes one group, and I take the other. I am glad he takes most of the experienced Maquis. I organise my group in a line, a Sten with each person and we practice taking them apart and putting them back together. Eve, Pierre, Eric, Giselle, join my group and two new young joiners from the town, brothers, Jacques, and Alain.

'Well done,' Eve whispers to me.

'Once I am concentrating, I am not so self-conscious,' I say. We're interrupted by shouts from Bear. He hoicks the gun to waist level and lets off a round of shots aimed at the straw man forty metres away. The insides of the straw splatter everywhere. We all stand still in shock and awe. Bear is revelling in his drama and suspense.

'You!' he points at Benoit. Benoit stands to attention and takes his gun, aims, and shoots a volley of shots off. The first volley of shots hits the straw man, Benoit is congratulated by his group. Eve shoots the next volley, and they go wide hitting a tree and sending shards of splinters shooting in all directions. I re-aim for her and set her arms right. Rat-a-tat-tat, the Sten gun shakes around, but she keeps control and this time she hits the straw man. Sweat running from her brow she is smiling from ear to ear.

'Well done you shot a German,' I tell her. 'The parachute drop dropped six Suppressed Sten guns. I am going to have one, and I think you should have one as well. Although noisy, you can shoot individual-like shots in *semi-automatique,* which will be more helpful to us.' I point at me then her.

'Why is that?' she asks.

'It's more precise. Slower, I think, more for shooting sentries rather than groups of soldiers. More for a one-on-one scenario. We would be best to keep it near the front door but hidden perhaps kept in your barn, for easy accessibility but not so Mauvais will see it.

Benoit calls us to follow him to the river. He takes us all to a point in the river where he tells us he and his friends have dropped a pile of stones years ago so that anyone can cross there at waist height. I can't see the stones because the water is dark, and the river flows rapidly this side of the river. But the water glints in the sun as it topples over from rock-to-rock tumbling downriver.

'It was a quick crossing when we were kids,' he explains. It saved us going kilometres out of our way around on the road.'

'Genius Benoit. But how do you cross with it flowing so fast?' asks Eve.

'In winter it's dangerous, one of my friends was swept away years ago. In summer, it's safer and it cuts off a lot if you're up to braving it. But by the look of all the rain we've had, it's too high to cross now. We'll have to wait until another day when it's gone down.

'I'll show you!' Girard suddenly dashes off and climbs down to the sandy bank where the oxbow cuts away into the bank and swerves off to the other side of the river further down. It looks deep here, unknown boulders are strewn down river, it's dangerous to even attempt to cross.

The river is wide here, I can see the vegetation clearly on the other side of the river, so near yet so far. It's about forty metres to the other side. Girard wades out to the depths and using his feet he feels his way at the bottom, his foot finds a hard rock and he gingerly makes his way across the swirling river from stone to stone. We stand in awe as he struggles to push his bulk against the flow, at one point he almost loses his balance, it looks like he will be swept away, but he reaches the other side and we sigh with relief as he jumps up onto the bank. He waves at us. Benoit decides to do it next, and he waves back to us and shouts when he gets across.

'Well done!' Eve shouts to them. She turns to me and says, 'I thought they was going to get swept away!'

We turn to hear shouts behind us and see Robert hurrying towards us from across the field.

'It's Laurent, he's disappeared!'

Chapter 19

I cycle over to Robert's house late afternoon the next day the sun has heated up the day and I'm perspiring by the time I get there and out of breath. Before arriving in Normandy, I spent several months of daily vigorous exercise in the highlands of Scotland training for SOE, I need to keep cycling to keep fit. It's taken me an hour to get to Robert's house only one road passes their house and I follow it from the edge of town.

I see Stephanie sitting on the bench outside in the shade. In her calm usual way, she is sewing with Mila playing with her doll on the floor. She looks up and points her finger to her lips as a sign to keep quiet. I acknowledge with a nod of the head. There's usually no outward sign of affection from Robert's *maman*, but she is a stoic and resolute woman. And the two times I have cycled over to visit her are genuine times I have come to seek her companionship and because I am lonely at times too. She seems to realise this, and we sit in the sun in a companiable way.

This time I hear voices raised inside. I hear a woman's voice raise to hysteria and the next minute Yvette comes storming out of the front door with Robert following her. Now I notice her bicycle on the inside of the gate. She has come a long way to see him, and I can guess what it's about. She doesn't even acknowledge me as she pushes her bike to the road with tears in her eyes and rides off furiously. I stand there with my mouth open and raise an eyebrow at him.

Mila watches Yvette with confusion on her face and she tugs at her father's hand.

'Yes, *mon enfant.*' He absentmindedly holds her hand watching Yvette cycle off.

'She is distraught,' he says to us. 'Laurent was picked up by the authorities, she fears he's been taken for *Services du Travail Obligatoire*. Because he's so tall they think he is older than sixteen.'

'What can we do?' I ask.

'I have promised to find him,' Robert answers, 'But I can't guarantee to get him out of the *Milice*'s clutches.'

I pull him back by his hand as he walks towards his van. 'But you can't go, they'll take you as well!'

'That's what I told him,' says Stephanie.

I stand in front of his van blocking his path. 'Think about this Robert! They won't believe their luck if you walk into the *Gendarmerie,* looking for someone who has been taken for STO. They won't let you out. Let someone else go.'

I know it can't be me, because the *résistance* can't afford to risk a radio operator arrested. He stands and thinks about it as Mila looks up at him holding his hand. She's upset by this outward emotion by the adults around her. I look down at Mila.

'Don't go. For Mila's sake.'

He looks down at her. Mila looks cute with her ponytail tied up with a big red bow, and a dress, made by her grandma. Mila looks up at her father and from him to me. She looks up at me imploring with big brown eyes, confusion clouding her little innocent face.

'But I'm the leader.'

'Let someone else do it for once,' I counter. 'You can't do everything.'

Chapter 20

Robert studies the Wehrmacht officers who sit outside under the colourful umbrellas eyeing up the women outside Henri's bar, as they walk past. He sits at the bar waiting for Henri to finish serving a customer. He comes back to Robert, and they look out, watching the German officers carefully.

'You didn't go to beg for Laurent then?' Henri says under his breath.

'No, Gaston has gone to try and find out where he is.' Robert shifts uncomfortably on his stool so he can see out of the window into the street.

'How are you doing for places to transmit from?'

'Emily is cycling around the countryside before curfew, she is finding her way around. She's doing very well, as I'm not always able to assist her. She has proven to be very resourceful. But then she runs the risk of getting caught with her radio. I take them with me in the van where I can. But she's less likely to be stopped if they think she just has food shopping in the basket.

'Can you pass this on to our friends when they come in?' He passes a message under his breath to Henri and Henri nods.

'We have to ask for another drop and some heavier artillery.'

Suddenly there is a commotion outside the café on one of the tables. Two men in blue jackets and brown trousers walk up to a patron at a table and seize him putting his hands behind his back knocking his coup de rouge on to the ground. The man protests vigorously, but nothing will stop the Nazi machine once the cycle gets going.

Robert cursed, 'It looks like the Milice are taking him for STO. Poor man must be my age, about forty?'

Henri goes outside to pick up the cup and see what he can say in the man's defence. But they ignore him and drag the man off before Henri can get to them, with the man struggling between them.

'He was in the wrong place at the wrong time.' Henri says to his friend. 'The Germans are desperate to recruit more men. Their losses were heavy in Stalingrad. I hear our young men are being used to reinforce the coastal defences against invasion.'

'That is ironic considering the Nazis were the invaders at Dunkirk,' Robert says, and in a lower voice. 'I will be disappearing today Henri, to join the Maquis.'

'Go soon, my friend,' says Henri.

Then Robert steps out into the bright sunshine. *Poor sod*, he thinks about the man that has been just taken. *Here one minute, gone the next*. Then he turns up the street and walks back up to his bakery. It was time to go home and see his family. As he turns the corner into the Rue de la Poterne the boulangerie is in view and outside waiting for him are two men in signature raincoats and Trilbies. It's Gestapo. It's too late to run, they've seen him.

Chapter 21

Major Hans Weber likes to study human nature. He sits in the corner of the bar his hat next to a glass of red wine which he feels has been watered down, it isn't what he's used to. He is used to drinking the finest reds nowadays. Those that have been taken from the wine cellars of the chateau that the Gestapo had just invaded outside Saint Just. But that doesn't bother him. What bothers him is the *résistants* evading capture.

They still haven't found out who had shot one of the soldiers from the garrison, although they've taken lots of young men in retaliation and shot them. That was his idea. Then he got his wrists slapped by his commandant and was told the *résistants* could have gone to work down the German mines; an even worse fate, from which there is no return. Those that are strong still may succumb to dysentery and disease, malnutrition, and dehydration.

Weber is in his element in a dark corner watching people as they come in and out of Henri's bar. He's watching some men talk to Henri over the bar. It gives Weber an opportunity to observe locals who come into the bar. He can't get the girl from Rennes out of his mind. He's not sure if she's authentic, but he decides it'll be fun finding out once he finds her, she seems to have disappeared off the face of the earth. Then he can't believe his luck when she actually appears in the bar.

* * *

The midday sun is overhead, and it's bright outside, coming inside you can't see for a while until your eyes adjust to the subdued light. I wave to Henri at the bar.

Henri notices Weber is in the corner of his bar today, someone else must have served him. Henri usually warns the locals when they came in with a flick of the head towards Weber in the corner. But he isn't quick enough with me.

'Bonjour Henri, have you heard anything about Robert yet?'

He shakes his head and leaning over he quietly speaks under his breath.

'Gestapo, twelve o'clock.'

With alarm I look behind Henri's shoulder and see an SS uniform but can't make out the face. Then I see it's the man Weber sitting in the corner quietly with his drink watching me. When he sees me, he moves towards us.

'Damn it. Wrong place wrong time.' I say to Henri under my breath.

'Friends have told me that Robert's not been seen yet being put on a train bound for Germany. As far as we know.' Henri continues under his breath. 'Eric told me the German train left last night, but he didn't think Robert was on it.'

'Well, that's good news at least. I have to go.' I walk away quickly, but Weber follows me out of the door.

'Mademoiselle Boucher, a moment please.'

It's too late to run away from him.

'Monsieur?'

'May I call you Emily?' His French is impeccable, with just a hint of German accent. I'm conscious of all eyes from the bar turn to watch us. I don't want to be associated with this man. No matter how nice he appears to me on the surface.

'You seem to know the man at the bar very well in the few weeks you've been here.'

'He's a friend of Robert's so he's a friend of mine.'

'Ah yes Robert. What brought you here today to speak to the barman? Because I saw that you came in specifically to see him.'

'No. Oh no, I am just asking him if the *Milice* have taken Laurent Sainson for *Service du Travail Obligatoire*. Do you know if they have? He's only sixteen, they shouldn't have taken him.'

Weber looks intently at my face, I hold my breath, they've shot people on suspicion before now. I look determined but he may also know the answer to my question. Can he see through me? He shakes his head.

'I don't know where he is.'

I don't believe him. I turn to go.

'If you do something for me, I could enquire.'

I hesitate, is it worth it? It depends on what he wants me to do. I look at his face seeing if I can see any truth in this enemy's blonde-haired, blue-eyed face. All I can see are some lines around his eyes which leads me to believe he smiles a lot. Probably when he's getting his own way.

'Accompany me this evening to *Le Strase.*'

There's nothing I'd like to do less. Particularly as it would be advertising the fact that I had likely become his whore. I know what *Le Strase* is; an up-market restaurant full of Germans, there's no shortage of wine or food there as they get it from the black market. I decline politely. Some girls would swear at him with insults, but I don't forget I am supposed to keep a low profile. If Robert found out, I'd been to Henri's bar and been stopped by Gestapo he'd be upset with me for making myself vulnerable. So I will have to rely on Oberleutnant Sachs, to hopefully get Robert out of danger. I decline. I have no intention of putting myself in danger.

'*Non*, I am not for sale.'

He is about to say something, and I interrupt and shout '*au revoir*' as I hightail it down the street towards the boulangerie.

I pick my bicycle up from inside the boulangerie; Robert left the back door unlocked. I check my radio at the bottom of the bicycle, I had brought it with me today because Robert was going to transport us to a rural location for me to transmit. It's now a liability and I have to get out of town quickly. I quickly cycle down the road towards the town square, realising I've just had a narrow escape from the Gestapo. He could have arrested me.

My heart is pounding as I take the road to Eve's house on the South side of the town, and I cycle at top speed going past two German soldiers in the town square.

'Halte!'

A soldier shouts to me to stop, which I am not going to do - or else they will discover my radio. There's a shout, and one of them sticks his gun out and knocks me clean off my bike. I yelp in pain as I topple over the handlebars. People in the town square stop and look. I land on the side of the road and on my side. I have torn the knees on my trousers, and I have scrapes all over my hands.

'I told you to stop!' the soldier shouts in French. I pretend to have hurt myself a lot more and stay on the ground. I am shaken up but give myself a minute to get my breath back. Out of the corner of my eye a big black Citroen pulls up the other side of the square. I take my time getting up.

'Everyone understands Halt.' He points his rifle at me. 'Get up!' he says in German. I pretend not to understand as my accident has started to attract a crowd. The onlookers come closer to us and are glaring at the two soldiers. I show the scrapes and the blood welling up on my knees so everyone can see. I rub my hip which is bruised so the growing crowd takes pity on me, they stand back to give me space. I feel the animosity towards the soldiers growing in intensity. I hear someone say, 'Quel enfoiré,' *What a bastard.*

I gingerly get up off the ground and try to sit on my bike. I see out of the corner of my eye a Gestapo in trench coat get out of the black Citroen, he leans on the car, and watches me as the crowd gets bigger. The two soldiers now warn the people to back off and I take that moment's loss of concentration from the soldiers to get back on my bike and zoom off towards an alleyway. They realise what I am doing.

Two shots are fired, but they miss me.

'Nicht Schiessen! Nicht Schiessen!'

Someone's shouting *Do not shoot,* in German. I don't know whose voice it is, but I don't stop, I keep going. I cycle down a street laid out for the markets as women in headscarves haggle with prices behind stalls that are covered in local produce. I pull in at a small entrance and hide my bike under a table draped with hand embroidered sheets. Tying a headscarf around my hair I bend down next to the woman seller as she looks at me askance. But she doesn't give me away as the German soldiers aren't far behind me, they shout at everyone to get out of the way. They run past the stall not seeing me, as a woman dressed as a local seller. In a moment I retrieve my bicycle and I nod at the woman and go back the way I came. Walking this time I turn towards my side of town and the embattlements. But then I see a black Citroen driving slowly towards me.

I cycle through the streets avoiding soldiers until I get to a rundown alley no wider than a small passageway, an area of narrow sloping lanes and crowded houses. On the corner is a small café used only by the local citizens and the *résistance*. Out of the alleyway the sun hits my eyes and I balk as the brightness bounces off the white wall. But it's dark in between the buildings because the roofs are askew and almost meet. It makes me blink a few times before my eyes can acclimatise to the shadows. The Ruelle du Nul is a run-down street, an area of narrow sloping lanes and crowded houses. It's a place where children run through chasing each other and hide away from the Boche. It isn't wide enough to run two abreast, but it's ideal to hide in the shadows, especially on a sunny day. If you walk past at the end of the road you can only see the silhouette of a figure.

That's why, when Madame Fisolee walks past and looks down the Ruelle du Nul, she doesn't see me squeeze up against a doorway. I peek my head out to see her marching down the street in the opposite direction. I breathe a sigh of relief. I knock on an unobtrusive door set back from the alleyway and hold my breath, is this the house they told me about? I am supposed to meet Robert here. A friendly face – but it's not Robert. It's Henri, with Giselle behind him.

'Emily. Something terrible has happened,' he says, and my heart sinks.

Giselle's pale face too shows anxiety.

'It's Robert. I saw the Gestapo take him away about two hours ago.'

'Oh no! He was going into hiding with the Maquis before that happened.'

Henri rubs his bald head.

'We think it's for STO. What can we do?'

'Where's his work extender permit?'

'I don't know, he'd have it on him?'

'Maybe not. I'll cycle to his mothers to see if she has it. They can't take him if he's been granted an exemption certificate, that's just not fair!'

'What are you going to do? You can't go into the *Gendarmerie*,' says Giselle ringing her hands. 'It's too dangerous. They could detain you.'

'Robert told you to keep out of sight,' says Henri.

'Maybe, but we have to do something. I'm going to see his mother.'

Before I know what I'm doing, I grab my bicycle and cycle off quickly towards Robert's house. It takes me thirty minutes to get there. Mila hugs my legs as Stephanie and I search for the permit. She finds it straight away.

'Here!' Stephanie holds it out to me and waves it. 'What will you do now?'

'Make sure he doesn't get transported,' I say. I hug them both and detach Mila from my legs. Wave goodbye and try and think. I'm not sure what to do. But as I cycle back along the road, a plan is forming in my mind.

I pass the bakery on my way to the *Gendarmerie*. A group of people are outside the locked bakery looking through the window, trying the door and looking for Robert.

Walking towards the town square is Oberleutnant Sachs. I cycle quickly towards him; I know what I need to do. I pull up in front of him, he puts his hands up as I almost cannon into him.

'Oberleutnant, please wait!' I get off my bike and step back. He frowns and moves a step away as if I might be a mad woman.

'They've taken Robert for *Service du Travail Obligatoire*, but he has an exclusion permit, you know. Well, I've found it. Please could you take it to the police station. I daren't go because the *Milice* hate me, and they'll rip it up. But they wouldn't dare turn you away with this proof.'

'I was coming to tell him that the garrison has its own bakers now.' He brushes the front of his uniform down as if I've tainted it.

'The *Milice* have taken him, but we hope he's not yet been sent on the train to the camps. You can help by stopping them!'

He hesitates. People are starting to slow down and look with interest at a woman talking in the middle of the town square with an Oberleutnant from the Abwehr.

'I could get into trouble trying to go against the authorities with this.'

'But we stick up for our friends, don't we?' I insist. 'You wouldn't want it to happen to any of *your* friends, would you?' I emphasise your and hold his gaze. He balks as I stick it in his hand as if it's repellent. 'We will do anything for our friends and loved ones. Am I right?'

I am trying to will some conscience into him.

'Please, I am desperate to try anything to help him. They'll listen to you.'

'All right.' He snatches it off me. 'But I can't promise anything!'

'Thank you!' I call to his retreating back. He doesn't look back.

Chapter 22

I watch the Oberleutnant as he disappears down the street and turn to see a black Citroen passing the *boulangerie* coming towards me. I don't know where to go at this point. I lean my bicycle against a shop window as I bend down to do up my lace and, in the reflection, I see a man in a raincoat watching from the other side of the road. He has the typical look of the Gestapo, brown coat, and trilby hat. Is he watching me or someone else?

I push my bicycle over to the base of where a statue had once been - The Femme d'lsigny – the bronze has been melted down at the beginning of the occupation for German arms. Out the corner of my eye I see him follow behind me, keeping his distance. I cross the square with my bicycle, take my bag out, and lean it against the wall of the church outside. I go up the steps. It's 13th Century with tall stained-glass windows of the Saints facing the square. I am just a young woman who has decided to go into the church to say prayers. Pushing through a curtain I find myself in the dark interior. As my eyes become accustomed to the shadows I look up at the roof and the Gothic structure, but down here amongst the pews it's dark and shadowy. I try to calm my breathing and look for a place to hide. There are only a few candles at the altar and down here, candles are too expensive to light all the time, so the church is locked at night. It's an ideal place to hide.

The skill is to throw the tail off without giving the impression that you know you are being followed. I look around at the glow of the flickering candles and the light streaming through the stained-glass window. It's quiet, there are whisperings and shifting shadows of people at their devotions.

On the right is a gilded sarcophagus, and the relics of a saint, on the left a side chapel where an old woman kneels at prayer. A priest is praying at the altar where there's a single candle. The medieval church is rich in history, and it is a survivor of the First World War and the French Revolution. I run up the aisle and through a door into the Chancel.

To the side of the altar is a door to the sacristy and to the opposite side tucked in a shadowy recess, a confessional. I walk round to the confessional, pull aside the curtain, put my bag inside and cram myself in after it. A musty darkness, silence, envelops me. I look through the gaps in the curtain forcing myself to calm my breathing. I see the Gestapo run down the central aisle, following my path. Did he see me enter the confessional? The man stands looking left and right. I hear the priest open the other side of the confessional and beside me the grille opens.

'Yes, my child?' The priest coughs, reminding me I must reply.

'Bless me, Father, for I have sinned.'

'When did you make your last confession, my child?'

It's easy to tell the truth in this situation. 'Years ago, Father.'

The man goes to the east in the shadows and stands indecisively by the tomb of the saint. I recognise him, he's definitely Gestapo. I can tell by the uniform - a raincoat and Trilby. He runs towards the sacristy and goes inside. He's panicking lest he should lose me. That would be embarrassing. Losing a girl? Should I make a run for it now while he is looking in the rooms there?

'What do you have to confess, child?'

A sudden sadness hits me.

'I don't love my husband.' There, the truth blurts out. There's no hint from me that he's dead though. Just a confession that's been needling me from the start. Did I ever love him? The answer to that is no.

The man comes out of the sacristy and looks around panicking. He screws his face up as if thinking. His shoes clicking on the stone slabs as he paces back and forth in front of the sacristy. He lurches off in the direction he came. My breath is more even. He marches back to the door looking left and right behind each pew. Then swipes past the curtain and gone.

The voice asks, 'Is there someone else?'

'Yes. Is that a sin Father?'

'It is my child. Do you love this other man?'

'I've changed my mind,' I feel obliged to say as I open the curtain and sneak out of the box. Putting my bag on my shoulder, I go out the sacristy door and out into the street. Leaving the priest behind me still talking to an empty box. I walk quickly away from the church without looking back, and quickly turn into a side street and into a doorway and look back. The man is not behind me. I wait five minutes; I can see my bike from where I'm standing. There are no men in long coats in the square as far as I can tell. I hope I'm merging with others in the square, I grab my bicycle and pedal as fast as I can towards home. I need to disguise myself, because the SS Major recognises me now with my coat and bicycle. It's getting late, there are less people in the streets now, it's nearly seven o'clock.

On the way home, I must cross the Vire bridge, there is a roadblock, cars and horse carts are queuing up to cross over to the other side. On the other side are German soldiers. They are checking people's cars and bags.

I start to walk over the bridge towards them. Then I see one of them wears a long coat and hat; it's Gestapo. I might fool the soldiers, but the Gestapo take a closer look at your identity card. I must find another route to Maria's house. I slow down unsure what to do, they may find my radio at the bottom under the clothes I have in my basket. After watching for a few minutes, one of them sees me staring from the other side of the bridge. Time to move.

Chapter 23

I turn back and cycle through the town to the North side of town and decide to lay low at Robert's house. It takes me nearly an hour to get to Stephanie's and it's dark. I'm exhausted by the time I reach the house and I knock on the back door, hiding my bike around the back. Stephanie immediately drags me in.

'I thought it was Robert!' she cries, and brushes away her tears, hugging me and trying not to show emotion at the same time. Mila comes out from hiding behind the door and runs to her.

'There's no news of him yet Stephanie. I've passed the certificate to a German friend, all we can do now is wait, and hope he's successful.'

Stephanie wipes her eyes, Mila is in her night dress. I smile at her, and she opens her arms to me and is trusting enough to come and hug me.

'Is papa coming home?' she asks me.

'Of course,' I say with conviction, 'It just might take a day or two.' What if he doesn't? What if Oberleutnant Sachs can't get the *Milice* to release him? It doesn't bear thinking about. I must trust my judgement and try to remain positive for everyone.

Stephanie smiles. 'I don't know what we would have done without you Emily. Thank you for trying to save him, whatever happens.'

I'm not so sure of that. Goodness knows what will happen. But we need our leader. I am fearful he may already be on a train to Germany. I have tried to stay stoic for their sake, but as time drags on, I'm worried. Am I too late to save him?

'It's after curfew Emily,' says Stephanie drawing the curtains. She takes my hand. 'It's too late to go back home. Please stay and have something to eat.'

'I am hungry so I may stay for a while, thank you. But I must get back to Maria tonight. She may wonder where I am.' I feel I should get back to see how she is, I feel responsible for her now.

'In that case, I'll show you a way to cut across fields, which is quicker and safer after curfew, and you shouldn't run into any patrols.'

Stephanie feeds me some ragoút she has left over she was keeping for Robert. It is dark when she draws a map on a piece of paper, it looks like it will save me time and angst as I'm less likely to run into Germans if I cut across the fields. It means following an old footpath that Stephanie used to take to Maria's house.

'It may be difficult pushing a bike in parts. But it's better than getting caught after curfew.' She says. I still have my torch in my basket, and my radio. I hug them both and set off to make my way westwards across fields to Maria's house.

I cycle for about five minutes down the road, the stars and crescent moon are hanging in the sky. Eventually my eyes get accustomed to the dark shapes of trees and shrubs looming up in front of me as I make my way carefully through a field making sure my torch is pointing down. I move slowly, it's a flat field but my front wheel meets tufts of grass, and this makes it difficult to push in the dark. It's heavy going and I'm perspiring by the time I cross the field. I'm unlikely to stumble across a sleeping cow here, all the Germans have taken them for food. I see the outlines of a cow with its feet in the air. It's dead and I can hear flies buzzing around it. The stench is awful. I bring up Stephanie's map with my torch and continue past another clump of dead trees, here the path narrows, I'm able to turn on my torch and show the narrow track following the line of trees for a while. The torch light is fading, I shake it and it flickers for a bit then goes out. I sigh, just my luck as I get to the most difficult bit. I seem to have everything pitted against me; Robert gone and the future of the réseau in jeopardy. I stop and let my eyes become accustomed to the shapes again.

I tread carefully westwards stumbling across fields and pastures with my bicycle for about thirty minutes until I come to an animal crossing. The effort makes me perspire even though it's a cool night. It's eerily silent as I push my bike across the road to the other side quickly and follow another track along the side of a field until I come to the start of some bocage hedgerows.

I hear droning in the distance, it's getting louder. Suddenly a large bomber passes overhead. It's so low that I gasp at the sheer size of it. It has no lights and I'm guessing it's an Allied aeroplane. I push on.

I vaguely recognise this area I've cycled past it before. It's the cobbled road that leads to the town from Maria's house. I turn northwards now get on my bike and my teeth rattle as I cycle over the cobbles down the road where eventually the dairy farm and Maria's house come into view. I feel very pleased with myself that my sense of direction hasn't let me down, and I've managed to negotiate across fields, away from the Nazis in the middle of the night without being caught.

Chapter 24

Maria is in her usual armchair in the parlour. She isn't well, she has a headache and tells me that the 'Milician pig has been here again. He told me he's coming back for you.'

A chill runs through me. It's time for me to move on. I may be better off making my way to Eve's. I change my clothes and cover the radio case with a load of vegetables from the shed. Watching me from the kitchen door she doesn't say anything, but her silence means she understands. She watches me packing my bicycle, and I feel guilty. I must leave her if I am to remain successful in my mission, and she knows this.

'You should come with me.' But I know she doesn't have the stamina to keep up. She'd never walk the distance to Eve's.

'I'll be all right. Just go and hide,' she tells me.

'I don't like leaving you.'

'Go!' she says.

'I'll be back as soon as I find somewhere. I'll come back and get you,' I tell her, but I am not sure how I will do that without transport to pick her up.

'Maria, let me make you more comfortable before I go. Will you go to bed?'

'No. Put me in my armchair near the kitchen fire.'

I sort her out making her comfortable and leaving some food and a drink next to her, I don't know when I'll be back and we both know this. Then I cover her with blankets, collect my belongings, light some candles next to her and leave.

'I was born here. I'll die here,' she says looking into the kitchen fire. Her eyes have lost their fight.

'You should leave now before they come back.'

I hug her and she tries to hug me back, but she doesn't have the energy. I get a lump in my throat.

'*Au revoir* Maria, you have saved an agent of France.'

I must leave her wrapped up in her chair her feet on a stool. I leave the curtains closed and ensure her rosary is wrapped around her fingers. I must get out of here before anyone comes. It's dark and I don't have long to get going before the enemy arrive. I make sure the front door is locked and the side gate accessible only to those who know.

Then I hear the car engine of a large car roaring its way over the cobbles and it's almost here. I go to my emergency exit behind the shed and lay my bike down horizontal and pull it through to the other side. The trees hide me from the dairy farm as I make my way behind them, I'm going downhill holding the front of the bike with the basket up and moving as quickly as I can. There is no noise coming from the farm or behind me. I move off noiselessly into the night.

The crescent moon lights the tops of the hedgerows, it is moving towards the horizon as the dawn approaches. I stand my bike up as torches shine across Maria's garden and I hear shouts behind me. The lights shine above the dairy farm wall, which means they're looking for me. Not a moment too soon, I think, if I'd stayed a minute or two longer, I would have been caught by the Gestapo. I keep going fearful they may be following me.

I push the bike through the long grass. The hedgerows are small here, it's hard going through, but I don't stop to look behind me. I can't hear anything now, and I say a silent prayer for Maria.

Running downhill now with my bag in the shopping basket and the bicycle is jumping drunkenly over the uneven ground. The weight of the radio in my basket is sending the bike bouncing in different directions. I'm trying to keep it altogether, then I reach a stream at the bottom of the dairy field. It's low, and possible to cross over. Thank goodness it's May, and it is slow moving and shallow. I push my bike over the stones to the other side of the stream.

I can see a road running parallel, so I get out of the stream, I get on my bike and cycle as fast as I can. The adrenalin keeps me moving. I can't hear anyone behind me, there is no one about.

The road is flat here and it looks like I'm cycling to the edge of town. Not really the place I want to be. I don't see much in front of me for a while as clouds move slowly over the moon. I suddenly hear a car and see the dim lights coming round a corner in the road in front of me. I jump off and quickly take my bike behind some hedgerows at the side of the road. A car goes sweeping past. I hold my breath. The hedgerow is part of the bocage. I push my bike along an ancient sunken lane, a *chemin creux,* the bushes either side of me will hide me for a while. It's an ancient cattle track that is low and covered by vegetation.

No sounds now in any direction. I follow the sunken lane for a while and lie down to have a nap, I am so tired I can't keep my eyes open. But eventually I get cold, and I have scratches all over me from the brambles scrambling through the hole in the hedge at Maria's. I hide myself in the hedgerow laying on my bag of clothes, I mean to rest for a few minutes, but I fall sound asleep.

I wake up after a while, cold and aching all over. The light of the dawn flickers through the bocage foliage. Looking into the growing light I recognise the castle ramparts of Saint Just are only two hundred metres in front of me and realise that I'm not far from Giselle's house. I need to get there as soon as possible before people move around and start their day. I make my way towards the town, cycling the rest of the way along the road. Nothing is moving and I can see the gargoyles on the west side of the battlements. I reach the outskirts of the town and hide in the remains of the battlements while I get my bearings.

Chapter 25

There are just two people in the street, but thankfully no patrols. I hope that Giselle is in. If I can wait out the day, then cycle to Eve's in the dark I may be able to escape the threat of the Gestapo on my tail. I knock as quietly as I can, careful not to alert anyone to look out of their window. I keep knocking until a hoarse whisper comes through the door.

'Who is it?'

'Giselle, let me in, it's Emily!' I hear the bolts pulled back slowly, and a tired face looks out at me. I push open the door and push her roughly out of the way as I pull the bike in after me and shut the door. She is angry.

'For God's sake! What are you doing here?'

'The *Milice* are after me and the Gestapo as well. I've had to leave Maria and I've got to hide the radio.' I still wasn't convinced she wasn't a *collaborateur* after I'd seen her with the Weber.

She bolts the front door behind me. 'You're soaking wet!'

'It's the dew, I had to sleep in the hedgerows, and I escaped by a stream from the back of Maria's house.'

'I'll get you a towel. You'll have to go upstairs.' She's unhappy about me turning up at dawn, especially as I'm bringing the mud with me, and my bicycle tyres make marks on her floor.

'Have you heard anything from Henri about Robert?' I ask in desperation.

'Nothing. We've heard nothing.'

'It's been two days,' I say forlornly. Perhaps the Oberleutnant wasn't successful in releasing Robert after all. I had been hoping he would be released. The full enormity of it hits me.

'It may be too late. I hope....' I get a lump in my throat, I am exhausted, and she looks with sympathy at me and leads me upstairs.

'You must lay low in here and stay inside while I go to work.'

'I am just so worried. About everyone. The *Milice* have been here already yesterday, looking for a whole bunch of people.'

She shows me to a small wooden bed in a small bedroom overlooking the courtyard out the back.

I had just gone to sleep what seemed like 5 minutes. And Giselle is shaking me awake.

'I am off to work. Do not answer the door. Do not make a transmission. There are RDFs around the town constantly. I'll see if I can find out from Henri any news.'

I breathe a sigh of relief. The sun is warm on the window, and I investigate the courtyard below at the back of her house, there's not many people about. I close the curtains.

I sit feeling numb trying to sort out my thoughts. I can't stay here I know that. I was right near the centre of town, a stone's throw from the *Milice* and the Gestapo. I will have to send my transmissions to London from somewhere like from a hilltop in the rural areas, at least I could see the enemy coming. I think if they can't contact Robert, I'll make my own way to Eve's farm to update her and then I'll hide in the forest. Perhaps even join the Maquis. I sleep until midday.

The curtains twitch as I look outside in the afternoon. There are some people walking through the courtyard. I am already going stir crazy.

Later, Giselle says goodbye to Albert, and gets on her bike and cycles to Henri's bar. As she gets there, she sees two German officers in his bar by the window. She tries to act casually and leaning in whispers to Henri over the bar.

'Henri, have you heard any news about Robert yet?'

Henri shakes his head. 'We haven't tracked him down yet. No one knows where he is. He may even be on a train headed for Germany.'

'You need to know that Emily is taking refuge in my house. You need to come and get her and move her out of the town. She's not safe in my house.'

Henri shakes his head. She sighs, says goodbye, and leaves abruptly, with the two German soldiers watching her go. While Emily is at her house, there is more danger for both of them.

Madame Fisolee suspects someone is inside Giselle's house. She's seen Giselle go to work. She thinks there are lights on. So she looks around the rear of the house in the courtyard which some of the taller houses back on to. She looks intently up at the windows; she is sure she can see a light on. She goes back around the front and knocks on the front door in the alleyway but there is no reply. She goes round the back, trying to look through the slats of the kitchen window at the back of Giselle's apartment.

It is late afternoon when Giselle gets to her front door as she pulls out her key to let herself in, a hand drops on her shoulder as she turns the key, she jumps, and quickly takes the first step up into the hall.

'Oh!' Madame Fisolee has fixed a hand onto her arm. Fisolee is trying to look through the hall to the kitchen beyond.

'I saw a light on at home, Giselle. Is it possible you left it on all day?'

'Possibly, I must have left it on by mistake. Thank you, *Madame.*' Giselle squeezes the door shut catching Madame Fisolee's arm in it. She retracts it quickly. Giselle storms through to the kitchen, lowering her voice, she is furious with me.

'What are you doing with a light on? Don't you know there's a war on?' she hisses at me. Giselle turns the single light bulb off in the kitchen, making it dark, so I light a candle. 'Fisolee was outside stalking up and down trying to see in. She suspects someone else is here.'

'Sorry Giselle, I saw you'd left it on, I didn't dare turn it off. Did you manage to contact Henri?'

'Yes. No one knows where Robert is. So, we have to wait.'

Chapter 26

While Giselle is at work the next day, I move the radio from the bottom of my bag of clothes to hide it. I still don't trust her, and I can't give her the benefit of the doubt. I hide it down the cellar inside a barrel and cover it with old bottles of wine. I thank Giselle's parents for leaving such an enterprising cellar. I hope it is hard to find if this place is searched. Anyway, if Giselle is acting as a double agent then it would be unlikely they'd examine her house.

That night as I lay on my sofa bed I can't sleep. I lay there listening to the crickets outside the kitchen window. I can't hear anything from Giselle's room, which is upstairs and has a nice view of the square at the back. It's warm in town, airless in this room, and I start to drift off to sleep.

Suddenly I hear loud banging on the front door. It's three am. My heart starts beating against my chest as I fling myself out of bed. I'm fully clothed as SOE taught us, so we can escape immediately in the middle of the night. The only people that force entry that time of the night are the Gestapo. It sounds like they'll break the door down. I must get out quickly. I look out of my window into the courtyard. The authorities don't know I am here. I am hoping that Giselle will hold off letting them in until I get away. I open the kitchen shutters and slip out like I had before, straight into the arms of a brown uniform. It's one of the *Milice*. He pulls my arms behind my back and presses me up against the wall. I feel sick, but don't say anything.

'Well, well. Look who we have here. Now why would you be trying to escape I wonder?' he says, handcuffing my arms behind my back. And shoving me in my back all the way round to the car at the front. He pushes me into the back of the car, and the next minute Giselle is pushed in beside me. We sit next to each other and try not to look at each other. She doesn't say anything. The *Milice* get in the front. We are both scared. Why have the *Milice* arrested her as well? Perhaps they don't know she is working for the Germans. We'll see.

Suddenly I see red and feel angry, it's not like me, but I start yelling at Mauvais.

'What is the meaning of this? This is an outrage!'

He looks at me behind him and smirks, which makes me even more angry.

'We are two hard working women trying to make a living and you are taking advantage of us.'

Mauvais smirks again as he looks at us behind him and Giselle glares at me.

'Mon dieu, shut up Emily.' She hisses at me. I am so tired and scared now, so I keep quiet. It was worth a try.

Deep in my heart I am hoping that I won't break too early, if they interrogate me, which they will undoubtedly. I automatically feel for the suicide pill in my pocket and realise it's in the lining of my coat pocket which I left behind.

As the police car drives us through the town, I wonder where they are taking us. They take us to a plain grey building with no windows next door to the Gendarmerie, where the Gestapo headquarters are, then I realise the reason they've chosen that building is because they have medieval dungeons that spring from next door's gaol, tunnels dug in medieval times. It's damp and dark down there, I've heard. There's one light bulb in the hallway and you wouldn't know it was Summer above. My heart sinks, I hate the dark. They're right. They drag us down steps to the depths of a dank, smelly gaol with small cells and thick walls and stick us in separate cells. I go flying in as Mauvais pushes me again and scrape my knees on the concrete floor. It's cold down here, it will never warm up. There's just a wooden bench to lay on, and my arms ache with being stuck behind my back the handcuffs. I sit on the bench and wait for what seems like hours but is probably only an hour. I decide to stick to my angry attitude and confess complete ignorance to anything they accuse me of.

Eventually, Mauvais bangs open the cell door and grabs me by the hair, before I know what he's doing he's pulled off my cardigan and skirt, I fight him off. But he hits me round the head and drags me out the cell with just my slip on, I become dazed as he forces me up two steps to another room. It is like a gaol cell, with a big bright light bulb in the middle of the room.

I look upwards to a small window the bright sunlight shines through the gap making me squint. There are metal rings hanging off the wall and a length of rope hanging from the ceiling. I swallow some bile, and my heart is racing. This scene reflects mock-up interrogations we did in SOE, so I know what's to come. Even so I am still shaking. Mauvais forces me to sit in a chair and ties my feet together. There's a smell of stale urine and sweat in the room. I see a bath filled with water in the corner. It's the dreaded *baignoire* – the Nazi version of waterboarding. An array of tortuous instruments lay on the table in front of us.

I swallow because now I realise what they have in store. There is another man with just a vest on, and blood-stained trousers, standing with legs apart. They are enough to tell me what is going to happen. He stares at me, waiting to inflict punishment. He reminds me of a hairy gorilla. Whatever I say they're going to inflict pain on me. I remember that the first twenty-four hours are the worst for torture; I know I have to hold out for forty-eight hours to allow my friends to escape. My heart is beating like a runaway train, my stomach squirms and ties itself into knots as I try to hide the emotion of fear.

A man stands before me in SS Major's uniform, he stares at me for a while. I recognise his face. I look him in the eye and stick my chin up to show I am not scared. He puts his hand on his hips.

'I recognise this young lady, Mauvais, it's Emily Boucher,' he says in English. This is to try and trap me, to get me to reveal who I really am. I don't fall for it.

'If that's who she really is.' His voice sounds silky smooth, and he looks at me. I frown as I pretend I don't understand the English he's speaking to me. I am not to be caught out. When I focus in on him, I see it's the Gestapo, Major Weber, who came to Maria's house. He is immaculately dressed, a clean pressed uniform which is at odds with the dirty, damp room. I can't imagine this Major getting his hands dirty.

'Why have you arrested me?' I demand in French, trying to sound confident. I notice the dried blood on the floor, and I start to break out in a sweat.

'My dear,' he continues in French, ''This is what happens when Mauvais is in a bad mood. You can make him into a better mood by telling us why you are in Saint Just. You are part of the *Résistance* aren't you? What is the address of your friends?'

'I don't know what you mean. Are you suggesting I am a *collaborateur*? Good heavens no,' I protest, trying to sound as innocent as I can.

'I don't know any. By the way, this man has hurt my Great Aunt. She is an old lady, and he should be punished.'

'She isn't innocent of anything. Except of harbouring terrorists over the years and of being part of the last war's *Résistance* movement. Of course, you would know their names and where they live. So you tell me, then I'll let you go, and you can go back to your aunt. We'll start with why you're here.'

'I told you, I came to look after her.'

'Why did you run away yesterday from her house?' he asks.

'Because I think he is going to kill me. He nearly did, manhandling me in the most terrible way, by pulling my hair, and treating me like an animal.'

Mauvais can't wait to have a go at hurting me. He grins and flexes his hands and rolls his sleeves up, watching my eyes get wider in a panic.

'You need to tell me Emily who you're *collaborateurs a*re. Then I will let you go,' says Weber.

'I really don't know who you're talking about,' I say. 'I think you have the wrong person.'

'We have your accomplice. She won't take long to break either. Make it easy on yourself.'

'Giselle doesn't know any *collaborateurs* either. We're just two working girls. I worked in Rennes for the council, I got sent here to look after Maria in her final years because my mother couldn't.'

Weber continues to look at me thoughtfully. I feel very vulnerable in just a slip. But I sound convincing even to myself. But before I realise it Mauvais steps up and slaps my face hard. The shock is immediate, and I try to recollect my senses.

Chapter 27

Robert is bruised and battered all over. He has been roughed up by the *Milice*. Mauvais particularly enjoys his moment of power, punching him in the stomach and hitting him round the head, knocking him unconscious. Then reviving him with a bucket of water. Mauvais doesn't ask him questions; he just enjoys hurting him.

'Why have you taken me? I have an exemption permit; I work as a baker.' Robert spits out blood from his mouth. His right eye is swelling up so he can't see out of it.

'I know what you do. Do you think a certificate can stop you from being sent to the German mines? Well think again,' Mauvais says exuberantly, swinging his fist wide to give as much strength to the next punch that he can. He enjoys this feeling of power over a person, especially as the recipient can't defend himself.

Then Robert's taken to a cell where he's left on his own without food or water for hours. He's lost track of time. Something is going on, but he doesn't know what. He can hear shouts and screams in the distance. But no idea where or who they come from. A few hours later the cell door is unlocked and pushed open. One of the *gendarmes* is thumbing him to get out of the cell. Robert gets up off the hard bed gingerly nursing his bruised stomach.

'What? Where am I going?

'*Salaud de veinard*! You lucky bastard! Get going. Someone's paid to release you. But don't leave town. We're keeping an eye on you.' He doesn't have to be told twice. He grabs his clothes and leaves.

Robert drags himself out into the sunshine. He struggles down the street bent over in pain. His clothes hide the majority of his bruises, but his face tells a different tale, his left eye is swollen and shut. But he still can't believe his luck. Mauvais, his sworn enemy, intended to beat the hell out of him, and he wonders if Mauvais knows he's been released. He wonders if his compatriots have paid a substantial amount to get him out of gaol. Perhaps the Gestapo released him to see where he went and follow him so that he leads them to the *Résistance*. Even so, Mauvais didn't suspect that he is the leader of the local *résistance* otherwise he would never have been released. First things first. Go back to the bakery to his van and then get to his mother and Mila and get them out of the town. Then he must remove himself from the town and go and live with the Maquis.

There's a roadblock leading out of town, he picks up his family and goes the long way round the other side of town via Eve's place.

Eve comes out of the barn as she sees his van coming down the hill to the farm. She rushes to him to hug and kiss them all. She is relieved to see them.

'Let everyone know I am out,' Robert tells her. 'I don't know who helped me, but I am grateful. Where's Emily? There's no one at Maria's.'

'Emily and Giselle have been arrested. They're in the gaol now.'

'When did this happen?'

'Yesterday.'

Robert's calm exterior disintegrates. He puts his hand on his forehead. '*Mon Dieu*, what on earth do we do now? Where's the radio?'

Eve looks bereft and runs her hands through her hair, 'I don't know.'

He raises his hands in the air and slaps them down at his sides as a sign of desperation. 'We've lost our *pianist*.'

Eve doesn't know what to say, she hates to see her friend upset.

'She should have come and lived here instead of Maria's. She could've hidden in my barn.'

'It's too late now.'

'I'll have to take my mother and Mila to Yvette's, she has room. Then somehow think how to get Emily and Giselle back.'

'You are welcome to leave Stephanie and Mila here, but it won't be safe if Mauvais decides to do a visit.'

'I know. They'll be safer at Gaston's farm. Then I'll go to the Maquis and get help. I don't want to put Yvette and Gaston in anymore danger.'

'What about Emily and Giselle?'

He wipes his hand across his brow, 'I'll have to think of some way of getting them out.'

They kiss each other on both cheeks, and he drives off with his family to Yvette and Gaston's farm. It's more remote here and the farm is at the end of a narrow road, it was once a prosperous farm. They should be safe here. He drives slowly down the track leading up to their farmhouse. Either side of the road are crops growing, it's a sea of greens. They used to have cattle but that's no longer viable with the Germans taking animals away for themselves. As he pulls up to the front door. Yvette comes out she has seen them coming down the road. She doesn't look pleased.

Chapter 28

Mauvais is excited to be able to finally inflict some pain and anguish on the woman in front of him. He's grinning and is in his element.

'You have been seen mixing with the bar owner and several *résistants* who we have now in gaol. I think you are one of the *résistants*.'

Major Weber slaps a baton against the table with a bang, and I jump. I shrug my shoulders, trying to remain calm. Deny everything. He is probably lying about already having *résistants* in gaol, he's trying these tactics to get me to talk. He hands his baton to Mauvais, and the man steps forward and hits me round the head so hard with it, I am knocked senseless. I am still tied to the chair, which tips over. Memories come flooding back to another place, another time, when someone hit my head against a wall. I feel dizzy, unsure where I am. I think I am with Luke again. He hits me, and I fall to the floor dazed, my hands and feet still tied. I am confused, am I in Normandy with the enemy, or Norfolk? There's not much difference. I gradually get my senses back. Oh yes, I am in Normandy. A sense of relief rushes through me that

Luke is dead. The memories strengthen me, and I don't move, I pretend to be unconscious.

'Oh, my dear, you do make it hard for yourself. You will tell me eventually,' the Major takes his baton and hits it against the table again in desperation. He is trying to scare me, but strangely it doesn't. This time the sounds and sights are blurred. He pulls my chair up and my head lolls on my chest. I open my eyes. And with a flick of his head which Mauvais has been waiting for he springs forward, and he and the gorilla drag me to the bath in the corner of the room, it's filled with water. I manage to take a big gulp of air before they push my head under and hold my head in the trough of freezing cold water. After what seems like an eternity, I can't hold my breath any longer and my lungs are bursting. I struggle and I take in water and come up coughing and spluttering. I am dragged back to the chair retching.

'I am afraid Mauvais enjoys his work. But you must tell us Emily who the other *résistants* are. I don't like to see a beautiful young lady like yourself being drowned.'

'I told you who I am and what I am doing here.' I gasp taking great gulps of air between choking.

'I came to look after my aunt, and I don't know of any *collaborateurs*.'

They take me for another dunking, and they bring me up at the last moment when my lungs are bursting, and I can't breathe. I can't think either. Things run through my brain. I come to realise that they are grasping at straws. They are guessing and trying to get me to admit guilt.

If Giselle were a double agent, she would have told them about our *réseau*. But they obviously don't know who's involved in our *résistance* group. If they have arrested some *résistants*, they haven't told them anything, because they wouldn't be asking me where the rest of them are.

The Major takes off his glove and dismisses Mauvais, who doesn't like it and protests.

'Leave!' Weber shouts at him, and he sits next to me as I shiver and shake.

'My dear,' he says. 'Don't make it hard on yourself. You must be hungry and cold. Let me dry you and we can start again; I can make you more comfortable.' He gets a small towel and tries to dry the skin that's exposed. It brings me to my senses. Suddenly my mind is clearer, I try not to gag.

'I told you I don't know. I don't know anything. I'd tell you if it was different.' I don't know how long I can stick to the story, and how many more times can this go on before I pass out? I lose all sense of time as he leaves me tied up and dripping wet on the upright chair, trying to get my breath back.

'Emily, please tell me what I need to know,' the Major says, slapping his stick against his thigh.

'Anything,' I try to say, in between choking, I can't put up with the *baignoire* anymore, I'll drown if they dunk me again.

'So, tell me about your *collaborateurs*,' the Major says putting his arm around my shoulders.

'But I don't know. Please believe me. I don't want to go through that awful baignore again.'

'Who is your best friend now? It is Robert Dusacq?' He walks up and down watching me, his once spotless uniform covered in specks of dirty water.

I decide to give him bits of information at a time, information that the Gestapo probably already knows, but it will seem as if I am reluctantly divulging information at last.

'Yes. He was helpful to me when I arrived in Saint Just. We knew each other before the war when I came with my mother to see my aunt. It was about ten years ago, when I met him. Maria was pretty old then. Look, can't you let me go? I don't know who these *résistants* are that you talk about. I don't know that any of my friends are *résistants*. If they are, they don't tell me, and I haven't overheard anything.'

He smiles benignly and infuriatingly at me, sipping a glass of water.

'If you let me go, I can find out for you,' I say as innocently as I can.

There's a subtle change in his demeanour, so small he thinks I don't notice it. He's obviously chewing this over in his mind and eventually says:

'And how would you find out who they are?'

'I could put it around that I am interested in joining the *résistance*. And I would think they'll find me. They are desperate I would think in enrolling more people.'

It's a desperate attempt to get out of the interrogation. And I can see he's still thinking about this.

'Ah, if it were up to me, I would. But you see Mauvais needs a scapegoat and you're it.'

'What for?

'He messed up with a train load of Jews. They got hijacked on the way to a camp, now he's in trouble so he needs to make up his deficit. And anyway, Mauvais will track you down until he finds you. He's like a dog.'

Weber calls Mauvais back in and he takes me back downstairs to my cell throwing me on the floor. My arms are still behind my back, my hair is sticking to my head and all over my face. I am in my slip and freezing cold with my hair dripping wet. It's damp down here and my lungs hurt. There's one thing I can do make it easier for my arms and I manage to slip my derriére through to the back and my handcuffed arms are at the front now I can wrap the blanket around me.

After a while I hear footsteps coming down the steps to my cell. I hold my breath, oh please no more. I'm exhausted. They've only just thrown me in my cell, surely, they haven't come to get me back up there. My head bent in misery. I'm cold and shivering. There is the turn of a key, and I hear a click. A gendarme whom I can hardly see, and it's so dark in here, enters the cell. I look at him waiting for what will come next.

'*L'eau sil vous plait.*' I ask.

He points to the door. 'Sortez.' Get out. The gendarme throws my clothes down on the ground. I can't believe it. I stand up and show him my handcuffed wrists. He sighs and unlocks my handcuffs.

'*Sortez. Maintenant!*' He doesn't need to tell me twice. As I scramble for the door, I pull on my clothes as quickly as possible, staggering as I go. He follows me at the next door he pulls me back and goes through the door before me and shuts it while I wait with bated breath, my face fixed at the door. It's pulled open and he manhandles me by the reception desk and pushes me out through a back door which is the basement entrance. He points up. It's a back entrance that I didn't come down before.

'*Vite!*'

My legs are like jelly as I climb up the steps on all fours. I am devoid of energy. It is difficult to walk. Thank goodness that at the top of the steps is Henri waiting for me. He doesn't give me a chance to speak.

'Stay down just in case there's someone about.' He grabs my arm and helps me into the back of his truck. He hides me behind some empty boxes and drives off quickly into the night. In a few minutes, we are at the back of his bar. And he helps me out and bustles me through his empty bar helping me up the stairs to the room above. I flop into a chair and breathe for the first time in ages. I can hardly believe what has just happened.

Henri lights a lamp on a table. And looks out the side of his curtains. A German unit passes by the end of the street.

'Phew that's a relief. Just in time! A few seconds later and we would have been caught!'

I'm still trying to catch my breath. I sit and try and calm myself.

'It had to be timed exactly. Or we both would've been shot as spies,' he says.

'Mon dieu Henri, how did you manage to persuade the guard? And is Robert okay? Where is he?'

'He's in hiding.'

'I somehow don't think if they suspected I was an enemy agent they'd let me go. How long have I been in there?'

'Forty-eight hours.'

'Good. I gave them just long enough for our comrades in the *réseau* to escape.'

'They didn't escape. Where would they go?' He spreads his arms wide and shrugs his shoulders.

'Those that are fugitives hide in the forest. Robert was released by the Chief of police with the help from some German officer, I am not sure who.'

'That must have been Sachs.'

'I arranged with a Gendarme friend of mine to leave his station in the middle of the night and unlock your cell. We have more citizens now sympathetic to our cause, with the threat of the imminent Allied invasion.

'Thank you, Henri. But where is Robert now?'

'He's gone to live in the forest with the *Maquis*. He wanted to come with me to release you. But it would not have been sensible.' He sits heavily in a chair his tired eyes closing for a moment.

'His mother and Mila are staying with the Sainsons' for now. But he's…all of us were worried about you.'

'And what did it take to get me out Henri?' I lean forward to anticipate this answer.

'Fifty thousand francs did it, from the money you brought over. It came in handy, and some Frenchmen suddenly decide to change loyalties,' he says with sarcasm. 'It is always best to go on the side of the Allies, especially if there's money involved.'

'Well, I am grateful that you got me out of that hell hole Henri.'

He lights a cigarette and leans back in his chair. We contemplate what has been happening in the past few hours, in this comfortably furnished room, it is tidy and clean, even though it smells of alcohol and cigarettes. And I wonder what is happening to the friends and family I have come to regard as my own. Where is Robert, Eve and Marie?

We sit quietly while I'm trying to calm down the throbbing in my head.. So, Robert was safe, thanks to London money to get us both out of gaol. Then I start to think of my priorities.

'I have to get the radio back from Giselle's house, Henri.' I tell him where it is hidden.

''I might have to get it for you. But during the day there is too much traffic about. What about using the one Jean-Pierre had?'

'I need to find out where they hid it. That's something else he did not tell me.'

I stare into space and wonder why I hadn't thought of this before., but there never seemed to be enough time.

'It turns out Robert left half the SOE money with Eve, did you know?' he asks me. I shake my head. He hadn't told me. But then I hadn't asked. I suppose it's safer with Eve if I am travelling the length and breadth of the area on my bicycle.

'I paid the Chief Gendarme, who has sympathies with local *résistance*.

'I remember he told me he was an old school friend. So, Robert has gone to the forest to join the Maquis then?' I ask him.

'The Chief let Robert out of gaol, hoping the allies will look on him favourably once they liberate our town.'

I am so pleased I get up to hug Henri, but he holds me at arm's length.

'I think Oberleutnent Sachs had something to do with it as well, thanks to your quick thinking.'

'Thank God Stephanie found the certificate.' I collapse in the chair. 'Two days in gaol!' The enormity of the last two days gradually sinks in.

'And another thing,' Henri says. 'Pierre has reported to us that a train full of Panzer tanks, and camouflaged, is making its way through the station yesterday on its way to Cherbourg.'

I sat up suddenly alert. 'I need to retrieve my radio Henri. How am I going to get it back from Giselle's basement?'

Henri looks out the window over the square to the Rue du Nul, and draws heavily on his cigarette, thinking.

'I need to sleep Henri; can I sleep here? But first I need to know, did Giselle escape?'

'I don't know. My gendarme friend hasn't seen her in the gaol. No one has heard of her. Now, how am I going to get you out of here, without you being seen?'

By sunrise there's an army of soldiers scouring the town for a woman who's escaped from the gaol. A hearse pulled by a strong horse is clattering along the main street at midday by Albert the undertaker on his way to a funeral. Albert is stopped by a roadblock across the road and two soldiers pull him up and demand he gets out.

'Absolutely not,' says Albert. 'A family is waiting for their dead relative, and we are not going anywhere but to the church. Let me pass to the cemetery, give the dead some respect!'

The soldiers fall back. And Albert makes the horse walk on towards the church.

At the Church of Saint Just the coffin is taken into the vestry, there is no one about only Albert. He lifts the lid on the wooden coffin and helps out a woman who disappears into the back of the church.

* * *

I am waiting for Henri to pick me up and take me in his vehicle to a safe house. After sitting and hiding in the digger's shed in the shadow of the church for several hours I am getting agitated. Has Henri been stopped by the roadblock? I watch for his approach. Finally I see him coming down the road in a gazogene truck. A vehicle altered to run off anything that's cheap and available when there's no petrol to be had, like charcoal or wood. Today, Henri's gazogene is burning wood and belching out fumes from the burner – a tall funnel behind the cab.

I am glad to see him. 'Did you get stopped?'

'I didn't have any wood, so it took me a while to obtain some, it is pretty slow and uncomfortable Emily.' I hop in beside him.

'I've brought the bicycle and the radio from Giselle's so that you can at least continue as our *piano*.'

'That's wonderful Henri, well done. How did you manage to get them out without Fisolee breathing down your neck?

'I saw her going past the bar earlier, so I drove the truck to the back of Giselle's house and the kitchen window was still unlocked.

I got them in the back of the truck pretty sharpish and came straight here.'

'Did you find the radio all right?

'That took me a while. I had to remove all the bottles on top!'

'Good hiding place though wasn't it?' I felt pleased with myself that the Gestapo hadn't found that. 'You are a marvel Henri, there is another radio somewhere, but Robert didn't tell me where they'd hidden it.'

'I don't know where it is. We will find out later when we meet up with Robert,' he spreads his hands. 'Now let's get you to this safe house. And you need to hop in the back, so you're not seen.

It's an uncomfortable ride with the gazogene belching out smoke from the burner, and there seems to be no springs in the chassis, fortunately we didn't have far to go. Henri turns off the road after about five kilometres on the Villedieu Road. There's an incline and we climb slowly the gazogene struggling with its small cargo. It is a cul de sac, Henri turns round and backing onto a wood off the road is a small house.

'It's perfect Henri.'

'The old couple who lived here were Jews. Gestapo pigs dragged them out in the middle of the night. We don't know what happened to them.'

He offloads the bicycle with my radio in the basket and takes me around to the back of the house. As we go into the back door, it's empty apart from a few pieces of old furniture. Presumable looted by the people who knew the couple had gone from their home. The curtains are closed. The atmosphere is dark and depressing. There are some cracked cups and a gas lamp.

'Here is some food I've wrapped up for you.' Henri shows me some bread and cold meet wrapped up in paper. 'It is best not to cook anything, that's why I've brought you some cold food. There is a candle on the side. But keep the curtains closed Emily. The house at the end is empty as far as I know, but I wouldn't open curtains just in case there are enemies about.'

'I must get back to the bar, I've managed to get out for a while but it I'm gone too long they will ask where I am. I must go now. Robert will be in contact with you. I sent a message that you're here.'

'Merci Henri," I kiss him on both cheeks. 'You risked a lot to free me from gaol.' It was Henri's genius idea to hide me in a coffin to take to the church and escape from Saint Just.

Henri sighed, 'Anymore arrests and we have no more bargaining chips. I hope the invasion comes soon.'

I change my clothes and am delighted that I can use clean water from a tap. I put the clothes back on top of the radio. It's no good getting settled; they're looking for a woman who's slipped out from under their very eyes, they will be searching everywhere for me.

Chapter 29

I slept for about two hours from when Henri left until the moon rose. The house at the end of the road is in darkness I can't see any movement outside anywhere and there are no lights. I get out my radio and set up the aerial out of the window ready to send my message. There is cloud covering the moon. The forest behind me is hiding its secrets – I hear no sounds, no nesting birds. Nothing. I have my window open and look down the road to view the turn off to this cul de sac. The wood behind me extends to the river Vire, a lone bird of prey glides above the treetops - a foreboding dark shape silhouetted against the moonlight. I get out my silks and start up my radio. The enemy will be waiting for me to send because they know I'm in the area of Saint Just. If the RDF van is in Saint Just waiting to triangulate my signal. I will have less than twelve minutes at best.

I tune in and send my call sign…. Dit dit da dit..dit dit da dit…I wait patiently. The response is finally returned… da dit da dit dit…

Ten minutes.

I send my message on recent military movements and the information on the Panzer tanks sighted in Saint Just.

…. Panzer tanks at St Just station moving on route to Cherbourg…. send instructions….

One minute.

No time to sign off with *Toodloo*. I'm ready to flee at a moment's notice. Something tells me to pack everything away ready to go, which I do, and I even go outside and put the radio in the basket and cover it up with my dirty clothes. If I am still here tomorrow I will wash them. I go back upstairs to clear any evidence of me; that I've been here. Perhaps tomorrow I will move on if Robert doesn't contact me. I feel an unease I can't explain.

I re-tie the Commando knife on my left calf under my trousers. Recently I've been keeping my pistol and knife hidden under my clothes but accessible. I don't carry a gun when I'm on the street, if it were found on me, I'd be arrested straight away. I can't relax, as I lay against pillows on the bed in the dark I wonder how Maria fared against the Gestapo and wishing I could see Robert and Eve. I am feeling lonely. The cat and mouse game with the Gestapo is catching up with me. My eyes start to droop, sleep tries to drag me under, but something makes me sit up and look out of the window.

A vehicle with no lights on has turned into my road about a kilometre away and has stopped. It takes me about two seconds to realise it's a German RDF van, disguised as an ambulance. It takes me ten seconds to scramble down the stairs and out of the back door and get on my bike. I am pedalling as fast as I can along the track by the time the ambulance has stopped outside the house.

The track inclines for a bit and I'm panting as I reach the pinnacle of the rise, it's an outcrop of granite rocks, and over the tops of the trees I see the river glistening below me as the clouds part to reveal the moon. It shows me the path I'm about to take, and I push off on a downward slope. My radio and I bump violently over obstacles on the ground. The trees envelope me as I slow down listening for signs that the Gestapo are following. I can't hear anything as me and my radio are being jostled all the way to the bottom of the hill. Trees and bushes scratch my arms and face as I continue to cling on to my bike, as we shake all the way to the bottom of the hill. I'm terrified I am going to fall off. I practically fly straight down a track that leads down to a barrage of bushes which kills my speed. My bike bumps all over the place with the valuable goods inside my basket banging the sides. I just need to get out of sight. Speed is of the essence here. I graze my face on some leaves that flick past me. Adrenalin keeps me going. So far I don't hear or see anyone behind me. All I can hear is the pumping of blood around in my ears. Obscure shapes appear in front of me which is a tree or shrub and I move direction at the last minute to avoid them. It starts to get lighter ahead as the trees thin out, and I see the moon straight ahead of me lowering itself towards the horizon. The riverbank slopes down to a muddy bank. It's taken me ten minutes to get to the river. I listen for sounds of men following me, but I hear nothing. Is it possible they didn't see me escape?

The track has disappeared somewhere, so I push my bike to my left along by the river. But it rained last night and it's swampy and the bike is starting to get stuck in the mud on the edge. I look back to where I came from a few minutes ago. I can see nothing, it is too dark back there, even though I have the moonlight before me making the river sparkle. It is a beautiful sight. I push on, I just don't know how far they are behind me. After struggling over the terrain and taking an hour to go several metres. I want to discard my bike, but I can't, I need it. I'm perspiring and panting for breath. Keep moving, I tell myself. This cat and mouse game that I play with the Gestapo is wearing me down. Without Robert and Eve, I feel alone.

After an hour of walking along a flat riverbank, rain clouds gather overhead. Within minutes there is a downpour, and I am drenched. I'm still struggling with the bike along the muddy riverbank, that seems to suck my shoes into a quagmire, they are covered in mud, I squelch along, hauling the bike over the obstacles. I come across a small pebble beach where the river is shallow and the ripples lap against the shore. Someone has tried to cut up a fish as I see its entrails lying on the shore. I look up the hill and see a house in darkness. It's a house set back from the river and if it's not occupied, I could sleep there a while. Exhausted, I leave the bike on the beach and haul my bag up some steps I reach the door. Then I realise I can hear voices from inside the house, there is someone living here. The light is fading, I'm tired and cold. I knock on the door, and the voices stop.

'*Laisse-moi entrer. Laisse-moi entrer!*' I plead outside their door to let me in. The door opens and a light shines on my face. I look into the shocked face of a middle-aged woman who has wiry grey hair as she holds up the lamp between us. She sees I'm in a state of distress, with my clothes covered in mud and my face and hair wet. She opens the door wide and beckons me in. There is a man and two children sitting at a table looking at me with their mouths aghast as I stand on the mat looking like a muddy rat. My back is stiff with the recent escape, and I bend with difficulty and take off my muddy shoes. I slowly stand up and sway with dizziness from lack of food and sleep. The woman helps me in to sit down on a chair. I start to tell them a story of why I am there in the middle of the night. I could fall asleep at the table. But she hurries to the stove and brings back some stew which is heaven and I eat it like a starving child. I haven't eaten fish for a long time. Then I look at my surroundings. The family sit and watch me from around the table. They take in my demeanour and my clothing. The father and children have ruddy faces and piercing blue eyes. But they listen to me and don't interrupt when I start to explain who is chasing me.

'Can you please shelter me for a few hours?' I plead.

'*Bien sur mademoiselle*. Don't say anymore,' says the husband. 'Anything we can do to help. The Germans don't generally tend to come this way as we're out of the way here. We will keep a good watch out to see if any cars come down the road.'

I try to tell them who I am, I am so exhausted, but I must let them know the truth. But they can tell I'm in trouble.

'My name is Emily. I shouldn't stay long. The enemy is out looking for me, I just ask for some water to take with me.'

'I'm Jeanette Doriot and this is my husband, Marcel.' She is the speaker of the family. Her hand indicates the people staring at me. 'Marcel and our two children.' They look like people who work on the river, they have sunburned faces. Jeannette has a kind face and I'm just too tired to ask questions.

'I can't begin to tell you how grateful I am, I've hardly eaten or slept for days; I'm trying to escape the Nazis.' Madame Doriot smiles and then sends her children off to bed. I try to tell her how grateful I am, but she waves it away and tells me to stay to rest until I feel I am able to leave. The children go very reluctantly, they keep looking back at me as they leave, they want to stay and hear what I am doing here in their house. Jeannette shows me to a wooden bed in another room and I fall into bed fast asleep within minutes. Later I find out that it was the parent's bed that I slept in. But in the morning, I wake up to find my trousers and blouse have been taken off me and my radio case is next to the bed. She gives me eggs for breakfast and fresh bread, I feel guilty that I am using their rations, but she shows me the chickens out the back of the house in the coup. I feel much happier and positive.

Later, I say goodbye to the family and feel sad to leave them. They did not ask any questions and accepted a complete stranger, whereas in the town I know some who would sell their soul to the devil. I feel better with food and six hours sleep. I have promised to come back and let them know when the *le jour de la libération* arrives. If it hadn't been for them, I might have given up and been discovered by the Gestapo. Madame gives me directions and I continue my way pushing my bike alongside me with the valuable radio in the bottom of the basket covered with clothes and food.

I decide to continue along by the river until I get to the wood the other side of town near Maria's house, which houses the derelict farmhouse that Robert and I visited for my first scheduled transmission. I push my bike along the rivers' edge, there's a track along the riverbank a bit overgrown with wet grass, but the ground is firmer here. Madame Doriot has put some bread and cheese in my basket on top of my radio. I decide to hide it in the barn next to the derelict farmhouse while I try to find Robert, Eve, and the rest of my friends. I walk for most of the afternoon on the edge of the river I can see the edge of the town in the distance. My instincts combined with memory of the town map I looked at some days ago makes me turn me left and I continue along a dry embankment, until I come to a wood I recognise, the angle of the trees and the sun make the area look familiar, I'm coming at it from another direction. It's the one that holds the derelict cottage.

The sun is low in the sky by the time I reach the edge of the wood. I fumble in my bag for my torch. It's dark in the wood and my eyes find it a while to adjust as I'd been walking towards the sun all afternoon. The wood is quiet underfoot, just an owl hooting in the distance and birds fluttering in the trees. I can't see or hear evidence of humans. I turn on my torch and walk with it aiming down on the ground. Going as carefully as I can I avoid the swampy areas leading from the river to the wood. I remember Robert had told me the fields often flood in the winter, and it is springtime.

I keep walking until I come to the edge of the wood. Now I make my way in the dark towards the barn with the broken ladder. It's just how Robert and I left it. I hide my radio and fall asleep instantly on the dry hay on the mezzanine.

I awake about five to see it getting brighter through the hole in the barn. Time to move. I put the radio under the hay. And make my way up the hill towards Maria's house. I haven't seen her for several days. I keep close to the edge of the field. There is no movement at the dairy farm. First check on Maria. I squeeze through the side gate being careful of the brambles and let myself in the kitchen door. As I go through the house, I see chairs are overturned and the candles have burned down. I go through the house calling her. The front door is broken on its hinges. I push it shut but it hangs there. I run upstairs. The bedrooms have been ransacked. Poor Maria, she must have been scared out of her wits.

There is no sign of her. The Gestapo must've taken her away when they couldn't find me. She won't survive a grilling from the *Milice* or the Gestapo. I run outside and put my hands on my knees taking deep breaths. Although I am sure she's been taken by the *Milice* I can't stay here in case they come back. The only thing to do is to get to Eve's house from here, and try and get to the dead letter drop, I can't risk going back to the bar. It's about three hours walk with my case to Eve's, but the safest way of avoiding the enemy in town. They'll be on the lookout for me. I decide to stay in the derelict farmhouse during the day and walk at night.

The sun is out and it's May, the insects are buzzing close to my head. Mosquitoes try to nip me. It's getting hot. Taking some food remaining from the pantry, I return to the derelict shed, climb up to the mezzanine and eat my food knowing with great sadness if it weren't for me, Maria would still be here.

Chapter 30

I awake to find it cooler and early evening. I sit for a while looking out of the window into the green fields and listen to the insects and birds making the noises around me. I keep an eye out for anything that moves. I eat the last of the bread given to me by Madame Doriot.

I haven't ever done a schedule in the middle of the day before, and in the same place. But I will have to do it, speed is of the essence, because they might take less than fifteen minutes to get a fix on my position this time. I will not be able to hear an RDF van pull up and the sounds of footsteps won't be heard until they have run along the field's edge to the broken gate. I will have to escape back by the river the way I'd come if need be.

Back in England the radios are manned twenty-four hours a day by the FANYS. I hope someone is listening out for me at this unscheduled time. The red evening sunset seems to dull the sounds of the creatures in the wood. It is quiet. Too quiet.

As I make my way over to the derelict farmhouse, my radio case in my hand, I don't register that the broken bit of wood stuck across the back door last time has moved. It seems aeons ago that Robert put it there for a warning. It was flat on the floor in front of me, and I almost tripped over it as I made my way towards the bottom of the stairs when I remembered it was a warning signal that someone else had been in. I stop dead in my tracks. Are they here now? My training kicks in and I start thinking like a trained agent. If there was someone upstairs, it's possible they could have seen me moving around.

Then it wasn't a friend. I feel for the pistol inside my jacket. I'm glad I listened to Robert and took heed of his advice. I feel more confident with it. I wrest it into my right hand as I quietly put my case down on the floor with my left.

I move slowly up the stairs; I'm careful not to tread on the creaky stair, so I step above it to the next step. Halfway up the stairs I pause to see a man's back. The setting sun is shining down through a gap in the trees and falls on the windowsill. I see a rifle leaning against the windowsill, and I can see the side of his face as he's bending down picking up something from the floor. I thank God Robert and I moved the radio to the barn. He's come to ambush me, and I'm not surprised to see who it is.

The light hits the side of his face. He doesn't hear me come up the stairs to the bedroom. It's Monsieur Chevrolet. I stand as still as I can. He turns slowly and sees me with a jolt. He is the Gestapo informer. I am in the shadows by the door. I have my pistol behind my back, and we stare at each other. No one speaks. I assess how quickly he will grab his rifle. Then he says a stupid thing.

'So, *you* are the spy. As I thought. Major Weber will be interested to see that it is you.'

'What makes you think I'm a spy?'

He holds up the piece of silk that I thought had burned from my last sked two weeks ago, and I curse myself for missing it.

'I gather this is yours?' His eyes are like slits as he holds it up.

'Why do you think it's mine?' I said, straightening up on the top step the pistol burning into my thigh. He's no more than three metres away and facing me.

'I saw you and your lover the other night come in here, and I bet you have a radio stashed somewhere. So right under our noses. Very clever. But you're a spy and they'll pay me lots of money for you.'

'It's not what you think,' I say, my heart thumping in my chest, and giving me a chance to think. But I am not to be distracted, and I will not be caught by this man.

'Tell that to the Gestapo,' he says as he moves to reach for his rifle next to him. A tide of panic threatens to overwhelm me. He's a big man, but I am quicker.

I raise my pistol and shoot him twice in the chest.

He doesn't even have time to grab his rifle. He shouts and holds up his hand as if he might ward off further bullets. He leans towards me. I fire once more at him. It's decisive, right to his heart. He slips to the floor and lies there with a vacant expression staring up at the ceiling. A pool of blood starts to expand underneath him and trails along the floor. I start to breathe heavily. It's a movement I'd practised time and again in training, but still it makes my hands shake with the sheer force of the gun. His rifle still leans against the wall.

I stand and listen, unless there's a radio detection van out this way, there's no one around. I don't move for a minute. All I can hear is the adrenalin pumping in my ears. I push him with my foot just to check. No movement. I check his neck pulse, nothing. Now I know he's dead.

I try to move him to hide the evidence and as I look down, I see my jacket covered in blood, my hands, and now my shoes. It's seeping through the floorboards. I feel sick. Keep going, I tell myself. The adrenalin will keep you going.

I feel no remorse because I think of the friends who have died because of people like him. He did not have a conscience about me being captured by the Gestapo. He was a *collaborateur* and it was either him or me, I keep saying to myself. Even so the act of killing someone and then watch their blood seep out as they die before my eyes is something I don't want to do again. It was self-defence.

There was just one thing I hadn't anticipated…how am I going to dispose of the body from up a flight of stairs. I can't carry him. I need to get his body out of sight.

There is nowhere to hide a bloody body in this empty house, if the Gestapo or *Milice* look here, the evidence needs to be hidden. I try to drag him to the window, but he is a tall man and a dead weight. I pull his coat and his body to the edge of the open windows. Then with all my might I lean his body over the windowsill and upend his feet and hurl him over the edge. My heart is thumping in my chest the adrenalin keeps me strong, but I am sweating with the effort it has taken to get him there. Only the fear of being caught gives me the extra strength. The body hits the bushes below. And I run downstairs and drag him by his coat, bit by bit over the overgrown garden to the well, several metres away from the house. Moving the broken plants of wood away and trying not to fall in myself I push his body to the edge and with my feet push him over the edge. There's a thump as the body hits the bottom of the dry well after a couple of seconds.

I hurry back upstairs to get the rifle. Stepping in the blood makes my shoes sticky. In the dark the blood is difficult to see, but I'm not sure if it's obvious during the day. I don't hang around to see. I grab the rifle and empty out the ammunition and throw it all down the well. It's too big for me to carry. The jangling of the shells echoes as they bounce off the sides. I put the rotting planks of wood back across the well. Not as it was but it'll have to do, I'm hopeful if someone comes looking, they won't think to look down the well. It will bide me some time. I wipe my hands and shoes on my jacket and bury it amongst the head-high nettles on the other side of the barn.

I grab my radio case and try and clean my stained hands on the wet grass outside. And puffing and panting after the exertion I go back up to the mezzanine preparing to do my last sked from here. Trying to regulate my breathing I hang out my aerial and send my coded message. I try to calm my beating heart as I transmit my message as quickly and concisely as I can.

Safe house compromised moving on and awaiting instructions re Panzers

I turn off the transmission and wait five minutes, listening to the sounds of the wood.

I try to calm the sense of panic now as it washes over me. Pulling things together, my radio in my bag, as the last rays of the sun set. I make my way towards Eve's farm in a southerly direction, keeping well under the hedgerows and prepared to throw myself and the radio in the ditch if a car comes my way. I've got this far, I'm determined not to be caught now.

I aim for the train station because I am not sure where her farm is from this direction. As I make my way along the edges of fields stumbling in the dark and trying to preserve any battery that I have left in the torch, I spend an hour sleeping in the shallow dip of a bocage hedgerow, its leaves sheltering and hiding me like a baby against the damp of the night. My last thoughts as I drop off through sheer tiredness, are how do I organise the sabotage of the Panzer tanks now Robert is not around.

I zig zag across fields avoiding roads that the Nazis could be driving along, and I reach the train station and it's about three hours later when I arrive. It's late afternoon and I'm exhausted. I sit in the shade of some trees, there are no trains and not many people around. I access the ladies' toilet easily on my side of the station, away from soldiers, and I wash my face and hands. I even wash my shoes. All the time asking myself, how will I get across the station with a load of German soldiers around?

Chapter 31

Lieutenant Schiller studies the triangulation information that he had worked on so diligently for the past few weeks. His RDF van has quartered the area, closing in district by district until now, finally, Schiller has got his lucky break. He excitedly shows his findings to his boss, Standartenfuhrer Riesel, as Major Weber stands by watching and listening.

'Very good lieutenant, what makes you think this radio operator is nearby?

'Sir, this is the operating frequency that he often uses, and this is where we compared signal strengths in different locations. This operator has started using the same place twice, which gives us the chance to home in on his location more securely having triangulated that section before. He never stays very long. I think he is running out of options it is only a matter of time before he goes back to one of his previous places and we will have him. I cannot pinpoint the street or the building, but I will.'

'Are you certain there is only one enemy wireless operator transmitting in the town?'

'Yes, sir. An operator's life is a lonely and fearful one. Hiding out and trying to find food and water on a daily basis is very taxing on the body.'

'Unless he has friends who leave him food and water. Of course, he could be hiding in their farm or barn? Or even in someone's roof in the town.'

'Most of the transmissions seem to come from outside the town, but they are spread over a wide area. I believe he must have transport of some kind.'

'This man is resourceful and energetic. He could be using a bicycle to transport himself and his radio about.'

'I will increase the searches of baskets including the women in the town.'

'Do we need to do that?'

'We have found women in the past to act as couriers. Never underestimate the enemy mind. He or she is desperate.'

'He could be a woman?'

'In Paris sir, I know of a case. Our man has the light touch of a female operator. It could be a woman.'

'Are there such women? Those who are quick enough and clever enough to escape our clutches? I had not realised such agents could be women! It would never happen in the Fatherland, women know their place for raising children, not as secret agents.'

'I have discovered that some of them are women, sir. I believe they are chosen because they are less likely to be stopped by our patrols.'

'Then we increase our patrols and stop all women and inspect their baskets.'

'The women of the town won't like it and it will take more time.'

'After this revelation it has to be done and see that no one is missed.'

'Yes sir.'

'What about the baker? And the man who runs the bar on the corner? I have been there when a woman comes in regularly to speak to him. I thought it was his mistress, but now I'm not so sure. She may be an informant. Get someone to disguise themselves and follow her home. The *Brigades Speciales* are good at doing that.

Schiller nods and turns to go.

'And don't let them interrogate him! I want that privilege. If we can find the wireless operator, it opens the key to the door to the rest of the circuit.'

Weber looks out of the window onto the town square from his vantage point of the *Mairie,* the town hall, and smiles, not long now to capture.

Chapter 32

Two figures wait amongst the trees on the edge of the forest. One dozing, one sitting fidgeting. They are waiting for a *rendezvous*. It overlooks the signal box on the railway line, it's a good vantage point. They stay still, well hidden. The night is clear, they can see anything moving from their position.

'There's been more Krauts around than I realised were in the garrison. If they're looking for us, they won't find us.' Robert says. 'We've all hidden away. But they might find Emily.' His comrade doesn't answer him. He feigns sleep.

'I hope she's ok,' he says to himself.

His comrade is still motionless. Owls hoots across the forest to each other.

'We've waited long enough,' his comrade says quietly.

'No!' he hisses, 'You go, I'll wait.'

'How do you know she's coming? She's probably been discovered by the Gestapo.'

'I don't think so. She'll get here. Somehow or other. I am waiting.'

His comrade sighs and closes his eyes again. At two in the morning the clouds have covered any clear sky there was earlier on. All is quiet except for small animals rustling through the undergrowth. No soldiers are about, Robert's sure of it. A fox screeches from across the fields in the distance. Suddenly Robert sits up alert. Gaston dozes. Robert gets up in anticipation and rubs his hands together and stamps his feet. It's getting cold sitting here for hours, but he still waits. A few minutes later, he almost misses an imperceptible dark shadowy figure making its way along the railway track.

* * *

I look about me, I am at the signal box for two o'clock. But I can't see anything moving. Where would I be to be safe out of sight but have a good view? I look up the hill behind the signal box. That's where I would wait and have a good view of anyone coming.

I decide to climb over the tracks and start climbing the track through the trees. After ten minutes I am puffing and panting. I stop to rest. Going uphill with my bag is hard going. The quarter moon comes out above me to greet me.

I see a momentary flash of a torch. It's him. I continue climbing and I see a dark figure coming down to meet me. Then he disappears and someone creeps up behind me and puts a hand over my mouth. I tread backwards on his instep.

'Ow.'

'Good job I knew it was you. I could've slit your throat,' I tell Robert.

'Good to see you too.' He puts his arms around me and squeezes all the air out of me, kissing me on both cheeks, and we give each other a long hug.

'I had to leave my bike at one of the station cottages…and the radio case inside a compost heap.' I tell him breathlessly.

'Of course, where else would you put it?' His face smiling down at me. He is glad to see me. We keep hugging each other. I don't want to let him go.

'I missed you.'

'I missed you too.'

Gaston appears behind me.

'I'd better go and get the radio then,' Robert reluctantly lets me go.

'Perhaps Gaston would like to go and get it?' I look at Gaston.

'No fear.'

'I'll try and retrieve the bike too. It depends on who is about. But I'll have to go and retrieve the radio now. Which cottage is it?'

I explain which one.

'It's best to go now. Stay with Gaston.'

'Emily…if anything happens to me or you...'

'Just shut up, will you?'

He takes me roughly into his arms. His ammo belt is slung across from shoulder to waist. It presses painfully into my chest.

'There's no time to say much now,' he says. 'But afterwards it will be different.'

Gaston makes a noise and stamps his feet impatiently.

'I am going, wait here.' Robert says. 'If I am not back in an hour, Gaston will take you to Eve's.'

He leaves us watching after him as he swiftly and silently disappears from view down the hillside into the shadow of the trees. We can't see anyone around, and I cross my fingers for the second time today.

'Let's wait under this tree. If there's anyone down there and they catch him. We will need to disappear instantly,' says Gaston.

We sit for a while, listening and waiting. The only sound is my heart thumping in my ears, and some bats flying nearby from tree to tree. The moon disappears behind some clouds. Thank goodness for small mercies. If he is caught again, it doesn't bear thinking about.

Time drags on we can't hear anything but then the station is not in sight.

Suddenly Robert appears behind us.

'Hoi,' he hisses, and startles us both. He puts the suitcase intact on the ground in front of me, smiling from ear to ear.

'Well, you two are a lot of good. I could have been the enemy creeping up behind you and slit your throats.'

I am so relieved I fling my arms around him and hug him.

'Oh, come on, you two, for goodness' sake!' says Gaston, descending the hill.

We walk for a kilometre before the van is found hidden well under an oak tree. I tell him on the walk about my new friends the Doriot's who want to help the *résistance*, and Maria's disappearance.

'Oh, and I had to kill Chevrolet,' I sound guilty.

'Mon Dieu! What happened?'

'He was hiding in the derelict farmhouse for me, he tried to take me in to the Gestapo. I had to shoot him.'

I explain as briefly as I can both Robert and Gaston listen quietly as I give a brief description. I am so pleased to be sitting next to him in his van. We don't say much more until Gaston is dropped off at his farm. On our way to Eve's farm, I have so much to say but don't know where to start.

'So much has happened since I last saw you,' I tell him.

I recognise the outlines of the empty cattle shed as we turn up at Eve's farm ten minutes later. A faint glow of dawn is showing on the horizon. No lights are obvious from outside, but when we go in the back door there are candles illuminating the kitchen. Within a few seconds Eve comes down the stairs at the sound of our voices.

'I thought I heard a car. Welcome back Emily.' She hugs us both and kisses us on both cheeks. 'I was so worried about you.'

'I'm so glad to see you too.' I hug her tightly.

As we sit down around the table. I am suddenly exhausted. I open out the radio case to see how my radio is faring after the compost heap. It smells of manure, but it looks no worse for wear.

'Poor Maria,' Robert looks out of the window, then sighs and puts his hands over his eyes as if trying not to imagine it. 'She would do anything to help the *résistance*, like she did in the last war. Don't feel guilty. You did what you had to do.'

'The bastards didn't need to take her away,' says Eve. 'Knowing Maria, she'd spit in their faces. She will stick up for herself.'

'It's probably what she did. But it won't keep her alive,' says Robert. 'She has an indomitable spirit for a ninety-year-old. Let's hope she's still alive somewhere. I'll check with my contact in the Gendarmerie and the hospital after I have dropped you off.'

I know Robert has it all worked out; we can all rely on him. What would we do without him? I think to myself; it doesn't bear thinking about.

'Eve has Jean-Pierre's radio hidden in the barn,' says Robert. 'Now we have two new crystals, and you'll be able to use two radios at different places without carrying two around and running the risk of getting caught.'

'I haven't eaten for ages Eve; do you have something to eat?'

'Of course!' She jumps up and serves me half a batard. I am famished and devour the dry bread before she can heat up some cassoulet on the stove.

Robert paces up and down. 'Right, we need to organise another drop and more guns and ammo before the Day of Liberation. I'll write out the message. I'll take you out to the shepherds hut on the hill Emily tonight...'

'No, it's too dangerous for you. I can walk or cycle during the day rather than after curfew. They may not be expecting me at midnight after all that's been happening, they know things are dangerous here, and I can't keep to that time now. Anyway, I'm less likely to be caught on a bicycle if I hear anyone coming, I get off and hide in the bocage. I can always see any car which climbs the hill from the Coutances road. It's easier to hide one person than two. I need sleep first, then I'll go.'

'I am so glad you're all right.' He starts to say something else, but I am too busy devouring food to answer. And Eve watches us from the end of the table and smiles.

Chapter 33

Henri and Robert are alone drinking a mixture of acorn coffee at Eve's table as I come downstairs after my first proper sleep. I wonder if they went home last night. I smell the strange aroma and decline a cup when Eve enters the kitchen.

'What has happened to Giselle?' I ask them all. 'Has anyone seen her since our arrest?'

There is an awkward silence, as if she were condemned already for being a *collaborateur*.

'I couldn't find her in the police station,' Henri says. 'I asked about her everywhere I could, Albert hasn't seen her either. The *Gendarmes* don't know where she's been taken. I knocked on her door this morning. And looked through the window. But it's all shut up - like she has left Saint Just. What is going on?'

'Did they let her go? Even if she told them the truth, they would arrest her and torture her, if they suspected she was a *collaborateur*. I wonder what she gave in return for her escape?'

'If she did escape,' says Robert.

'No one's seen her,' says Henri.

'Didn't you say she was close to Jean-Pierre, your leader? What if they used him as a bargaining chip? She'd do anything to release him.'

'It is assuming he's still alive. Unlikely, even in Germany. She should realise that,' says Robert.

'Some people will do anything to hold on to love,' I say I am so tired I put my head on my arms and close my eyes for a few moments.

I hear Eve clear her throat and I realise she is trying to tell us something.

'Maria died two nights ago,' she says. 'Albert told me yesterday, she died at the police station. Her heart he thinks. God knows what they did to her, he wouldn't say. He has her at the funeral parlour and will let us know when her funeral will be. It was Gisard Mauvais who brought her to her end, you can be sure of it, the bastard!' Eve bangs her hand down on the table and makes me jump. I've never seen her this angry before.

'She was still walking the day before he turned up.' I tell them.

'He'll get his come uppance you'll see,' she says. The men look pale as we sit in silence, contemplating her last hours.

'We'll need to be inventive on how we get to the church without the Boche finding out.' Says Robert.

'I don't think Giselle informed on our *réseau* Robert, otherwise we would have been arrested by now.'

'Then, where is she? Would she still be in the cells? My contacts tell me no.' Robert runs his fingers through his hair. 'Where on earth is she?'

Chapter 34

The little church outside Saint Just has a large, unkempt graveyard. The grass is long and wet. Since the graveyard diggers were sent to Germany the priest has had to dig some of the graves himself. The rest are dug by the relatives of the deceased. He stands in his cassock on the front steps of the Church of Saint Marie. It has been drizzling all night and continues into the morning, giving the morning a dismal depressing feeling. Eve, Robert and I have walked from Albert's funeral parlour to the church, trying to keep hidden from German eyes, the weather is mild but wet and windy. It still doesn't seem like summer even though it is the end of May when the sun should be out. The weather reflects how we are feeling as we come in through the sacristy door, just in case the police are watching and waiting for us at the front.

The undertaker has laid Maria out in some fine clothes, she doesn't look like Maria. She looks calm and peaceful as we say our goodbyes and Albert closes the coffin. We are a forlorn small group. We are drenched through after a few minutes of prayer. The undertaker has kept it quiet as he doesn't want the Gestapo or the *Milice* coming to arrest us at the church. Robert and Albert lower her coffin into the ground. The priest leads Eve and I under his umbrella back inside the church. He has warmed some red wine for us, and we sip it gladly as he says some kind words about her.

'Did she have children?' I ask.

'Yes, although I believe they were killed on the Somme. Two sons. And her husband died of the swine flu which killed thousands after the war.'

'My goodness, how sad,' I reflect on how much sadness she's had in her long life.

'That is harsh,' said Robert. 'I remember the family; she was a different woman then.'

'It's probably the right time to go. Things will get worse from now on,' says the priest. 'You'd better go.' He looks out of the door so he can see who is on the path leading up to the church. 'I told the *Milice* there was a funeral tomorrow for an old woman. But they may find out we brought it a day forward.'

We leave the way we came in. Scurrying across the graveyard towards the lane behind the church looking left and right in case any spies of the Gestapo are out and about. The lane leads through some alleyways until it reaches the road to Albert's funeral yard. From there we get into Robert's van. I see a black police car speed past the end of the street. Timing is everything.

'Quickly let's go,' I say.

Robert drops us off at Eve's farm, gives me a hug then without saying a word he drives off into the distance along the back lanes towards the forest. As he goes, I breathe a sigh of relief. We manage to evade the Boche by the skin of our teeth.

I sigh and Eve puts her arm around me. 'Try not to worry. I'm sure he'll be all right.'

'I'm just so worried. About all of us.'

'And he's worried about you. He feels helpless that he's not here, but he has to be with the Maquis, to help organise and arm them for the Day of Liberation.'

We sit at the kitchen table and sip tea as I stare through the window at the view outside but feel depressed.

'You are in love with him, non?' She smiles sympathetically as I put my head in my hands and close my eyes. I am tired.

'Robert has been the best friend to Antoine and me. The three of us were inseparable when we were younger. I think Robert feels it's his responsibility to help me now Antoine is not here.'

'It's good you have Pierre too.'

'Yes, he's my darling child, what would I do without him? I worry about him on the railway. What if he gets caught?' Her eyes look to the window, as if waiting for him to come in the back door.

'His mother has been the role model for him,' I smile at her. She shrugs her shoulders and sighs.

'But I can tell Robert also will do anything for you too.'

'Tell me more about him.'

'He is trustworthy, loyal, a good friend. Plus he has good looks as well. If I hadn't met Antoine...' She shrugs her shoulders and smiles at me. 'Who knows?'

I look at her with raised eyebrows willing her to explain. But I trust her judgement. In a way I'm a bit jealous of the bond that they have. I wished I'd known him before.

'He met Chantel, his wife, at school. They didn't marry until 1940, before Dunkirk, but she died giving birth to Mila, and he was imprisoned by the Germans. He escaped and came home. When he found out, he was distraught, he went back to the Maquis and didn't come home until last year. I think he regretted going away and leaving Mila with Stephanie. But at least he tried to make up for his absence when he returned.'

Unwelcome pictures appear in my mind of Robert and his wife but I try to shake myself out of it. I came here to help win a war, not to fall in love. I want to ask more questions about him, but instead I try and think of my tasks ahead and my mission. London wouldn't be happy with me if I got distracted, especially by the *Chef du Reseau*.

Pierre arrives home on his bicycle after work, he's wet with the rain we've had today, his face covered in grease and soot. But he can't wait to tell us;

'You'll never guess what? The tank transporters have arrived in Coutances, they are there for two days. Eric and I think we can sabotage tomorrow night, we have a run there and then back in the dark. One of us can keep guard while the other one does the carborundum. I'll need the grit grease. Where is Robert?

'Pierre be careful,' Eve tells her son. 'He is back tomorrow. Where is the carborundum? How will you do this without getting caught?' Pierre tells us Eric's plan but Eve is still anxious about this I can tell. Pierre is excited he is at last doing something meaningful against the Nazis.

That night I make a bed of hay at the back of the mezzanine in Eve's barn and hope the rain doesn't come through. I have some shelter, but at least if the enemy turns up I have my knife and pistol on me and I can defend myself. I look out of my spy hole at night, I look out over the flowing river below the farmhouse, it is still flowing fast after all the rain we've had in May. It is staying lighter at night now and even at ten o'clock I can see the end of the lane and any suspicious vehicles. But I needn't worry, I only recognised Robert's van that day.

I make myself comfortable to sleep on a bed of dry straw and wrap myself in one of Eve's warm blankets. There is an occasional scurrying of a small creature as I look up, I see a mouse running along the slats below the roof struts. It's completely oblivious to me, and I'm glad it doesn't stop. I hear the clucks of the chickens below, one occasionally flies up to see what I'm doing up here, but once night comes they settle and roost. I need to do another sked but the Gestapo are on my tail. I feel my luck is about to run out.

Chapter 35

In the afternoon, I say goodbye to Eve as I cycle out into the countryside and up to a shepherds' shack which has been used for years for sheep farming in past winters. It still has a roof on it and three sides which give protection against the wind.

I am looking from the hill to the main road into Saint Just. It's an ideal place to transmit, away from the town. There are plenty of places to hide the radio in the undergrowth now it's summer. And the shack has a window I can look out of and if an RDF van disguised as an ambulance is coming this way, I'll see it in plenty of time. I can hide in the bocage hedgerows on the way back to Eve's farmhouse. It's a cycle ride away from the town the trick is not getting caught after curfew. I decide to go during the day so I can see what I'm doing.

Today, I need to transmit the requests from our leader for more ammo, guns, money, and this time mortars, grenades, and heavier guns. Gaston has an old 85 mm canon from the First World War, which he plans to use once the Allies invade and he has 'the Hun on the run.' It will be this summer and soon when the weather is more suitable to land armies on the beaches. But where? In France no one is yet sure. The weather forecast is cloudy and windy. It's warm but rain is threatening the air. Only London can tell us the secret messages that all resistant groups wait for, which is the second stanza of the opening lines of the 1866 Verlaine poem *Chanson d'Automne.*

'Les Sanglots longs des violons de l'automine.'

I cycle with the radio in my basket as usual it's covered with food – this time some vegetables from Eve's garden. I am hoping the German patrols won't be out. The day starts sunny and warm but ends up becoming cold and rainy. I don't like sitting in a draughty old shack very much, looking out for the enemy and transmitting in cold, wet clothes. Considering the alternatives, like a cold, dank, empty cell it's not too bad.

As I position myself in the window and open out my radio case setting the aerial onto a hook above my head, I see some Allied aircraft flying slowly towards my position on the hill. The hill is about 500m above sea level. I am astonished at how low they are flying. I wonder where they are going. I don't hear any anti-aircraft guns from the Germans; they must have taken everyone by surprise. I feel the vibrations in the hill as I look up and they pass overhead. I can almost touch them. They obviously mean business as I recognise Hudson bombers.

I send my call sign and commence with the message asking for more guns, ammo and cigarettes. The Maquis are starving yet they seem to live on cigarettes.

After thirteen minutes of transmitting I wait an hour for a response, which confirms the drop. I confirm the details then switch off and put the radio away. I look for a place to hide the radio, I walk past deep bocage hedgerows that are dry after the recent rain. A fine misty rain today hasn't penetrated the place. The radio will be dry and safe and only a few metres from the shack. The Gestapo won't think to look there, will they? I say to myself.

Satisfied with this I cycle back down the hill, another two kilometres along some country lanes and then I come to the start of the road leading to Eve's farm and as I start to freewheel down the drive towards her farm I see a black car parked behind the farmhouse. It's a car I've seen before. My heart is in my mouth, what do I do now?

I quickly cycle into the barn with my bicycle. But I can't stay here in case he's up to no good. I knock on the front door and make my way round to the side of the house looking to see if the front door is open. No one opens the front door and that worries me. That means Eve hasn't managed to get to the front door. But I can't see or hear anything. I edge my way to the kitchen window through the vegetable garden by the back door and try and look through into the kitchen. I can hear muffled voices.

Suddenly there's a thud inside and I can't restrain myself. I burst in the back door and at the same time the door is pulled back and a hand comes from nowhere, slamming me into the wall.

It's Mauvais. He is surprisingly strong holding me with toes barely off the ground with one hand at my neck. I gasp for breath unable to speak.

'I know who you are,' he says in English. 'Nice of you to deliver yourself like this.'

He wears his grey and brown dirty uniform. The mist clears from my eyes, I see Mauvais' face swim before my eyes. I can see the fine lines around his eyes, and the odd patch of hair scraped from the sides. He smells of garlic and bad breath. I want to speak but I can't breathe in, and my heart is pounding so hard in my chest.

'Where is your lover?'

I try to speak again but fail. Without waiting for me to reply, he smiles.

'In many ways this is much more fun than if I had shot you, you won't get away this time.' He pulls out a knife and sticks it against my cheek. I feel a trickle of blood down my neck. Then he bangs my head against the wall, and I drop to the floor and see stars in front of me. He thinks I'm unconscious as he turns to attack Eve with the knife. I'm dazed and motionless. I can hear clothes ripping. I can hear someone screaming in the distance. I'm not sure if it's Eve or me. Gradually the fog in my head dissipates but I have a headache that sears through my skull as I try to get up. I see a blurred vision of Eve on the floor with Mauvais on top of her and a knife in his hand, I can hear her clothes being torn. I try to activate my brain to attack, and I stagger over to them and wrench his arm back. But I'm still fuzzy and he swings round and fights me off, leaving Eve and turning to pin me down on the floor with his knees in my stomach. The wind is knocked out of me. Suddenly he falls on me, his full body weight on top of me. I hear a gasp from Eve, I realise I'm still alive and Mauvais is unconscious, as she leans over us with a poker in her hand. I throw him off me onto the floor, I crawl away from him gasping for breath. She looks at the poker in her hand and I crawl to a chair to pull myself up. I just realise she saved my life.

But Mauvais is still conscious. With blood dripping from his head, he pushes up surprisingly quickly, and lurches round and grabs her while she stands there with poker still in hand. She shrieks. They struggle with the poker, but he pulls it from her. She tries to escape from him, he hits her across the head from behind with the poker. She falls to her knees. Out of the corner of my eyes I see he is angry and determined to kill her. He ignores me trying to get up from the floor, I think my ribs are cracked. He doesn't give up, it's like he's insatiable for blood lust and revenge. He's using his fists now, hitting her like a maniac. He is excited. The only sounds are his grunting as he hits her and her cries. I try to remember my training but I'm not thinking straight. He is trying to kill my best friend.

I launch an almighty attack on his back. But he is strong, and he laughs as he slews around and flings me onto the floor, for a small man he is stocky and strong. He takes my feet from under me. I am trying to reach my knife tied under my trouser leg, with my right arm. As he bends down I grab him by his collar and send my right foot in between his legs. He falls on top of me. The air is forced out my body. And he is so heavy I can't breathe. I gasp, trying to push him off. With a superhuman effort I bend my right leg and kick him as hard as I can again between his legs. He groans. I push him and he falls off me, his hands go to his painful bits between his legs.

I reach for the knife and retrieve it from its strap around my leg. He is on his knees, bent double, as he tries to stand up from the pain in his groin, I stand over him. He tries to stand up, and with all the strength I can muster I stick the knife in his neck just below the clavicle with both hands and force it down as hard as I can. I pull it out as blood spurts everywhere. If I've done it right, he'll be dead in ten seconds. He looks up at me with a look of confusion and I stand there staring down in disbelief that I've actually done it. I watch him drop to his knees with the knife in my fist as blood drips down onto the floor. Then his whole body crumples and he goes face down with a crash and a pool of blood on the floor getting bigger.

I stand watching over him trying to understand what I've done. It's all over in a few seconds.

Eve and I stand there trying to get our breath and I stare at the body at my feet, with the knife still gripped in my right hand, dripping with blood.

'Is he dead?' Eve asks, and she starts shaking uncontrollably. My heart is racing with adrenalin, but I calmly walk over to a cloth on the table and wipe my hands and the knife on it. The relief is palpable. She laughs hysterically. I try to regulate my breathing and think.

I test his pulse. I can't feel anything.

'He's dead,' I tell her. 'What do we do with him?' I look at her. I still can't believe I killed him. The training paid off then, I reflect with irony.

'Have you got any brandy?'

'Erm.'

'It's for you, Eve, not me.'

She goes to a cupboard and takes out a bottle and takes a swig out of it. She offers it to me. I take a swig too. I must think clearly now, as clearly as I can. What if someone comes looking for him?

'Let's think, where can we put him for now?' I look at her.

'I've been wanting to kill that sadistic bastard for years since he raped me at thirteen.'

I let her talk for a bit as she shakes and I put my arm around her shoulders and she says, 'I feel sick.'

'You did well. But now we must dispose of the body. Before anybody finds it.'

'Stick him down the cellar.'

I try to pull his arms, but he's a dead weight I can't shift him. We struggle for a few minutes.

'Wait, I've an idea,' she says. She gets a mat from the hall, and we roll his smelly and bloody body back and forth until it goes under him. Then we both use the mat to move him towards the cellar. Touching him makes me feel sick. His clothes have a smell of sweet sticky garlic and something else.

'Pull together! Now!' I command. We make our way slowly across the wooden floor. Eve opens the cellar door. And slowly, we manoeuvre the mat to the top of the steps of the cellar. We both heave and push him from the top of the step and, with little effort after that, she puts her boot on his backside and pushes him and he topples all the way down to the bottom of the steps. If he wasn't dead, then he would be now. He lays there, neck turned sideways and his legs laying in odd angles.

'Wait!' I shout and run down the narrow steps as quick as I can and feel for any weapon that may help us. A German revolver is found inside his jacket and I tuck that in my trousers. I cover him with some dirty old sacks Eve found down in the dark and we go up and lock the cellar door.

We are both breathing fast, and I lean against the wall my heart heaving, while she staggers into the kitchen and flops down onto the armchair, her face bruised with a cut lip and torn trousers. Her face is as pale as a ghosts. I don't look much better.. We are both still reeling from what's just happened. I try to detach myself from emotion, willing the training to take over my thought processes.

'We need to clean the blood up and I need to wash my hands,' I say. 'Where can we dispose of the body? Robert would know what to do.' I lean over and breathe slower, although I'm still shaking. Suddenly the front door slams and Pierre walks in in his oily dungarees.

'Where is he? It's Mauvais' car, isn't it outside?'

'Oh God, his car! How could we forget?' We both turn to look at each other in horror.

'How long will it take them to follow him here? If he doesn't return today? Perhaps we have until tomorrow.'

We explain what happened. Pierre goes down to the basement and checks on the body.

'I'll drive it to the plateau and let it run down on its own from a great height. It'll look like an accident,' Pierre says.

'No!' Eve finally becomes alert. 'You'll get caught in the daylight. We need Robert to advise us.' She walks over to the window and looks out. Decisions. I know we can't shift him on our own.

'Pierre, go and find Robert and see if he can help us to get rid of his car and the body. We may be able to hide the body for a few days which will buy us some time.' I tell him.

'I'll cycle to the dead letter drop, it's closer than Henri's bar, and safer.'

285

'I'll hide the car in the barn, in case cars passing on the top road see it.' Eve says.

It's dark when Pierre gets back.

'How long do you think he'll be?' I ask him. We try to eat some supper but only Pierre has the stomach for it. I sit up most of the night, worrying, what we should do. In the morning I am still worrying - what if Robert doesn't go to the dead letter drop until today?

By morning, I go into Eve's bedroom.

'I'm going to drive the car out into the countryside.'

'No, you'll be seen! At least wait until nightfall.' I sigh and feel useless. I just want the dead body gone.

Nightfall comes and we sit listening to the BBC radio station. There's a quiet knock on the back door and Robert comes in, I jump up and we hug each other. His face is a picture of worry, and he is breathless.

'I had to cycle; we have no petrol left. But I came as quick as I could.'

Pierre jumps up. 'The body is in the cellar. They just threw him down the stairs.'

'I'll get rid of the body and car,' he says to Pierre.

'It would've been us if we hadn't defended ourselves,' I tell him. 'He just came at us both like a mad thing! He seemed obsessed on getting revenge, there was no stopping him. I didn't have my gun on me.'

We follow him down the cellar steps and he removes the sackcloth to look at Mauvais. Where the knife went in is marked in dried blood, the body is pale and a dead weight as Pierre, Robert and I try and take the weight.

Robert says, 'His neck is broken.'

'Probably when we flung him down the cellar steps,' says Eve dispassionately.

'It's no more than he deserved,' I chime in. 'But I'll come with you, Robert. If we get stopped by the police, we can say we're out for some romantic time for ourselves.'

'I wish it were true,' he says.

Rolled inside the old sacks Robert and Pierre manoeuvre Mauvais onto the back seat of his car. The smell of the body makes me put a scarf over my nose. Pierre and his mother watch us leave from the window. She has her hands over her mouth.

'It will be a long walk back.'

'That's all right. As long as I am with you, I don't mind.' I smile at him, and he drives off slowly down the road.

Robert drives the car in the direction of the river Vire, with no headlights on. We're following the route of the river. The area we arrive at a few minutes later is thick with undergrowth and suddenly he turns off onto a small road, it's a road leading out up into the hills and crossing the river that makes its way down to the sea. I see in the moonlight an old wooden bridge and underneath it the Vire river running swiftly under the bridge. A slope goes down into the river from our side.

'Will it be deep enough?' I ask him. I realise what he's going to do now. 'You've been here before.'

'As a boy, I used to come here with Henri, he used to live over there in that derelict old farmhouse.' He points in the distance. 'And we'd play in the river all Summer. I never thought I'd be using it for a trick such as this - hiding a dead body.'

Robert stops the car at the top of the slope.

'Get out now,' he says and roughly pushes me out. I shut the door and he immediately rolls the car down towards the river. I am expecting him to jump out before it hits the river, but I'm wrong. He's still inside as he aims for the middle where it flows fastest. The flowing current sparkles in the moonlight as it swallows the car and Robert whole. After I count five seconds his head appears then his body. A splash and I can breathe again as he scrambles to the bank and gets out.

'I had to go for the deepest part.'

'I was worried for you. I thought you'd gone down with the car!'

'I meant to get out before it went in, only I misjudged the flow of the river.' He laughs and shrugs. 'In a month it'll be low. It's just because we've had a lot of rain recently.'

'What if the body leaks out into the river?'

'Let's hope they don't find it before Liberation Day,' he says with a grim smile.

We are both breathing hard, and my heart is beating rapidly, when I realise how dangerous that was. I hug his sodden body.

'I got stuck a bit coming out the window, I'm not as fit as I once was.' He grimaces. 'But I am soaked. Let's go home.' He starts to shiver. I put my arm around his waist. We walk as quickly as we can the way we came. After about a kilometre we slow our pace. The wind picks up and the clouds scud across the moon.

'I was so worried about you,' I say to him. 'I thought you were drowning.'

He laughs, 'I knew what I was doing. And it is nice walking along with you, it will warm me up. How could I be cold with you here?' He puts his arm around me.

As we walk home in the moonlight, Robert keeps looking around us to see if anyone is about. There's no one, lucky for us. And I don't feel the cold, as we walk arm in arm now, and Robert is warming up. We walk past field after field along this country road, the hedges are getting higher as they join the bocage hedgerows. We seem to have been walking for an hour, when he goes through a gate and pulls me after him as we walk along the inside of a field. High hedgerows make it feel safer because they shield us from any patrols.

'We can relax a bit without checking for cars, I've used this track before, it's not so well used these days.'

The smell of cows is strong, and the grass smells of the recent shower of rain we had today. It's long and thick; it smells of summer meadows, I drink the smells in deeply. We come to an area I recognise. We're not far from the farm now.

He suddenly stops and sighs, he puts his arm around my waist and pulls me to him.

'I suppose I could have drowned.'

'You could have.' If only he could see my face. My voice is hoarse.

With his hands on my shoulders he seems to cast around for what he wants to say but can't find the right words. He puts his arms around me.

'Ow!' my ribs are still sore.

'Sorry.' He lifts my face up to kiss me.

'I'm not sure I want to live in France after the war if you're not here,' I tell him.

'I'll be all right. I won't get shot. I was in the Army for a long time.'

'What if you get caught by the enemy? No one's infallible.'

'If you get shot, we'd be stuck. You are the most important part of this group. You're indispensable. Without you we wouldn't have communications or resources from London.'

'They'd send another wireless operator, but you're our leader, without you to tell us what to do, we would be helpless.'

'You would take over. You have more guts than you think. Living amongst the enemy has toughened you up.'

'I'm not as brave as you think I am. I'm forever looking over my shoulder when I do my transmissions. I don't go out into the street now I realise how important it is to lie low.'

'That's good. That's how it should be. That way you live longer.'

I think about this as we keep walking. No one would know how to work the radio. Robert had watched me, but he wouldn't be able to use the silks. He was right. We walk quietly side by side. We are sheltered from the wind along this track and there's only the occasional dog barking in the distance. There are no lights on anywhere, but we pass an occasional farmhouse enveloped in darkness. Are they empty dwellings or people shutting out the enemy?

'Do you miss home?' he asks, startling me with his sudden question.

I cast him a bemused smile. 'I am home.'

'Your former home. England, Norfolk – your family, your friends?'

I was about to dismiss this question out of hand. Softly I admitted, 'Yes, there are some things I miss. My parents, my brother.

'What happened to your husband?'

291

'I couldn't go anywhere without his say so. He was twenty four, I was only nineteen.'

'What did your parents say about this?'

'They loved him. He wore a uniform and had a regular income. What was not to love?'

'Until he was killed.'

'Until he was killed. But by then I had begun to hate him.'

'You were so young.' He took my hand and squeezed it. 'What are you doing after the war?'

'No idea. Let's get this over first, shall we?'

'It might take some time. We have a lot to do.'

'Admittedly.'

'Then don't go back when you've done your job. Like I asked you before, stay here with Mila and me. She needs a mother. I need you,' he says quickly.

I stand still in the shadows of the bocage and look at his outline for a few moments. This is probably the most romantic moment I've ever had with anyone. He runs his hand through my hair. That pleases me immensely.

'You might have to practice that.'

Again, he kisses me. We put our arms around each other, and I don't want him to let me go. It's a moment in time I'll remember.

'Will there ever be a time when we can be together for good? How long will this war go on?' He sighs.

We walk across the field towards Eve's farm. I'm thoughtful but wide awake. We walk hand in hand and I realise it's still the early hours of the morning.

'I hope no one saw us walking back from the car,' I say.

'If they did, people round here won't say anything. They aren't loyal to the *Milice*.'

It looks like there is no light on in the farmhouse. But as I open the door, the smells from the kitchen entice me. It's warm and dry, the stove is still alight, and the smell of soup pervades throughout. Eve comes down the steps as if she's been waiting for us.

'Take your clothes off,' she says to Robert. 'You'll catch your death of cold.' She gives him a towel. He grins at me and goes upstairs to the salle de bains.

I go to the toilette in the outhouse. Then sit outside and look at the clear night while I smoke the cigarette Eve gives me. It's as if she understands everything I'm feeling. The first time I ever smoked it was one of Luke's cigarettes, before he left for the war. But I never smoked while he was at sea. My hand shakes as I breathe out the smoke, I start to cough. I'm not used to the nicotine and start to feel light-headed. Even so, I feel more relaxed now the worst is over. Or is it? What a lot has happened to me since landing here. I have seen another side of life. Life and death. I seem to be escaping at the last moment from the enemy wherever I go.

Robert comes out in Eve's husband's trousers. They are short in the leg, and he takes the cigarette off me. He has no shirt on. I busy myself lighting another cigarette conscious of his bare chest close to me. My hand isn't steady, he just smiles and takes it from me lighting it.

'Was I that obvious?' I asked honestly. I am too conscious of his muscular arms. It doesn't take much imagination to feel them around me. I look and smile at the trousers that are too short, and the shoes that are too big. He puts on a faded shirt that is too tight, pulling a jacket around his chest that doesn't fit. I can't help but laugh at him, he looks comical.

'Don't say anything…Emily.' He says to me, I am grinning from ear to ear.

'Eve is going to dry my clothes over the stove. He takes a drag from the cigarette and breaths it in heavily, as if it's a lifeline. I am glad he is staying here tonight.

'What a night - getting rid of a body.' He looks down at his new clothes. 'At least these are clean and dry. I hope Eve's husband won't mind.'

'I'm sure he doesn't.' I say.

'Are you staying the night?'

'Yes. It's too late to travel now. I'm so tired. I'll sleep with you in the barn.'

'Oh will you?'

Robert flicks the end of the cigarette onto the ground, and treads on it in the dirt. 'Come on, Eve has some cassoulet on the stove.' He grabs my hand, and we go inside. The clouds roll as the wind picks up speed. A storm is brewing.

Chapter 36

I see the body of Mauvais in the car and it's floating out of the window and downstream into the town and in front of the Germans. The face of Major Weber appears and points the finger at me, I run but can't run fast enough away from him. I turn to see him point a machine gun at me. He has me cornered. He fires. Bullets tear into my back as I wake up in a sweat. The rain pounds on the metal of the roof. It's been a nightmare.

For a moment I wonder where I am again. Another different place to put my head. Then I realise Robert is next to me in Eve's barn. I feel relieved he is there, and enormously happy. I stretch my limbs trying not to disturb him. Light is beginning to come through the gaps in the roof and the noise of the rain eases. We are lying on collapsed bales of hay, which are nice and dry. I am awake for an hour, not moving, as the light of day starts to grow stronger through the gaps in the barn.

I guess it's about six o'clock. It had become windy in the night and the whistling through the gaps had kept me awake, but now it's calmer. The rain is playing softly on the roof. I stay where I am just enjoying the moment of Robert breathing quietly next to me and his arm across me. I look at Robert's untroubled face in sleep.

I wish I could sleep like him. The truth is I never relax. But with Robert I feel calm, even considering all the events of yesterday. Even when Eve and I had been attacked, even though death surrounds us daily, I feel grateful I've lasted this long as a radio operator. I can tackle almost anything at this moment. My life has changed completely since I have been in Normandy. Looking at this man breathing gently beside me I feel more than I've ever felt in my life. I don't know what it is, but I just know that I can't live without him.

I can feel Robert stirring. I move and he does too. He scratches his head, and yawns.

'I don't like her husband's scratchy vest, it's rough. And she cut my hair, which I didn't ask for.'

'At least you can see out from under your hair now.'

I go to get up and he tightens his grip around my waist and pulls me back down on the hay, as he kisses me from above. I feel warm and happy, and a long way from England.

'Your family will be wondering where you are,' I say.

We kiss each other a bit longer. I try and drag it out because I don't want him to go, and I will have to get back into the cat and mouse chase with the Gestapo constantly on my tail.

'I wish the war would end,' I sigh. 'So we can get back to normality. I'm fed up with always trying to be one step ahead of the Gestapo.'

'It's lucky for us that you have a cool head and a strong nerve.'

I think about that for a moment and sit up. 'Do you really think I have a cool head?'

'Of course. Anyone going through what you have done recently wouldn't have kept their nerve I'm sure.' He sighs. 'I should go…I'll be back later.'

'Where are you staying?'

'In the forest with the Maquis. I've taken my mother and Mila to her aunt's house in a village in the south. They're safer where they were at the moment. There's too much going on at the Sainson's, and it doesn't feel good there. I must go as they'll be wondering what's happened to me. And you don't need to worry,' he says brushing my hair from my face. I reluctantly pull myself up from the straw.

'I worry more about you hiding from the Gestapo and for Eve too, it's all a deadly game,' he says. 'Keep low and in the barn today. It won't be long before they come looking for Mauvais. Let's hope we hear the call to arms from the Allies,' he says. 'Then we won't have to worry.'

Chapter 37

I am making my twelfth transmission in three months and feel elated as I look down from the top of the church tower of Saint Marie. Not bad for someone who was told six weeks would be my total life expectancy before the Gestapo catch me. I have received a transmission from London and show Robert the message from Baker Street.

Saint Lo train station sheltering three German tank transporters, request they be put out of action by June 1

'I think it should take three or four of us,' he says reading the message.

Couldn't Pierre and Eric do it from inside?"

'No, because they will be suspect, and we need them to continue to work for the *résistance* from inside the train station. We need to cut a hole in the perimeter fence, so it shows it's not insiders that have done the job.'

'There will be German guards?'

'Oh yes. Tell London we accept the request and will do the job.

'Mm' I see him churning a plan over in his mind, and I send the reply. This is the second time of transmitting from this point. I look at my watch it's been thirteen minutes in total.

299

'Time to go.' I tell Robert.

He is looking down on the town below. But we are hiding just out of sight of the people. I pack away my radio and antennae and stuff the case at the bottom of a basket.

We have one final look, as Robert puts his arm around me. 'You make everything better, even if you think you don't.' He takes the basket off me.

A warm feeling enthuses through me. I put my arm around him. He appears to be searching for the words he wants to say.

'You know I am trying to protect you.'

'Yes. But I'm trying to protect you too.'

'I'd never get over you. If something happened – you've meant more to me than...'

The revving of an army truck entering the square makes us move quickly down the steps. Our feet clatter and we almost bump into a priest who is ascending the stone steps. He asks us what we are doing.

'Just admiring the bells Father,' says Robert, and we laugh as we descend the rest of the way in the dark. Robert opens the door at the bottom of the steps to the outside. I am still digesting this comment as we make our way outside into the brilliant sunshine. And wonder what my mother would say to me if she knew I had fallen in love with an older man with a four- year-old daughter.

We blink as we come out into the market square which is bustling with people coming back and forth. The army truck has parked on the edge of the square. A young woman passes by and instantly recognises Robert. She says his name loudly and he says her name.

'Juliette!'

He has forgotten I'm here while they chat about how long it has been since they have seen each other. She is sorry about his wife passing. Watching her I realise this woman had feelings for him at one time, perhaps even now? Surprisingly, a spark of jealousy ignites in me, as I watch them kiss each other on the cheek.

It's then that I catch a quick movement out the corner of my eye. It's an ambulance driving towards us. I push Robert in the back to alert him and he falters and sees it. I don't have time to think, so I take the basket with my radio which he still has in his hand, and I merge quickly amongst the crowd. It's the most sensible thing to do as I am the least likely person to be stopped carrying a case. The woman has her back to the ambulance and she continues to talk to Robert while it stops in front of the tower. I turn back to see her put her arm on his arm as Major Weber and a subordinate get out of the ambulance – it's fake, as I suspected, it's an RDF van. They look around and see Robert talking to his friend, and that's the last thing I see of him as I disappear across the square and turn the corner into another busy street.

If they search him they will find nothing. Although my bicycle is in the back of his van. But that can be explained away. However, it is a long walk back to Eve's without transport and carrying a heavy basket to Saint Just all the way may alert suspicion.

There's a group of German soldiers at a barricade at the Vire bridge. A man in long trench coat and hat is searching a woman's basket. I turn quickly and go down another street, there are German soldiers coming up the street. As alleyway goes back to the main square, I walk quickly and they walk even quicker behind me. I see Henri's bar up ahead on the corner. I make my way towards his bar and go to the back of the bar and slip up the stairs to the room above. I close the curtains and watch the street to see if I'm followed.

Henri has seen me slip quietly through to the back of the bar and follows me upstairs.

'What's happened?' he asks in earnest.

'I just escaped arrest, an RDF in the guise of an ambulance stopped at the tower where we were just transmitting from. I slipped away but Robert saw an old friend and stopped to chat. He was still there when the Gestapo jumped out the RDF van. Thank goodness I managed to bring the radio with me.' I hold up the case to show him.

Henri moves to the window and looks out through the net curtain into the street.

'I don't think I was followed. But I need to hide for a while until Robert turns up to take me back to Eve's.'

'What if he's been arrested?'

'Then we're stumped.'

Chapter 38

Weber stands to attention in front of his superior's desk. The painting above the desk is stolen from a local chateau, showing an ancestor from pre-revolution times. Standartenfuhrer Riesel observes him from his seat the other side of his desk.

'I hope you have some good news for me Weber after yesterday's fiasco.'

Weber shifts a bit, his confidence dented just a bit. 'It was unfortunate that we were unable to catch the terrorists in the church tower. However, we are finding the people we took from the square helpful in bits of information about the *résistance*.'

'Titbits are no good to us, we need real information. Riesel bangs his hand down on the desk. 'I need results!'

'My spy in the résistance keeps me informed about the next parachute drop,' Weber says to his boss. 'There is a drop organised for tomorrow night on the road to Coutances. I will take the Gestapo and Fieldgendarmes. We will have the *résistance* terrorists in gaol this time tomorrow.'

'Good. How did you manage to get the spy to report on his comrades?'

'Oh, I have my ways. It's working well.' He shines his hat badge with his sleeve. His confidence has been dented temporarily. Under this plan he will regain favour with Riesel and more importantly with his Fuhrer.

'At last, finally we might be seeing some results. Let us see how you handle it,' says Standartenfuhrer Riesel.

* * *

Robert and the *Maquis* are hiding in wait. The moon is full, and it has been spluttering with rain. The wind is picking up - it's not ideal weather for a drop. Robert wonders if it's still on. He's got a bad feeling in his gut about tonight. But the *message personnel*s report the phrase after the news at 7.15 that night, '*The goat is eating grandpa's vest,*' And at 9.15 p.m. it is repeated and signals that the drop is on course to go ahead.

Robert wishes Emily were with him tonight. After narrowly escaping from the Gestapo yesterday in Saint Just he doesn't want to endanger everyone even more. It had been his idea to transmit from under the Nazis very noses. It was a close call. If his friend Juliette hadn't taken his arm and they'd moved quickly out of the area, and Emily hadn't grabbed the radio and removed it out of harm's way the day might have ended differently. As it was the Gestapo rushed up the tower to find they had missed the *résistants* by seconds, they then rounded up a group of men that were in the square and took them back to the police station.

Robert feels terrible, he feels it is his fault the innocent men have been arrested. He has heard nothing in twenty-four hours of what has happened to them. Although he and Emily got back to Eve's eventually last night, she had asked him to include her in the drop, she felt guilty too, but he had said no. He was making mistakes. Even if it's to confirm his suspicions aren't founded, he needs someone he can tell his fears to, he has an uneasy feeling about this *parachutage*.

Robert drives Bear and his cousin Jacques in the baker's van to the drop area. Jacques is seventeen and a recruit. Jacques is so excited about going on his first parachutage. Bear worries that he doesn't see the dangers in his excitement, he warns him that he must follow their instructions to the letter. The Maquis are driven in a truck that belongs to an older man, called Marcel who wants to join the Maquis - now his wife will let him - because it looks like the tide of the war is turning in favour of the allies. The truck is a wood gasifier. The man uses wood from the forest to fuel his truck because there is no petrol to be had. Although it belches out fumes into the faces of the men in the back of the truck, it helps them get from place to place. The ammo and arms can be loaded into it and driven away quickly to a safe place. Vehicles are in short supply for French citizens, petrol even more. They meet at the old barn like before, near Coutances, and Robert goes over the plan of action.

'Do you have your guns?' asks Bear.

They nod. Some have hand grenades hanging from their belts. The men from the forest look dirty and dishevelled. They wear their pistols cocked aggressively above their trouser tops, the rifle on the shoulder, the Sten on their backs. Months of living off the land with handouts of food from local villagers has made them hardy but hungry. Many are smoking cigarettes. Even some of the new recruits some as young as sixteen and seventeen, are smoking and trying to look confident. Many more people are joining the *résistance* after escaping from the *Milice*.

Laurent is not going on this drop, Gaston suggests Robert take some of the new recruits instead, as his wife gets upset each time Laurent leaves the house with him. The tide is turning in Europe and people are waiting for the Allied invasion which will come soon, citizens are just waiting so that they can help the Allies kick the Nazis out of their country. Robert chooses a man about his age, Maurice, and has experience of fighting in the army. He has joined the Maquis after his wife and son were shot for running away from a blockade, he hates the Nazis with a vengeance. He wants to fight alongside the *Maquisards*. Robert has heard of lots of stories like this, of women and children fleeing the Nazis, but they shoot them anyway. It makes him sick to his stomach. But because of the good news that the Russians have pushed the

Germans back after the Battle of Stalingrad, morale has increased. At last there's been a successful battle that has gone the Allies way, like El Alamein. It has revived the morale of the Allies and consequently the local inhabitants of Saint Just after we find out on the 7.15 BBC News. People sense freedom is coming and soon.

The clouds' part at midnight and a group of *résistance* gather in the damp field next to a river estuary which makes its way to the sea. They hear the droning of a medium sized aircraft as it flies slowly beneath the cloud cover. The noise of the engine comes and goes as the wind passes over its contours and it continues on its path towards them. The reason they're going slowly is because the wind has picked up and is throwing the pilot off course. The aeroplane is bucking in the wind, as if objecting to its destination.

Robert beckons to Maurice and Bear to light the paraffin lamps and stand in the L configuration. He signals the pre-arranged letter as the aircraft flies over them. Robert holds his breath. The aircraft has overshot. That's all right. It does a U turn and flies back over the area dropping its cargo of ten containers. Its engine revs up and sails up and away into the clouds and out of harm's way.

All ten parachutes open this time. But the wind blows up and catches some of them and they get blown towards the beach some distance away. Some of the team are new recruits, they shout and run after them. Robert tells them to gather nearer the beach and run towards the trees on the edge of the field where the sand dunes start. He sees the parachutes billow out and flap about as four of the containers sail over the dunes and out of sight.

Robert and Maurice hear a machine gun firing and look back in horror as some of their comrades are being mown down by German soldiers.

'It's a trap! This way!'

They hear shouts and cries but run for their life.

They get to the trees and run left along the thickest parts of shrub where there are hiding places. They have a head start. They keep running parallel to the trees and the beach. Weber and the Gestapo have captured some of the Maquis. A machine gun goes off amongst the trees and some of the *résistants* fall but some keep running.

'Run Jacques!' Bear shouts at the top of his voice as he dives into some dense cover. Jacques is one of those running towards the beach, he doesn't look round he doesn't stop.

One Maquisard stands still, he turns round to face the soldiers, his hands up in the air in a sign of submission. Don't shoot!' he shouts. Gunfire explodes all around them. He is shot in the chest and falls flat on his back.

Weber shouts to his soldiers 'Don't shoot them all. I need some for interrogation!'

The soldiers rush towards them firing in the air.

'Hands in the air! Surrender, or you will be shot!'

It will be his pleasure to inflict even more pain on them back at the police headquarters. After he's reported to Standartenfuhrer Riesel of course. He has a plan to make them talk this time.

Robert and Maurice keep running out of sight behind the sand dunes and are about a kilometre away when the machine gunner stops. They keep going with two Gestapo on their tail.

Weber shouts; 'No *résistants* are to escape!'

Robert pushes Maurice one way, and he goes the other as he shouts to him.

'Split up - use your Sten!'

The two Gestapo are dressed in dark clothes and now the moon has gone beyond the clouds Robert strains to see the outlines of their pursuers in the grey darkness, as he hides behind one of the dunes. They must have split up too. Robert sees one of them crawling along behind some undergrowth. Something flashes in the dark as something on the man reflects in the partial moonlight. The man coming towards him can't see him although he guesses he's hiding, and Robert crawls slowly forward behind the bushes until there's a gap. The flash again. It could be a medal on his chest or even glasses. He's about thirty metres away. Robert takes aim and fires a round into the man. He slumps down to the ground. There is no sign of the other one, but you can bet he's hiding here somewhere.

Robert keeps moving low towards the Gestapo that he's shot. He gets to the body and pushes it with his foot, his Sten aimed at his head. It doesn't move. He's dead.

Suddenly a figure appears about ten metres away, emerging from his hiding place. He aims at Robert and in an instant, a burst of fire behind him and the man falls flat on his face. Maurice stands up and waves at Robert. The moon comes out and Robert stands up and checks the two bodies are dead. He does a thumbs up to Maurice. Neither of them speaks. They run off into the night.

Back at the forest hideout, Robert is checking who is still alive and who isn't. Bear is the only one alive who managed to escape. He ran to the dunes and hid in the dark for hours, while they searched the area. But Bear has escaped soldiers before and knows the area well, so he knows where to hide and keeps still until they've gone.

The field is full of dead Maquis. They killed seven and wounded five and took them away with them keeping them alive just long enough for interrogation.

Robert tells Gaston and Henri that it was a trap and the *Maquis* who were taken are mostly young men, who don't know anything about the reseau.

'Who would give us away like that?' He demands of Gaston and Henri. 'Who would be a traitor to France?'

Chapter 39

D-DAY minus 1

The second verse of the French poem is repeated in the evening's British Broadcasting Corporation's broadcast to the *Résistance* movements listening on their radios all over France. It is the opening lines of the 1866 Verlaine poem "Çhanson dÁutomne,' it's the second stanza we're all waiting for.

'Les Sanglots longs des violons de l'automne.'

At Eve's house, we lean in closely to Robert's radio, as he tunes in past the static. A voice booms out:

'Blessent mon coeur d'une langueur monotone' — *the landing will follow within forty-eight hours.*

'The second passage has been spoken! The second passage has been spoken!' Pierre exclaims as we sit round the table looking up at the radio and listening to the midnight news, hardly daring to breathe. Eve and Robert sit opposite me at the table. There has been rain and wind recently, and we didn't think the Allied landing would go ahead with such bad weather in Northern France.

Now we need to get ready for sabotage and formulate our plans so our *réseau* flies into action.

'Oh my God,' I said. 'It's happening.' I push my drink away from me and look at everyone's faces around the table. At last, after three months of playing cat and mouse with the Gestapo the time is finally here when we can get out into the open and fight for France and liberty.

'Then let's get to it,' Robert pushes his chair back and stands up.

'Now perhaps we can get our men out of Gestapo gaol!'

We look up at him as he goes to the door.

'You all have your instructions. We know what we must do now. Go to your groups. Good luck everyone.'

Robert leaves to notify the Maquis while Eric and Pierre notify the railway workers that are part of the *résistance*.

'It's here at last,' says Eve. 'Le jour de la liberation!'

'Le jour de la liberation!' I shout with her in triumph.

* * *

As the sun goes down, Robert is changing into overalls, a jacket and cap brought in by Eric.

'Put a bit of grease on you Robert,' Eric grins. 'Then you'll look more unrecognizable.' Eric smudges some grease from his can onto his face.

Eve and I look at him, 'You'll do,' she says. He looks different in railway workers' clothes.

'Come on, Gaston and Bear are already camouflaged,' says Eric. 'They're in the barn.'

In the barn Gaston and Bear are handling the plastique carefully as they lay them out in a row on bales of hay. Thirty-one-pound charges of plastique lie neatly to attention, with pencil detonators lying next to them.

'I'll go over this once more,' Robert says to Bear and Gaston, while Eric looks on.

'Crush the copper end of the detonator. This releases a chemical which burns through a wire inside. When you've done it pull out this safety strip.'

'This is all new,' says Bear, his huge hands handling things gingerly. 'It's not like when we were in the army.'

'When the wire dissolves it releases a striker which hits the detonator, Robert continues. 'Put two of these timers into each block of explosives in case one fails to work.'

'Do you have your Stens primed?' I ask them all, they all nod. At that moment Laurent turns up from across the fields from his house. He looks into the barn and sees the men stuffing their plastique in their engineer bags.

'Hey,' he says looking at his father. 'How come you didn't tell me you had a mission going on?'

'You do not need to know, Laurent. I've told you about this before.' Gaston spreads his hands earnestly trying to get his son to understand. Robert makes Laurent face him.

'We can't go telling everyone about every secret mission, or every German will know about it.'

'I won't tell anyone.' He says.

'Too late.' I say to Robert. 'We could have a look out.' I say ruefully.

'All right, you can help Eve as a look out down the other end of the rail yards.' Laurent does a celebration dance.

'But! You are to tell no one of what is happening tonight. If the Boche find out, innocent civilians will be killed.'

'There's just one thing Robert,' I say before he gets any further. 'I am going instead of Eve.'

'What?'

'She's not well. I think it's the after-effects of the other day with Mauvais.' Robert's shoulders sag a bit, he looks angry.

'It's too dangerous to take you, something could go wrong and then we've lost our *piano,* our only way of communicating with London,' he says despairingly. He thuds his equipment into his van. It's the first time I've seen him angry.

'I'll be all right,' I tell him quietly. 'My ribs are healing after the fight.'

'No, it's too dangerous, Laurent can go instead of Eve.' And he bangs the van door shut after Laurent and Gaston get in the back of the van, Bear and Robert are in the front. He winds the van window down and smiles at me, 'Anyway, you should rest and help the ribs heal.'

'At last, a sabotage mission!' Laurent is beside himself with glee.

'Try and be quiet. A lot of it will be waiting, we can't do anything until it's dark.' Gaston says.

'Perhaps I'll better go and tell *maman* where I am first.'

'No!' I push him back into the van before he can jump out.

'Absolutely not. No one is to know. Like Robert said, it's on a need-to-know basis. He will explain what you do on the way Laurent.'

'But what if *maman* comes looking for me?'

'We will say you passed through looking for a friend, or something like it.' I tell him and Robert pulls away, giving me a last wave.

Laurent looks uncomfortable, but his keenness to participate in his first sabotage mission is overtaken by any qualms about his mother wondering where he is.

Saint Lo is the main hub for trains in the area. Near the perimeter fence the men get out and hide the automobiles in the trees next to a track running parallel to the train tracks. A tall barbed-wire fence separates the two. There is no climbing over this one. Before the Germans there was no fencing to keep people out. Now the railway yards are secured with fencing and has twenty-four-hour security. We will enter about a kilometre and a half down the track, where there is a padlocked gate. They crouch down in the undergrowth on the edge of the wood.

'There's a group of German soldiers inside the sheds at the end of this track as it curves into the station,' Robert points in the distance. We see a glow of light as the door opens and some soldiers come out and go in the opposite direction to the saboteurs.

'They do their rounds from there every half an hour. We don't have long in between midnight and 12.30 to set the plastique. So, let's be as efficient and as quiet as we can.' Robert whispers loudly. 'Laurent you will hide here and keep in contact flash your torch if someone comes out of the shed.' He nods.

'Silence from now on,' he says. 'Just use your torch, if they come our way, flash it at us and then hide. No sounds. Got it?'

Laurent nods again. There is no moon tonight. Some owls call to each other across the wood behind them.

'Off you go, down there.' He points to an area closer to the main platform and parallel to the soldiers' shed. Laurent hides down amongst the bushes. Robert, Bear and Gaston go to the other end of the compound and hide amongst the undergrowth by a sealed gate. Two soldiers come out of the hut, the light shining behind them. The door is shut.

The two soldiers walk down the track and disappear into the dark next to the ghostly bulbous black shapes of the tank transporters. They don't stay long to check them over as they make their way back almost straight away. Laurent remains hidden in the darkness of the bushes as they make their way back to their hut. One of the soldiers walks up to the perimeter fence as he unzips his trousers near where Laurent is crouching and pees through the wire fence, the smell of urine seeps into the night air. Laurent turns up his nose at the smell of strong urine. He is hidden under the protection of a big bush in the darkness.

At last, the soldier joins his friend. They light cigarettes and then walk slowly back to their shed. At the train station two single lamps glow dully giving a narrow cone of blurred light. Not much can be seen on this moonless night.

The saboteurs go to town with bolt croppers cutting a doorway big enough for a crouching man to crawl through. They move through the gate noiselessly. They crouch down keeping on the dark side of the train track towards the two swan tank transporters, they disappear behind them, the transporters loom ominously under their black shrouds of camouflage.

The minutes tick by. Laurent starts to sweat even though it's a cool night. At twelve thirty, Robert comes back through the hole in the gate, crouching low. Gaston and Bear are a few metres behind him.

Then everything happens at the same time. Immediately there is a flash of light from Laurent's torch as the soldiers' door opens and light spills out. Suddenly they hear a droning sound in the distance, the sky lights up with anti-aircraft gun fire. Realisation dawns on Robert's face. The bombers on the horizon are getting closer. Some soldiers come outside to look up at the sky. There is a row of Allied bombers coming towards them like huge birds of prey. The noise is deafening. Then Laurent comes out of his hiding place on the edge of the wood. His torch is on and he's waving it back and forth anxiously so that his comrades the other side of the trains can see it. Robert sees him do it, as they're already crawling through the wire fence. They will escape into the woods, and all he he's done is alert the enemy to his position.

But then suddenly someone shouts, and it looks like Laurent is running now down the track towards them, with his torch still on. It flashes up and down as he runs. A shout again and two shots are fired, and the torch light disappears. Laurent has fallen on the path and is out of sight. Is he shot? Dead or alive?

'Nicht schiezen! Nicht schiezen!'

'Don't shoot! Don't shoot!' Robert shouts.

The *résistants* crouch unsure what to do while Robert, crawls quickly, commando style, parallel to the boundary fence. The soldiers shine their torches at Laurent, who is covered in blood and doesn't move. He could be dead. They hear some shouts the other end of the compound and they raise the alarm and run down to the end where Gaston and Bear are. Meanwhile the troops spill out of the shed searching to see where the dangers are. In the confusion Robert gives Laurent a fireman's lift and runs into the forest towards the van. He shouts to Gaston and Bear; '*Vite!* Hurry!'

The *résistants* disappear into the wood, just as two bombs explode one after the other behind them. The allied bombers have made direct hits on the railway tracks in the middle of the station.

At the same time at 12.32 the plastique explodes dead on cue, further down the track it blows the two transporters to fragments. It's chaos as metal and wood fly everywhere. Debris lands all around them. The air smells of burning and cordite.

In the confusion the *résistants* escape. Shots are fired through the metal fence, but the soldiers can't see in the dark and the torches don't go far enough into the wood. An automobile roars into life and they hear a car roar away.

Robert bangs incessantly on Doctor Jacques' door, until a man half asleep opens it. Bear and Gaston half carry half drag Laurent inside and lay him on the doctor's sofa.

'This is the first place they'll look. Fix him as soon as possible, then we'll take him out of here.'

The doctor strips off Laurent's shirt. 'The bullet has just missed his heart, and he's bleeding internally. He needs blood - he should go to the hospital.'

'Neither of which we can do. Do what you can doctor, and we'll take him back to his mother to look after him.'

'He'll die without proper treatment.'

'He'll die anyway through torture when the Boche have finished with him!' Bear exclaims.

The doctor sighs and treats his wounds and bandages him. They carry Laurent back to the van, he's a deathly grey colour. Between them they lay Laurent gently in the back. Gaston gets in the back with his son and holds his head. Laurent is quiet and pale. Blood covers the sacks on the floor of the van. The doctor shakes his head as he watches them drive off.

Robert takes the back streets avoiding the town centre and the destruction and bright fires highlighted against a black and smoky sky.

The last RAF bomber has flown over and the scale of the fire and noise around the train station shows the scale of the destruction. They are two streets away and determined to avoid the main road where soldiers and men in plain clothes are everywhere. A German fire engine is trying to put out the fires.

Robert dodges the destruction and fires as he comes to the East side of town where most of the Allied bombs have been dropped. At last, he comes to a small back road which will lead to Laurent's farm. He screeches to a halt. A bomb has blown a huge hole in the road in front of him. The longer the van is on the road the more chance the Germans have of catching them.

'How is he? 'Robert demands from the front seat.

'Not good.' Is Gaston's reply. 'Take it easy now. Laurent is unconscious.'

'This one on the left!' Gaston shouts from the back. Robert reverses and drives down a side street. They find another back road which will lead to Gaston's farm. He is too close to the bomb dropping zone, but he drives slowly with the window down and no lights on. As he comes out of the town, he puts his lights on so he can see the road in front. It's down a small lane from here.

Laurent is quiet, and deathly pale in the back. Gaston is holding his head in his lap; he has tears in his eyes. Within a few minutes, they go up the drive to their farmhouse. Yvette is waiting at the door when they arrive. Robert can see the white of her headscarf against the dark front door. She breaks down in tears as Robert, Bear and Gaston carry Laurent out of the van.

'Oh God, Robert, I thought he was dead. They promised me he wouldn't be harmed!'

Supporting him either side, the men carry Laurent's slight frame between them inside the house, Bear waits in the van, while Yvette makes up a bed for Laurent downstairs. Robert straightens himself up as Gaston gathers towels to put around his body to soak up the blood, and Yvette starts to fuss around her son who is unconscious.

'You have to go, Robert. Now.' Gaston tries to push him out the door.

'Who said he wouldn't be harmed? What are you trying to say Yvette?' He insists and won't be pushed out of the door. Something slowly dawns on him. They've been set up.

Yvette is crying. 'I am sorry. So sorry.'

'What are you saying, Yvette? Have you informed on us to the enemy?' Then as she hangs her head and fusses over Laurent.

Robert stands his ground as realisation dawns on his face. He grabs Yvette by the shoulders, and he makes her face him.

'What the bloody hell have you done?' he shouts at her. She tries to pull away, but he won't let her, he grabs her arm.

'The Gestapo let him go last time because you promised to give them information about the us, didn't you?'

She pulls away from him, ashamed, trying to look away and towards her son.

'What?' Gaston is incredulous as he gets up from the bed. 'You've been a *collaborateur* Yvette? He stares incredulously at her, his mouth open.

'I didn't know about this Robert. I swear it!'

Laurent groans on the couch. His mother bends down to hold his hand.

'I couldn't help it. One son is gone, I don't want the other to go. It's all right for you Robert, you don't have sons!' She bends her head down above Laurent's body and weeps.

'You'd better go before they come!' Gaston shouts to Robert, 'You need to warn the others, the Maquis… Emily. Yvette, did you give them the details of the *parachutage*?'

Robert stands there taking all this in. He hadn't suspected a thing. He starts to shake with anger. 'They will still take him,' he says to her.

She shakes her head. 'I'll do whatever I can to save him. He's my life.'

'Go Robert. Go! I'll sort things out here.' Gaston pushes him towards his van. Robert drives off a horrible feeling in his guts. The whole *réseau* is in danger.

Since the explosions at the train station, Eve and I have been waiting by the kitchen window looking out at the smoke and fire. None of us bothered to sleep except Pierre, and he came downstairs as soon as the bombing went off.

My ribs still throb from the bashing Mauvais gave me. Laurent is at death's door, Giselle has disappeared. And we don't have enough *résistants* to fight back on the Day of Liberation. What on earth are we going to do?

We hear a van pull up outside Eve's farm. If it's Robert, he'll come in by the back door.

The back door opens, and Robert stands there, he looks tired, but he has news he wants to give us. He is covered in dirt and grease from the carborundum. He looks at us all and flops down on a kitchen chair. We wait for him to speak.

'Laurent's in a bad way. He got shot. I took him back to his home after the doctor tended to his wounds. I don't think he'll survive the night.'

We look at each other with worry edged on our faces..

'And I just found out who the traitor is.'

Chapter 40

D-DAY - 6 JUNE 1944

While Laurent was fighting for his life, the Allied invasion was under way. After midnight airborne landings are reported on the Orne and the Cotentin peninsula. Weather conditions and tides are unfavourable and many German senior officers in the area go on leave because they think the weather conditions are too dangerous for ships and men. Little do they know that a flotilla of a thousand ships had set sail from England.

By 0300 Eve and I are climbing over the telephone exchange's barbed wire barrier which rests on top of a metal fence. We use wire cutters and jump to the ground with bended knees, which is about two metres. Eve hurts her ankle and I have scratched myself on the barbed wire. We clamber to a door hidden from the road. Eve limps to the back door and we wait for Robert to open it from the inside.

'Are you all right?' I hiss.

She rubs her ankle and screws up her face in pain, 'Ouch!'

We hold our breath and listen intently in case someone hears us. Secrecy is vital here. The enemy must not hear us coming in their back door. Something only Eve knows of because she used to work here a year ago.

The telephone exchange is a central priority building which must be disabled permanently if we are to win the war. Unfortunately, it's right next door to the German garrison which is a municipal building commandeered by the Nazis and one of the nicest buildings for miles around. It's been completely re-purposed to house two hundred German soldiers. The exchange is now in German hands, surrounded by a fence and barbed wire. Two soldiers guard the entrance gate at night and operate from a sentry hut next to the gate. We know the night routines of the guards due to inside knowledge from one of the telephonists, who is sympathetic to the *Résistance* movement.

Robert is dressed as a French electrician with his box of tools in his hand, arrives at the gate, a sentry comes out of his office.

'I have no knowledge of anyone arriving this late,' he says in French.

'It's a problem with the teleprinter, they've only just reported it. I was on my way home from work.'

'I have nothing on this detail.' The sentry looks at his clipboard.

'Well, I'd rather be at home in bed. I am fed up with them calling me out to fix things at any time of the day or night. If I am not needed, I'll be off home. You will have to sort it out. Don't expect me to come out again in the middle of the night.'

The soldier hesitates. 'I need to contact your base to check.'

'Here you are.' Robert gives him Henri's telephone number and he goes inside his sentry box to make the call. Henri answers it on the second ring and gives the correct information that he's asked by the German sentry.

The sentry comes back. 'All right. It's been confirmed. But I have to escort you.' He lets Robert in and shuts the gate after him. He goes to tell the other sentry where he's going.

Damn, thinks Robert. I don't need him following me.

'It'll only take a minute. I am hoping to be in and out in five minutes.' Robert sighs with relief that Henri was awake to take the call so he can verify that he is a telephone engineer.

'I will accompany you,' the sentry repeats.

'Please yourself,' says Robert, shrugging his shoulders.

He takes Robert through the door into the building, and down the corridor to the main room. Robert leads the way although he's not been here before Eve has explained the layout by a diagram. At the point of entering the main room, Robert starts to make a detour down a small flight of stairs.

'I have to go to the main switch down here.'

The sentry's thrown off course. 'What switch?' then rumbles him.

'Hande hoch!' he sticks a pistol in his back.

They're two steps down into a dark staircase. Robert pulls out his pistol from his jacket and twists and steps back to the sentry knocking the barrel end of the pistol sideways and shoots him in his side. The sentry crumbles forward with a gasp and Robert trips him and pushes him down the rest of the stairs. As he hits the floor his head is knocked askew. His neck is broken.

Robert pulls him out of the way under the stairs by his boots and takes his gun. He runs upstairs and unbolts a back door at the end of a corridor opposite the toilets and lets Eve and me in. One of the ladies inside the exchange comes out to see what's happening. When she sees the guns, she goes to scream, but Robert has his hand over her mouth in a moment and drags her back into the exchange.

We follow him into the exchange where another woman is working on the ground level at a large switchboard. While Robert lays the charges downstairs. Eve and I stand with Sten guns at our hips our guns aimed at them. Eve recognises the women on the night watch; she motions them towards the door.

'Madeleine, don't scream, and Genevieve, don't speak. Take off your headphones and step away and leave here now.'

Genevieve looks aghast at her, her hand poised to answer a call. Eve pulls the plug out of the switchboard.

'Just in case you decide to call someone.'

'What's happening?' Madeleine asks.

Genevieve and Madeleine look at each other. Genevieve gets up slowly.

'Do as I say, ladies, and you won't be harmed. Step down now. Pick up your bags and jackets and walk out of here.'

Madeleine is confused but is beginning to get the idea.

'What are you doing?'

'Nothing which need concern you. It'll come clear tomorrow. Now go home both of you.'

The second sentry appears through the door to the main frame and asks Madeleine what is happening where's his friend? Then he sees us with guns drawn and he grabs his rifle slung on his shoulder. There is a shot, a scream, as he crumples to the floor face first. Robert enters the room with the German pistol in his hand still smoking.

'Why did you do shoot him?' demands Madeleine.

'It's either him or me. And the success of The Liberation depends on it.'

She stares at him with mouth open. Robert pulls the soldier's body down the stairs with the other dead sentry.

'Don't say or do anything until tomorrow ladies,' I tell them. 'Tomorrow will be a different day. Don't come into work.'

'But I need to...'

'No you don't.... It won't be here.'

I bundle Madeleine towards the door. She grabs her bag and coat. Genevieve walks quickly to the door with her bag and joins Madeleine.

'Don't say anything to anyone.' I zip my mouth. They get the gist. 'There's another room off there,' Genevieve points along the corridor. 'It has the amplifiers for the long-distance lines to

330

Germany.' Then she rushes out her coat flowing on her shoulders behind her.

'Quickly! Before someone realizes they're missing.' I say in earnest.

We spend the next ten minutes laying the charges amongst the main distribution frame. Two sets of terminals on long racks. Robert goes along the corridor to the room with amplifiers. We've already discussed how we're going to destroy the building – and Robert's gone over this with a telephone engineer. We work swiftly setting the fuses, the ticking of the clock dictates how quick we do this.

'Emily, set the fuses under the record cards,' he shouts.

I run into the next room - I know what I'm looking for. They're the duplicate records which show how the cables are connected, if they're destroyed there is no chance the exchange will be back in action this year. I am anxious and I shake as I set the fuses. But not because I've seen Robert shoot a soldier in the back. I've killed people too; it's been a necessary evil. I know that I won't survive if I don't use my gun to defend myself. My hands shake - it's the adrenalin rushing through my body. I finish setting the charges.

'Hurry!' I shout to them. The telephone is ringing off the hook in the sentry office.

'I've set the fuses for five minutes.' Robert says as he comes back into the exchange. He appears calm, while I observe Eve is anxious.

'That should give us plenty of time.' Eve bustles the rest of plastique back in her bag. She knows what she's doing.

Suddenly, another soldier has entered through the door behind me. Eve and Robert stop and freeze mid crouch and Eve has her hands on fuses. He takes in the picture of the two of us in black camouflage gear and a bag of plastique and fuses and aims his gun at Eve.

'Halte!'

I am closest to him but I'm kneeling, my back to him. My hands close over the gun in the bag. Robert and Eve stare at me. I try to think how I am going to stop him from shooting my friend. I spin round quickly and shoot him in the stomach. It's not my best aim, he doubles up and looks up at me, his young face looks shocked. I shoot him again right between the eyes, this time he falls forward to the floor. We're taught to shoot twice in SOE, in case the first one isn't deadly.

'Go!' shouts Robert.

We all run to the gate, Madeleine and Genevieve are in the sentry shed looking for the key to unlock the gate..

'It's locked!' I shout. I panic, 'Where's the key?'

We stand for a millisecond in despair, the bombs are going off in four minutes. Robert has already run back to the dead sentry.

Madeleine and Genevieve are panicking still looking for the gate key, it cannot be found.

Robert runs back with a key. 'It was on him!'

He undoes the gate and we run out of the gate.

'Run!' Robert shouts and they don't waste a second, realising what is about to happen. Madeleine and Genevieve run to the right while we run to the left and into the alleyway across the road and into the darkness beyond.

Running through the Rue de Nuelle into another narrow street where Robert has hidden his van behind wooden double doors. The van takes three starts of the ignition, and with a look of relief, Robert drives out of the garage, I close the doors and hop in the passenger seat, as Robert drives out of the narrow street and into the main street and past the Gendarmerie and police station. There are no lights on and no moon. It's pitch black and quiet as a morgue, as the tyres screech as Robert puts his food down on the gas and we drive off at top speed.

'That's thirty pounds of putty,' says Robert, a little bit puffed, 'The place should go up like a tinder box.'

Behind us the telephone exchange explodes, the roof flies off like a volcano. Several blasts go off one after the other inside. When it's finished the flames take a hold on the wooden structure. The flammable electrics catch alight and add to the heat. More shock blasts ring into the night, people start to wake up and wonder what the noise is all about. As the debris disperses across into the garrison, lights come on and the embers float like little flaming islands as the dry wood encourages the fire to spread. The flames lick up into the sky as high as the garrison as the flames spread across the building like a tinderbox.

'It's payback time,' says Robert.

0330 hours

A few ships are sighted off Port-en-Bessin at 0300. Admiral Krancke has ordered sea reconnaissance by surface vessels. At 0430, torpedo boats put out from Le Havre.

Many of the officers have gone away for a long weekend and the Allies have caught the Germans napping.

On this morning of June fifth, the weather is wet and windy, the waves are choppy, and the German army is not expecting an attack from the English Channel by a fleet of warships.

There is, however, a window in the weather today and the Allies set sail for Normandy; a vision of choppy seas, grey skies, and seasick sailors are the first wave of invaders on the Normandy beaches. It's the Allies invasion of France. Most German officers are visiting their girlfriends. Himmler is seeing his mistress and Rommel is seeing his wife in Germany for her birthday.

All is going as planned. Phone calls are trying to be made, but no telephone calls are getting through. The sabotage at the main communications centre is a success.

Meanwhile, outside Saint Just, the *Résistants* are getting ready for their sabotage.

'They'll have difficulty getting through to Hitler now,' says Bear. We get up to go and we hear an explosion some distance away. We look towards the horizon from our vantage point, we can't see but we can hear bombs in the distance. The excitement is unbearable, Eve and I hug each other, at last the Allied invasion force is on its way to rescue France from the Nazis.

* * *

Two British Mosquito fighter-bomber aircraft fly low over the Normandy coastline. They approach the German defences at high speed. Two German soldiers in their bunker watch the glow of the fire as the kettle hanging over it starts to boil. They are well dug in and hidden in the depths of their bunker. One of them looks through a window slit and sees the aeroplanes flying towards them at a dangerously low level.

'There's only two of them. They're just reconnaissance,' says the first one. He turns to his friend, who says.

'Maybe. But I don't like the look of them.'

A mile further along the two Mosquitoes home in on two aerials and blast them to tiny pieces. They see the obliterated aerials behind them as they fly back over. Triumphantly they zoom off up into the sky and head for home.

0400 hours

It is still dark with a speck of light on the horizon. It's cloudy and the wind is picking up. Three figures in black, the typical camouflage of the *Maquis*, are fixing the final wires to the row of overground telegraph wires. They each have a Hurricane lamp to see things by. The telegraph wires stand majestically with the loose wires swaying more and more as the wind picks up. The men have finished wiring up the detonators to the explosives which are wrapped around the bottom of the poles. They jump down and run down an embankment as a German armoured car goes past but doesn't see them. They hunch behind trees as it goes past looking for the *résistants* who blew up the telephone exchange.

One of the Maquis fixes the end of the wires to a box, and he primes the box. After a nod to each other. He pushes down the handle and the end telegraph pole blows up at its base, then the next explodes, then the next. The wires are all sparking like November 5th fireworks and the telegraph poles fall one after the other like a set of dominoes. The last pole crashes to the ground.

336

The figures run off into the shadows. Another communications network has come down.

Another group of Maquis is working on underground wires at an electrical box at the end of an enemy compound. Out of sight and unseen. The combination of these sabotage groups will mean that Franz who is trying to get a call through to his superior will not be able to get through. The German communications system is being sabotaged at different places and they will not be able to communicate with each other or German High Command. This will drastically hinder the Fuhrer's plans to obliterate the Allied advance.

The plans are working well for the start of D-Day and for France 'le jour de la liberation.'

0530 hours

As the dawn light spreads across the sky we hear guns in the distance. It has stopped raining in Saint Just, but it is cloudy and the wind has picked up to 20 knots increasing the size of the waves on the ocean and making it dangerous on the beaches as troop ship carriers evacuate their cargo of Allied soldiers.

'It sounds like the big ships...destroyers...are firing at the German gun defences.' Robert says. 'It's the start of the day of liberation, who knows what's in store for us all.'

The barrage of bombs is getting louder and more frequent. We can hear the big guns of destroyers on German positions. An armada of ships appears on the horizon, and large flotillas, destroyers and landing craft of all shapes and sizes get closer to the beaches of Normandy.

At the top of an escarpment Robert, Eve and I are looking out over to the horizon. We can hear the guns from the Royal Navy landing on enemy positions on the coast. The booms are continuous but muffled, they come in surges on the back of wind gusts. As we strain our eyes, we can see plumes of black smoke against the growing grey light of dawn.

As time goes on and the clouds scud across the sky the bombing gets louder and more prolific. Aircraft fly amongst the clouds, firing on enemy positions. We can hear the booms from our position on the top of the plateau and realise that we are witness to the start of the end of the war.

The first men of the US First Army hit Omaha and Utah beaches at 0630 and British and Canadian troops begin landing on Gold, Juno, and Sword beaches at 0700 hours. Operation Overlord lands 150,000 men and 1,500 tanks in the first forty-eight hours. This covers the whole of the Le Havre area from Cherbourg to Cabourg.

Senior German commanders are trying to get through to the Fuhrer, but his generals know not to disturb their leader on just a suspicion that the Allies are advancing onto Normandy. They thought it was coming across from Calais anyway.

It's chaos on the Normandy beaches. The smell of cordite fills the air. There are bombs exploding, bullets flying, and blood and bodies on the ground. Barbed wire entanglements, the booms of the overhead big guns from the warships. The machine guns desperately rat-a-tat against the enemy who are taken by surprise emerging from a stormy sea, they are now defending the Third Reich. On some beaches the Germans are picking the soldiers off like ducks in a row. It is heavily defended and although low tide, some of the amphibious vehicles are churning out their soldiers too early and some weighed down in the wild seas drown with equipment still on their backs.

The ebb of the tide has exposed the mass of beach defences. Mines and obstacles have been built by the French slave labour from *Service du Travail Obligatoire* used to fortify huge stretches of open beaches.

Chapter 41

An Allied aeroplane flies over Saint Just and Saint Lo and drops a pile of leaflets telling the local population to get out of their towns immediately. Their town will be bombed tomorrow. But it's a windy D-Day. The wind and rain send the leaflets off course, and they land in villages a few kilometres away. The towns of Saint Lo and Saint Just do not get the warnings and the population stay in their houses, unaware of the bombings to come.

Meanwhile Robert, Maurice, and two other Maquis are en route to sabotage the bridge at Vire to see if their earlier sabotage has worked. It has - the bridge is in pieces, bits of wood and metal spread out over the stones, sending stones and boulders downstream. The river is blocked and split into different routes with boulders sending the river into two different paths. Mauvais' car that was pushed into the deepest part of the Vire River by Robert, is exposed. The windows are open. The car is full of water inside. There's no body inside the car.

Robert and Maurice drive up to another bridge outside Saint Just a few kilometres away at the River Suzanne. They get out and see a group of Maquis standing under some trees. Their pistols cocked aggressively in trouser tops, a rifle on the shoulder, a Sten gun on the back. One man has a string of grenades hanging from the belt, two of them are smoking, while two others are setting charges and fuses. Robert jumps out and helps the two under the bridge to set the charges; it's Benoit and Gilbert. The wind is against them, and no one hears the truck full of German soldiers come growling around the corner. The soldiers leap out of their truck and start shooting the Maquis who are taken by surprise. Some Maquis manage to shoot back but some are shot while still smoking, they fall down their Stens still on their shoulders.

Robert sees this all happen in seconds. The truck stops at the bridge and the officer in charge and another soldier aim their pistols at Robert. Robert and Maurice put their hands up it's too late for them to make a run for it. They'd be shot in the back. But the German soldiers don't see the two under the bridge at the other side hiding in the bushes. They hadn't finished connecting the charges. Robert drops the fuse he has in his hand and bent down he comes out from under the bridge. He nods at his friends to pull back. It's Benoit and Gilbert on the other side of the bridge and they manage to slip amongst the bulrushes on the edge of the river where it's thick and hide.

Robert comes out from under the bridge with his hands up. A litter of Maquis are laying dead on the ground under the trees. The German soldiers walk amongst them, kicking them to make sure they're dead. On the ground one of the Maquis groans and one of the soldiers shoots him in the head with his rifle. Robert and Maurice gasp, they are shocked.

The German officer states, 'We don't take prisoners. What are you doing under the bridge?'

'Why would we tell you when you're going to shoot us anyway?' He's upset and angry at seeing his comrades gunned down.

'Take these two for questioning,' he tells the other two soldiers.

Robert and Maurice are surrounded by soldiers. They are arrested and led towards the back of the truck. An officer and his sergeant walk towards the bridge to inspect it for wires. They pull the plastique and charges out and take them away. The truck drives off with Robert and Maurice in the back with the German soldiers.

But the two remaining Maquis - Benoit and Gilbert, creep out from the bulrushes when the truck has gone they hurry to see if there are any of their friends still alive. But they are all dead, killed by Nazi soldiers. Benoit spots more plastique and charges in a bag amongst their dead comrades. They start again setting the charges under the bridge to blow again.

After a few minutes, Robert and Maurice with their hands tied in the back of the German truck, hear an explosion in the distance as the truck careers back to Saint Just. It was the bridge detonated by their friends.

'I hope they destroyed it,' Robert whispers to Maurice.

* * *

Albert, the funeral director, dresses another deceased person at the *mortuaire*. He hears a knock at the door. When he answers, he doesn't see anyone. Then he sees what looks like a dead dog wrapped in a blanket, all bloodied and mashed up. When he undoes the blanket, he realises it's not a dog but a human body. It has terrible torture marks on its body; the body has cigarette burns on it and fingernails pulled out. The bottom part is difficult to see, it is twisted at an angle to the top part. He jumps back when he sees what and who it is.

It's a woman. And it's Giselle, her face swollen with black and blue bruises.

Chapter 42

On the Day of Liberation the people are waving French flags out of their windows as word has spread that the invasion is happening. In Bayeux, the crowds cheer as the Allies take over the town. The Germans here have surrendered.

Where French citizens had welcomed the Allies by running out into the street in Bayeux, a few kilometres away in Saint Just and Saint Lo, the Germans hold on stubbornly to the towns. They are key ground to the south at the centre of a major road network of Saint Lo, and German troops need to command the crossing of the Vire bridge. A vicious battle is fought for Saint Lo the next day.

In the town square of Saint Just - a crowd is gathering. There are two men tied to stakes their hands tied behind the execution posts. They are not blindfolded and are terrified. Some women are crying. There is a row of German soldiers standing to attention.

'Fire!' a German officer shouts above the noise and wails of their relatives and friends. The two bodies slump down against the stakes, as their bodies are riddled with bullets from the soldiers' rifles.

The crowd is angry, and a woman and children cry and shout at the tops of their voices.

The German officer shouts above them; 'These are traitors and collaborators - reprisals will happen daily if you continue to harbour terrorists! You have brought this upon yourselves!' he shouts to them in French. He doesn't mention the Allies at the door. He's been told by the Fuhrer to defend the town at all costs. He will do so.

'Anyone who knows of any *collaborateur* or is knowingly working with the Allies will be shot. If anyone knows of any such information and comes forward, they will be paid handsomely.'

The townsfolk mutter angrily amongst themselves. They've heard all this propaganda before.

'The Allies have tried to destroy your towns and cities. Soon there will be nothing left for you to live,' he continues. Everyone watches with hatred as their citizens are treated like dogs. Several people run up to the dead men and take them away for burial.

There is shouting by the river and some people run over to see what is happening.

'What is it?' the German officer demands.

'There's a body in the water, Sir. It has a *Milice* uniform on it.'

1600 hours

Pierre and Eric are returning to St Just from Coutances. A train is due later today with more German armaments. They have decided instead of blowing up the railway they can sabotage it, it'll still slow them down, maybe even derail the train, if the driver doesn't see it ahead. If the Germans don't see obvious evidence, like an explosion, then there is less chance for there to be reprisals on the local population.

Five kilometres from Saint Just in a rural part far away from the village, their train stops half-way along the track. The Germans will execute anyone they suspect or anyone near, so they must do this quickly once their train has passed. It has passengers on it, as they pass a signal box Pierre stops and gets off and runs back to the spot they have chosen. Eric stays at the engine looking out for German soldiers. Pierre hops off the back, he is young and fit and has strong arms. He pulls out the pins on a section and, with a sledgehammer, knocks the points wide apart. The next train will be a German one. Either way, the next German train won't be able to get to the next town, which is Saint Lo.

Pierre jumps back on board with his sledgehammer. He hides it in the rear van and runs back to the front of the engine. It has taken ten minutes. The steam discharges slowly, and Eric releases the brake. They move forward. The passengers look out of the windows but don't notice Pierre run past the window. They wonder why they've stopped.

But these days, with the enemy stopping people and transport and the *résistance* derailing trains, it's not surprising. Two people in the rear carriage notice Pierre run back to the front of the engine.

Chapter 43

D-Day + 1

0700

It's the first morning of no rain and Eve and I cycle to the hill where I left my radio case under a grassy tussock. It's still here wrapped in a sheet and that's covered in mud, protecting it from the wet. It has rained a lot since I last hid this radio. The ditch under the bocage is sopping wet. Our shoes and trousers get covered in mud. The rain's stopped, but it's still windy and grey. It's definitely not summer weather. We push our cycles up the hill and hide them under overhanging trees. I show her the shepherd's hut where I did my sched transmission to London a few days ago.

'I haven't been here in ages,' she says.

'It's dry under here. I've used it before, so just watch out for the RDF van for me. It's even more important now that the allies have invaded.' I look at my watch. It's 0700 hours.

Eve watches as I set up my radio and dial in to deliver my information.

Local comms have been destroyed however Jerry has dug in and using citizens as protection against allied bombers.

My reply from London HQ comes back a few minutes later.

Fierce resistance at Cherbourg the Allied beach head is moving south Bayeux liberated American bombing raid at 1700 in St Just and St Lo area leaflets have been dropped to warn citizens imperative you get out

'Mon Dieu Eve, we have to get out of Saint Just - a bombing raid is set for 1700 hours!' I start putting my radio away.

'We'll never get there in time.'

'We have to go and warn them now!'

We run down the hill to put my radio back in its hiding place then cycle quickly over the bumps of the uneven ground and over the cobbles back the way we came.

'Leaflets were supposed to have been dropped. But I haven't heard or seen any planes this morning, have you?' She shakes her head.

Eve and I frantically cycle into the town as fast as we can. People are out and about in Saint Just, they've heard the allies are on the way to liberate them, and Bayeux has already been liberated. It will only be a matter of time before the Germans are gone. But we see a lot of German activity, and I realise the enemy are not going to hand Saint Just back to the allies. There's lots of German military activity in the town. The high street bustles from the garrison to the edge of town. The blockades on the exits to the town have been strengthened, the number of German soldiers has been doubled on each sentry post.

As we cycle past the blockade into the town, we see the Gestapo and soldiers are letting people in, but not letting them out.

'Get off the streets!' the gendarmes are shouting to people.

A family is trying to leave but the Gestapo won't let them. The father is arguing with the Gestapo. One Gestapo officer aims his pistol at the father, who backs off.

The engineers are desperately trying to repair communications. It is chaotic in the town square where the town hall is, German officers are up and down the steps of the *Mairie*. Gestapo cars are in and around the town looking for *résistance* and any men they don't recognise as an excuse to detain and arrest them. Fear is starting to bite the enemy, now they know the Allies are pushing their way forward through Normandy.

As we cycle into the town square Eve and I shout to everyone congregated there that bombers are on their way. There are lots of groups of people banding together, they are angry, they don't listen to what we tell them. One of the women I recognise from the bakery tells us:

'They've taken two men and shot them in front of their families for holding up French flags outside their houses!'

We are shocked. The Germans here aren't backing down. Hitler has told them to hold fast and defend the towns and cities. The Germans are digging in and holding the citizens as hostages in the town of Saint Just.

A man next to her says: 'They need to hang onto Saint Just. It's the main communications hub between Cherbourg and Saint Lo. They won't give in so easily.'

Then we see German soldiers dragging four men into the town square. There are execution posts put in right next to the church. With horror we recognise Pierre, as two soldiers pull his slight frame along with them, he is struggling. An older man in front doesn't struggle against the young soldiers. It's Eric. There are four men in all, all railway workers, they have coal dust and grease on their overalls. But the worst thing are the cuts and bruises that are evident on the men.

'It's Pierre!' Eve sees him at once. She cries out his name. It looks like they've all been beaten up.

Two soldiers drag Pierre who is handcuffed, and struggling, towards the execution posts. Eric walks upright, appearing to accept his fate. The other two men are also struggling. Oberleutnant Sachs appears with a band of soldiers with rifles. He disdainfully watches the crowd.

'I didn't tell them anything, mama!' Pierre shouts to Eve as we rush up and try to pull them off him.

'Oh, my poor boy.' She screams at the soldiers. 'Let him go!' Tears fall down her cheeks, she is distraught.

'He is innocent, he's just a young boy, let him go!' she calls to Sachs. One of the soldiers strikes her at the side of her face, the other one lets go of Pierre as he gets his rifle and threatens to shoot us. Undeterred, she tries to pull Pierre away from him. While the tussle goes on, I go up to Oberleutnant Sachs who is standing there surveying the scene.

'For pity's sakes, let him go, Oberleutnant. He hasn't done anything wrong.' He stares at me as if seeing me for the first time.

'Have some compassion. The woman has lost her husband, don't let her lose her son as well.'

'There will be reprisals for our dead soldiers,' he says.

I try to wear him down with reason.

'He's just a boy. He works hard on the railways, so he serves the Germans as well. He isn't a saboteur, he's a simple boy, he hasn't even fallen in love yet. Give him a chance.'

Sachs looks at me thoughtfully, then he looks back at the growing angry crowd. One woman shouts at him and throws a stone at one of the soldiers. It is chaos. This could turn into a blood bath, with the crowd turning on the soldiers, and the soldiers shooting back to defend themselves.

'Let him go. The citizens have watched Pierre grow up alongside their sons. If you kill him, you'll have the town rise up - a blood bath will ensue.' He looks around at the growing angry crowd and the anxious soldiers, some aiming their rifles as the crowd closes in.

He nods almost imperceptibly to me. While two soldiers are tying Eric to one of the posts. I tell one of the soldiers who is holding Pierre to release him.

'The Oberleutnant has said release him, he's innocent of any crime.'

The soldier looks with confusion at Sachs who nods briefly, and they reluctantly let him go. Eve and I take hold of Pierre's jacket and pull him away before he realises what is happening. Two other women who know Eve bustle him through the middle of the growing throng. It all happens so quickly.

Pierre shouts: 'No! Save Eric!' I put my hand across his mouth, and the four of us scramble to pull him away through the frenetic crowd, as he struggles to get back to his friend and mentor. If he shouts any louder, he will get shot, or Sachs might change his mind. We must get out of here as quickly as we can.

The crowd is getting bigger all the time as people filter into the town square. I try to follow the others pushing one of the soldiers out the way, who is separated by the crowd. He tries to push his rifle into my face. He is getting more anxious. Some of the crowd gather round me and the soldier. It just takes one shot, and it could end in soldiers firing off their rifles into the crowd.

'Don't be a fool,' I say into his face. 'If you want to get killed, go ahead.' He looks scared at all the murderous faces around him. The main square is full, and people far outnumber the execution squad. Sachs brings the squad into line in front of the execution posts. By this time we are nearly at the exit.

Pierre is sobbing and doesn't want to leave his friends.

'You can't save them, but you can save yourself,' I hiss into his ear and dragging him along Eve one side, I the other, he trembles with emotion. The path closes behind us as citizens crowd in to vent their anger on the Germans. There are shouts of 'Let them go!' And 'German pigs!' A woman screams for her husband's life. There are shouts of '*Vive la France!*' Not many people see us go down the side street.

Behind us I hear the shots. There is chaos behind me, women screaming and crying, children wailing. Pierre is scurried away down a street into somebody's home, with Pierre crying and remonstrating all the way. With the help of Eve's friends in the town and pure luck, we have managed to whisk Pierre out of harm's way.

'Hurry my son, it's no good crying. Eric gave his life so you might live. Let's hide in my friend's house over there.'

But I don't follow them. I'm still looking for Robert and the Maquis and I hope to God they're still alive.

Chapter 44

Some of the crowd surge down towards the river. There is excitement on the riverbank. I can at least try and tell them to take cover before the bombers come. I call to groups of people, but they are intent on getting to the crowd that has gathered I lean over between people on the wall overlooking the river foreshore and I gasp involuntarily. The body is of Mauvais. It's bloated contents and smell makes me involuntarily gag, the warmth of the sun has brought the flies and they hover above his bloated face. I turn away and try not to vomit.

A German unit has turned up and the crowd is growing. I see Henri from the other side of the crowd trying to catch my attention. I suddenly realise I am right in the centre of this excitement, and I should fall back out of sight. It's too late to tell everyone bombers are on their way they will want to know how I know this. Madame Fisolee and a group of Miliciens appear and I see her talking to them and looking at me. I make my way quickly to the back of the crowd. I'm watched all the time by Madame Fisolee. Some men from the *Milice* pick up Mauvais' body up and put him on a cart, the body drips with water.

German soldiers and the *Milice* start rounding up a group of bystanders; women and men who are looking on at the dead body and talking together.

A German Officer appears and takes charge.

'Get these people rounded up and into the town square. This act of murder will be avenged.'

The unit of soldiers prod us like cattle with their rifles moving a group of us up the street towards the town square. I am one of them in the group. I try to separate myself from the crowd, but there are soldiers behind us.

Within a minute the crowd starts to turn ugly, there are angry shouts, a stone is lifted, and a man's arm is ready to throw it at the *Milice*. I can see where this is going. It's becoming dangerous for the citizens. Tempers are running high, and some children are starting to cry as they are dragged along by their parents. The soldiers look nervous and are looking at the officer to follow him. Henri is the other side of the road with some of the *gendarmes* who are watching us, he is trying to get my attention. I can see him, but I can't let the crowd be rounded up and used as scapegoats.

I hear the droning in the distance of bombers and try and alert people's attention to them by pointing up into the sky. I can't see what types of aeroplanes they are. People are starting to look up and realise there are bombers coming. I try to encourage the crowd to disperse by talking in a low voice to some of them. Then I see Madame Fisolee behind the German soldiers.

'She is a *collaborateur*!' Fisolee shouts pointing at me, standing with a group of *Milice*. The *Milice* are not sure what to do. They wait for the German officer to take charge again.

Fisolee keeps pointing at us and there's shouts of '*Collaborateurs*!' from her and from people behind us. Things are turning nasty.

A *Milicien* shouts to the crowd; 'Who knows about the death of the officer Mauvais?'

A German officer shouts in French above the noise of the crowd; 'Anyone helping murderers and terrorists will be shot including their families!'

Our group start to shrink; we start to huddle together. Half of us are women, mostly old men. There are two children clinging to their mother's skirts.

I shout out: 'That is ridiculous. Madame Fisolee knows more than she says. *She's* the *collaborateur*!' I point at her. Henri is wringing his hands and pointing, willing me to shut up and go to the back of the crowd. The Allied aeroplanes get bigger, the growling of their engines sound like angry dogs as they approach their target.

All eyes turn to her. Angry comments rumble amongst the people in the crowd. People move towards her. She backs off and looks frightened as I step towards her. The crowd is with me. She stands on her own now. She tries to back off towards some of the gendarmes who have gathered, but they're having none of it.

I move slowly to the back of our group and whisper to the women to escape as the bombers are coming. I walk towards some of the ramparts out of view of the crowd. I look over at Henri who is looking anxious.

'They did it!' Madame Fisolee points randomly, not sure who she's pointing at now, she frantically looks for me in a group which is dispersing.

'She killed Mauvais!'

I've moved to the back of our crowd and alert Henri by pointing to the aeroplanes in the distance. Above the shouting I hear the low rumbling of bombers.

'We can't all have done it, *madame!*' I shout from the back of the crowd. She is looking wildly through the crowd, searching for me. I look from Henri to the soldiers, to Fisolee, and back to the bombers, it's not safe staying here. A squadron of bombers is coming towards us. Some people point upwards as if they can't believe their eyes. On the east side of town the aeroplanes drop their bombs; we see them descend in inclined strings. Then we hear the whistling – we see explosions hit buildings on the other the town, buildings collapse near us and some catch fire. At last people realise that they are in danger, and the crowd quickly disperses in all directions.

The soldiers jump in a truck and quickly disappear.

As I run towards Henri I say to the women,

'Get under cover!'

'Are they Allied bombers?' Henri shouts in disbelief.

'Yes - get out and take cover!' I shout at him.

Some of us run to the nearest shelter in a woman's back garden, seven of us squash in together in a tiny space only big enough for four people. She shuts the door as the impact of the bombs blows a man off his feet behind us and rents the air with debris and smoke. The noise and devastation thunders above us. The ground shakes. A gendarme is in here with us, we all look at each other anxiously, as the mayhem continues. After a while the noise of bombing fades but another sound takes over, one of hissing fire and buildings collapsing. As the woman opens the door the smell of cordite hits our nostrils. I stare in horror at the houses in front of us two have had direct hits and those still standing have roofs missing. We run towards the cries for help.

We unearth children and parents who are covered under a tangle of beams, rubbish, windows and electric wires. It's hot and dusty, we try not to cause a landslide climbing over the rubble in case there are more people underneath us as we move across the devastated houses. The fight against fires is difficult as the means to fight them are scarce, the municipal water pumps have been carried away by the Germans a few days before. The scenes are heartbreaking as we see mother's looking for their children. A woman is looking for her husband and grabs me by the arm asking for my assistance. I lose track of time searching for people through the rubble. There are no signs of Gestapo or German soldiers about now, they have disappeared from view. My throat is sore with the atmosphere of dust and heat around us. I lose all track of time and tell Henri that I must go to find Eve.

I run up the hill towards the town square, I see my bicycle after scanning the area, it's fallen under a tree. The area I left Eve and Pierre remains unscathed and Eve's bicycle has gone so I hope they've escaped from the town. Some people are carrying their injured or dead to the hospital at the end of town. A long thin line of people are leaving Saint Just, where there was once Gestapo and German soldiers are now broken roadblocks. I hope against hope that they have left our town. I breathe a sigh of relief as I come out into the countryside, I cycle down an empty road.

I'm exhausted and covered in soot. I pull in at the dead letter drop on the way home, to see if there are any messages from the group. There are none. I haven't heard from Robert. It's evening now and I'm hungry. I cycle back to Eve's farm by dusk. But as arrive, I see two bicycles outside which I don't recognise. Perhaps some of the Baker *réseau* have evacuated here. I let myself in the back door and call out:

'Eve, Pierre, are you here?'

To my shock two German infantrymen are raiding Eve's larder. They peer out from the larder, one of them has a loaf of bread and a half bottle of wine in his hand. But he's not that young, the other one is no older than twenty. The older one talks to me in German, walking towards me.

I shout at him in French:

'What the hell do you think you're doing?'

I back out into the vegetable garden. As he continues towards me, I turn and run towards the barn across the yard where my Sten gun is hidden. He doesn't run after me; he continues to walk and follows me swigging from the wine bottle. I hide behind the broken wooden cart at the back of the shed and unearth my Sten gun from its hiding place underneath the hay cart. A chicken comes up to me clucking around asking for food. I am thankful the soldier is taking his time following me to the barn. There doesn't seem to be any other soldiers around so I'm guessing there are only the two of them who are absent from their unit.

He continues to swig his wine from the bottle while holding his rifle horizontal in the crook of the other arm. My heart is hammering in my chest. He appears unperturbed and confident in his ability to frighten me and hunt me down, but it's him or me and I have the element of surprise on my side. My SOE training takes over. There's a reason I hid my Sten gun in the barn, it's at hand to grab and defend myself and Eve, against the likes of Mauvais. He looks around the barn then sees my head bobbing up and down at the back as I check the magazine in the Sten. The soldier steadily makes his way round to the back of the cart. I move around and slip behind a pile of hay bales. I can get a better shot here. I hear the remains of the wine swishing back and forth in the bottle. He is completely unsuspecting of what is going to happen to him. As he reaches the back of the cart expecting to see me cowering down behind it, I come out from behind the bales and let him have a barrage of bullets in his chest. The Sten gun only stops when it jams. I tut, clear it, ready to fire again. I watch as he staggers towards me, a surprised look on his face. He drops the bottle and his gun, then falls onto his knees and onto his face.

His friend, the younger soldier, can't have missed the shots, and I wait for him in the barn, deciding the element of surprise gives me the upper hand for my survival. The younger soldier starts tentatively to cross the yard with his rifle a few seconds later. He is unsure, he is wondering what is happening as he stands outside the barn, his rifle aimed straight at the ground.

'Hans?'

I step from the other side of the bales and walk slowly towards him with my gun aimed at him. He sees me and stops dead. He raises his rifle unsure as if to shoot. He's too slow. I aim for his chest but hit him in the head. He stares at me, while he falls to the floor, dead with one shot. My heart's hammering in my chest now. Whether it's because I shot a young man who hadn't appeared to shoot anyone before I'm not sure; he is someone's son. But I can't think like that, it's debilitating, and I must move the bodies out of sight and quickly. I pull the younger one by his feet into the barn, he's surprisingly light, and I cover them both with hay. I feel a pang of remorse for the young soldier, but I couldn't take him captive. I hang the gun over my shoulder, ready for the next

German. I hold my hand out, it's shaking a little. I start to breath steadier; I'm surprised how calm I am under the circumstances. If it had been a whole unit it would have been different. I understood during training I may have to kill the enemy. I'm certainly getting more practice just lately. There's a reason why we were trained to kill; to defend ourselves. I'm glad I paid attention. I've come a long way n four months.

Chapter 45

D-day +1

The second wave of American bombers flies over Normandy dropping bombs on Saint Just and Saint Lo because the Germans refuse to surrender. They are determined to retain their stranglehold on the citizens of Normandy. The first bombs of the second wave hit the gaol and the police station next door. The explosions kill everyone inside the gaol. The *Milice* and the German soldiers have evacuated and are hiding in citizens' houses.

Robert is being interrogated in the building next door, in Gestapo headquarters. The cell is full of torture paraphernalia. Weber has his jacket off. Blood is dripping from the cat-o-nine tails which a man looking like a Gorilla has in his hands. Robert's back and sides are swollen with welts from the leather strips. He hangs from a metal circle from the ceiling of an interrogation cell. His wrists tied together his lungs extended with rapid breathing.

His tormentors watch Robert squirm in pain as Gorilla raises his hand and whips him again for the twentieth time around his body.

'You might as well tell us who your compatriots are, you will only die needlessly otherwise.'

Weber is enjoying watching Robert suffer, and the gorilla reminds Weber that they need to leave before the next wave of bombers return.

'What a shame I was enjoying myself. We will have to continue this at another time.' He puts his jacket on and straightens it. Weber is not one to run away from a few Allied bombers. 'Go and put this man in his cell.'

Robert is let down by a single cut of Gorilla's knife and he collapses on the floor, his legs no longer able to hold him.

'I leave for the chateau now, and by the way, the Allies will not bomb it. They think that a French family is still residing there. They don't realise the Gestapo have killed everyone.' Robert looks up at him through the one good eye which is not swollen. Now he has Robert's attention he adds; 'They weren't being helpful. So, we shot the children in front of the parents.'

He grins at Robert's bleeding body as he exits the room, he revels in the rush of power it gives him seeing a Frenchman's bloody body on the ground. Gorilla tries to drag Robert to the cell door by the rope that ties his hands together. But Robert has a new lease of life, and he's not going to make it easy for Gorilla. His hands are still tied, but now they're in front of him.

He can hear the thunder and vibrations of a wave of big bomber's coming over the town. Robert pulls back on Gorilla. Bombs whistle as they fall overhead and the next minute there are explosions outside the cell, and his attacker is hit by a falling wall and part of a ceiling which falls in on them. As if in slow motion Robert sees the way the room is falling around him, he rolls under the heavy table which is holding the gross instruments of torture. When the thick medieval wall collapses Gorilla is crushed. Robert huddles under the table as debris is blasted across the cell, the collapsed wall reveals daylight. He looks out to the ruined remains of the room next door which has been completely flattened. The daylight grows stronger as the dust begins to settle. It's eerily quiet, it's his chance to run.

When Robert investigates, the whole one side of the police station is down, there's no movement anywhere apart from floating dust and debris. He has been saved from the worst of it by the medieval oak table, that's been here in this police station for years. It's a mess of bricks and rubble on the floor now. The other side of the wall is swaying one way then the other. The roof is in pieces around him. The wall and part of the ceiling his side of the room is still standing. But only just. There's rubble, smoke, and the smell of cordite all around him. He coughs up dust and dirt which has penetrated right into his lungs. There are some Germans under the rubble. His hands are still tied. He shakes his head. He is covered in brick dust and waits until the dust settles. Then he makes his escape.

Bricks and parts of buildings lay waste in the centre of the town, and all the while there's the droning sound of bombers in the distance. Have they gone or is there more to come? He must get out of here. He takes his chance and bent double he climbs over the smoking rubble with his hands still tied he makes his escape. He looks up at the setting sun which is shining orangey red on the horizon, and he sees the remains of the broken Church of Saint Marie on the horizon. Just the sacristy end remains, with its coloured panes of saints and martyrs.

The next wave of bombers continues its relentless deluge. He looks amongst the rubble for the knife that Gorilla had in his hand before he was crushed. He can't find it so makes his precarious way with hands tied still, clambering over the rubble and to freedom.

He runs towards some trees and hides behind them looking back and trying to strain to see if anyone is coming out of the building next door from the jail prison. Some gendarmes are emerging out onto the street. He wants to go and see if his friends are in the cells, but it's buried in bricks and mortar. He doesn't want to go back amongst the police. He hopes his friends survive

The bodies of twenty résistance fighters are found later in the gaol under mounds of bricks and rubble. They were locked in the cells underground; they didn't stand a chance.

Chapter 46

As the sun is setting over the blood-red horizon, there are thousands of Allied soldiers establishing a beachhead on the Normandy beaches. All the way along the Normandy coast there are thousands of men from different parts of the world fighting against the German army. The Fuhrer has told them to dig in and defend the towns and cities at all costs. Some will surrender easily. The Germans further south and west of Bayeaux dig in and prepare to defend their territory. While the *résistance* groups spread across France have been galvanised into action - bingeing on sabotage at train stations and on the roads, destroying bridges and telecommunication systems.

I wait for my friend Eve and Pierre to return. But Eve returns on her own, she is happy and relieved that Pierre wasn't shot, she tells me he's gone to the hills with the Maquis, they plan to sabotage the train station.

'He is overcome with grief at what's happened to Eric and his friends. He wants to get his own back.'

I hug her. There's nothing much one can say when lives are lost.

'We lost many brave *résistance* today.'

'Eric gave his life to the résistance so that Pierre could live. But where is Robert?'

'I don't know. I am worried.'

'The Allied bombing raid has done little to expunge the Germans dug in, but it's killed hundreds of people. The Gendarmerie has been attacked by bombers, apparently a group of *résistance* have been killed in the gaol cells, they've been crushed.'

As we sit at the table, I tell her what's happened in the past few hours, including shooting the German soldiers.

'But I shot them in self-defence.' I tell her.

'Mon Dieu. I came back thinking it would be all right now that Mauvais is dead, and the Allies are on their way, but things couldn't be worse. Who is bombing the town? Is it the Allies? I just can't believe it. Why would they kill us, the citizens?'

'The Germans don't want to let go of their stronghold here, they could hold out for weeks, months, especially if they're hiding in the peoples' houses.'

'It's just not fair,' she says, shaking her head. 'It goes from bad to worse. When will it all end?'

'We should leave too,' I say. 'It's not safe living so close to town. The Nazis are trying to find houses out of town where the bombs won't be dropped. We've already had two unwelcome visitors. What if we have more? They say they're killing the inhabitants and taking all their food. We're not safe here Eve.'

Eve looks out of the window and into the distance at the hills.

'I've lived here all my life.'

'I know, but it's no good if you're dead is it?' I go and put my arm around her. 'I think we should try and find Pierre and Robert in the forest, and the Maquis. And we should get out now because we could get bombed at any time again.'

'But where in the forest? It's a big place. Wouldn't it be better to stay here?'

'What if we go into the forest and join the Maquis? Here, we're just sitting ducks for the Allies to bomb and the Germans to seek revenge.'

Eve is reluctant to agree. It would mean crossing the river in the dark.

'All right,' she says, 'But we do it tomorrow in the daylight. It's sheer madness to do it in the dark. The river is swollen and flowing fast with all the rain we've had recently.'

We start to get ready.

I put the radio in the basket and cover it with a blanket and a small amount of food Eve has left in her pantry. We decide to go as soon as it's light. I put the two bicycles at the back of the barn out of sight leaning against the outside walls.

'Hopefully, the Germans will be gone by the time we return back to your farm, and the Allies will have won and chased the Boche out of the area,'

'Have you got your gun in your bicycle?' I ask her - Eve doesn't like carting a gun around.

'I'll put it in my basket.' And she takes it from a drawer and takes it out to do it. She runs straight back in.

'Germans coming! What do we do?'

I look out of the window and my heart sinks, another German truck bringing a whole load of soldiers down Eve's drive.

'Merde Alors.'

'It's too late to run. They've seen us.'

'We have to get out Eve, they'll find the other soldiers I shot!'

The truck is driving slowly over the bumps and avoiding the holes down the long track towards the farm.

'Let's run now.'

'Too late,' I say as we stand watching the truck from the back garden pulling up and the soldiers disembark. My heart is racing away again.

'How do we keep them out of the barn?' I ask her, trying to think of a plan. Worse scenario is we just make a run for it, and probably get shot in the back.

I look around me for inspiration, we nervously stand waiting as the officer in charge jumps down from the front of the truck. His uniform is dusty, and he looks dishevelled as do the group of soldiers who jump down from the back.

'We need to take shelter in this farmhouse,' he says in bad French. Eve pretends not to understand him and keeps shaking her head.

'*Non. Non.* We have no food.'

He ignores us and looks about him.

'Anyone else here?'

'*Non, non.*'

He pushes past her into the hallway and goes through to the kitchen. The others follow with Eve and I looking on and at each other. We follow them in.

'Stall for time,' I mouth at her. 'Stall them.'

The officer mimics eating food, and Eve and I reluctantly look in the pantry. It is empty. He sees this. I point to the veggie patch from the kitchen window and indicate we will cook them something from there. We both can't wait to get outside. He sends two soldiers to the barn. I follow them across the yard. I have my Sten gun in the basket. Our bikes are hidden from view the other side, but if they go round the outside, they will see them. I must somehow stop them from going to the back of the barn and finding the two bodies. I try to divert them from searching at the back.

'Food?' They ignore me.

They jump up to the mezzanine level. From the ground floor I look nervously at the pile of hay in the corner. I'm glad I put the bodies at the back of the barn they haven't looked here yet. It's dark now anyway. But someone will find them eventually, we can't still be here.

I can see them looking out of the window on the upper floor. And I wish for once it was already dark. Here in the Northern hemisphere, it won't get dark until 10pm, June has the longest days of the year.

I hear the low rumbling noise of two bombers flying over the town. I try to identify its markings but already know that it's Allied bombers flying over as the next wave of bombs are preparing to be dropped.

The Germans are not giving an inch they are well hunkered down on the outskirts of local towns and villages. The citizens of the town will be confused they haven't seen the flyers dropped by the Allies warning them to escape the town of Saint Just and Saint Lo. People who haven't been hit are grabbing their belongings and leaving, they realise at last that the Allies are not coming to emancipate them today and the Germans are digging in and using the town for a conflict battleground with the Allies.

It's getting dark but the red haze of fire lights up the sky on the horizon. I can see three German soldiers in the yard carrying an anti-aircraft gun from their truck towards the old cattle shed. With its other level in the roof the soldiers will have a good view of

Allied bombers underbellies as they fly over. They keep lights out so as not to illuminate their position to the enemy bombers.

Eve and I bend over in the veggie patch starting to look for vegetables. 'What shall we do?' She asks, her voice full of fear. 'The bombers are coming back.'

I say to her, 'This is what we'll do. You go and make the soup while I take the bikes out and then come outside and meet me when it's clear. Then we'll cycle to Gaston's farm along the road.'

But we don't get the chance, because at that point we hear the humming of another wave of bombers coming towards the town. We look up and on the skyline are black bombers looking like huge black birds of prey set against a red flaming sunset. And they're coming this way. My heart is constricted, fear is making my heart pound.

'Eve, we need to make a run for it,' I say urgently. 'We should leave the radio and the bikes. It's almost dark. We can slip away now. Just run towards the river. Follow it along until you get to the stepping-stones if we split up. Then cross there.'

Now we do it. 'Run!'

Eve and I run hunched as low as we can towards the river. We reach the long grass, and the sun has almost set. I see out the corner of my eye the soldiers taking their anti-aircraft gun up the steps to the top of the barn. They will aim at the under bellies of the Allied aircraft when they fly over Eve's farm. They do not see two women darting low along by the river which is now in deep shade. I give them thirty seconds before they realise, I am escaping. I hear the officer come out of the back door looking for us. We have slipped out from under their noses and am diving through the long grass towards the river. And it works because they don't see me at first. I reach the river where the reeds and grasses are longest, and turn as they realize we are escaping, and someone shouts;

'Halte! Halte!'

Twenty seconds. Eve is running ahead of me. I reach up to her and lift her elbow to help her keep running at speed without looking back. Instinct makes me run like it's a race to keep alive, at the same time trying to avoid the clumps of grass and river-swept logs as we run and jump over the obstacles.

'Keep going to the stones - we can escape over them in the dark!' I gasp.

Boom! Boom! The sky is lit up with explosions as Allied bombers pass overhead, I can hear the whine and whiz of the bombs falling onto the town.

Ten seconds. Another soldier yells, *'Halte!'* and starts shooting at us. But they miss because it's difficult to see figures fleeing in the semi-dark and we have a head start.

As I struggle to keep up with Eve, I hear men shouting. They see our silhouettes running towards the bend in the river. Soon we'll be out of sight. The first row of bombers sweeps above us, I feel I can almost touch them.

We are running like the wind. Upright now, and the sound of rifles shooting. But we are too far away. With any luck we will have disappeared into the twilight. I hear some shouts in the distance and guess that some soldiers are chasing us. I take a quick glance around, they are fast, but we have a head start. We just have to reach the first trees after the bend in the river, and I know the stepping-stones are there. Not far now, just a few metres.

'This way!' Eve shouts to me.

I hear the ominous rumbling sounds of a second wave of Allied bombers flying over the town, I hear the German 380 anti-aircraft guns crackling in the distance trying to bring them down. The bombs are being dropped ever closer. Some explode on this side of town. One aeroplane passes over-head, and we hear the unmistakable sound of screeching as the wind whistles over it. It explodes remarkably close, and I hear wood, splinters and shrapnel being sent in all directions. I look back quickly. Eve's barn is being blown to bits. There's wreckage splaying out on a wide area across the field. We got out at the right time.

I reach the bend in the river. It's dark now, and as I glance back quickly, the town is red where the fires are blazing. We're breathing heavily. The fires are taking a hold on what's left of Eve's barn.

Some of the German soldiers are already on their truck following us. At this rate if they get to the bend in the road next to the river, they will get there before us. We are going the long way alongside the river before we break off.

Eve slips over in the wet. I stop and haul her up.

'Keep going. Keep going. It's not far to the stones.'

The problem is - will we find them before it gets dark? I am panting by the time I reach the trees round the bend. I can hear the Germans' truck hammering down the track towards us. I'm surprised they are continuing the chase. Or are they trying to escape the bombs?

Behind us, there is carnage as more Allied bombers hit their targets and Saint Just is suffering destruction on a huge scale, as we hear explosion after explosion. The skyline goes dark as the red sunset we saw is extinguished by the rows of bombers filling the night sky.

'It's so dark amongst these bushes and trees to see where they are. All I can hear is falling water,' says Eve.

'Where are the stones?' I ask in desperation as we continue to run and dart in and out of the bushes by the water. I know they're around here somewhere, hiding in the dark. More fires are spreading in the town behind us, the noise is deafening as the bombers pass us overhead, lower this time. There are shouts as the soldiers close in on us. They are determined to catch us. Explosions seem to be chasing us as the sky is filled with the rumbling of aeroplanes. Some fall on the forest and bocage in the direction of Saint Lo to the East.

'We must be near the stepping-stones, but I can't see where they are!' I shout and suddenly I trip over something and land face down in a ditch.

'Emily! The soldiers are here!' Eve says, nearly falling on top of me. The truck pulls up with a squeal. In a minute they will capture us for sure.

We keep running along the side of the river. The men stop and get out, not sure where we are. Amongst the trees it's too dark to see us. They shine torches amongst the bushes looking to catch a glimpse of us hiding.

'Where are they?' she hisses. We've run out of breath. My heart is thumping in my chest. I have no energy to run further. There's nowhere else to run. We run towards the edge of the river, Torches are shining up and down in the dark and aiming ahead as they follow behind us.

'Don't look back Eve. Follow me quickly.'

Suddenly I hear the fast section falling of the waterfall, I recognise the huge boulders that narrow the river at this point, making a gushing waterfall almost drown out the noise of the mayhem behind us. The stones must be in front of the waterfall, but I still can't see them. There's no time - I jump in anyway, hoping my feet will make contact with or without the stones. Have I got the right place? Eve is right behind me she must have recognised it too. The water is freezing it takes my breath away, and I hear the shock on my breath, but adrenalin keeps me going.

The river is a torrent here, it seems deeper than when I last saw the area in daylight. I keep quiet to avoid giving our position away. My life depends on keeping quiet and concentrating on keeping my footing on the stones. Eve follows me gingerly trusting in my instinct. I hear her gasp as she tries to steady herself. The force of the water threatens to take my legs from under me. There is nothing to grab hold of and the water picks up speed as it hits the steppingstones and takes my legs from under me when I'm barely halfway across. I flail about trying to catch hold onto something. The current drags me, but I twist, raising an arm to throw myself face up and then kick and struggle to the riverbank twenty metres further downstream. I buffet into some stones, and I hold on for grim death choking and coughing the water I have swallowed from my lungs, the current trying to pull me back into it.

I'm disoriented until I feel Eve next to me trying to pull me back up. It gives me momentum to scramble across the stones. As I try to peer through the darkness and tumbling water around me the water is deeper here and I'm up to my neck. I panic as I can't see Eve and I can't shout out to her in case the enemy hear me. Eve is right behind me. But I miss my footing and fall into the depths of swirling water, I go under totally submerged, I can no longer breath. I try to remember how SOE taught us to swim strongly, so I give up trying to come up and kick my feet sideways, using the strength in my arms and legs to keep me level and swim until I reach the other side, holding my breath it seems like an age.

And as I try to submerge my head and get a breath, I am caught in an eddy.

The next moment Eve is pulling me up by my collar and I scramble around trying to get my feet in contact with the ground. She drags me out coughing and spluttering. Eve half lifts half drags me to some boulders which have come down the river eons ago. As she helps me out, I try not to choke the river out of my lungs as she puts her head close to mine and puts her finger over her lips in a silent *sshh*.

This side the river has sloping banks to climb up on. We crouch down and watch and wait as the soldiers shine their torches in the river and can only see a swirling mass of dangerous deep water; two women couldn't possibly have swum across this deep, fast-flowing water in the dark.

We sit shivering and watch the figures of enemy soldiers about forty metres away from the other side of the river. They are frenetically looking for us, with the German officer shouting commands up and down the river, they're trying to find a way to cross. Now they're trying to get their torches to reach our side of the river. But it's too far, they shout in frustration because they cannot find us. We have disappeared.

The town of Saint Just is burning. The sky is suffused with fire behind the trees in the distance, which is all we can see from here on the edge of the river next to the forest. Another wave of Allied aeroplanes goes over, the roar of each four-engined heavy bomber thunders towards the East, they don't drop their bombs here in the forest this time, they're searching for another target.

'The soldiers will probably be able to cross further down river,' Eve says, as we come out of our hiding place and crawl our way up the bank digging our fingernails into the mud. We crouch in the undergrowth. I am coughing up water from my lungs, but trying to smother the sound, as my friend helps me up and to safety.

'Come on Emily, we'll have disappeared into the forest by then.'

We lean on each other as we make a distance between us and the river and plunge deeper into the darkness of the trees. Our clothes and hair are dripping with cold river water, and we shiver as we make our way into the forest to see if we can find any of our friends who are still alive, with the sound of aeroplanes thundering overhead, and the blood-red night sky lit up with fire behind us.

END OF BOOK ONE

Getting to know Janina Clarke

What made you write about female Resistance fighters in World War Two?
Researching the women who worked for Special Operations Executive and what they did for their country against all odds makes for an astounding read – fact is stranger than fiction. Did you know that women weren't allowed bank accounts until they were thirty? Their husbands had to sign for everything financial, yet they were allowed to put their life on the line and fight for their country at such a young age. It wasn't until much later after the war that they were allowed the medals that the men were bestowed; many were made posthumously. Survivors like Pearl Witherington, the leader of the Wrestler network, was recommended for the Military Cross, but as a woman she was ineligible, instead she was offered a Member of the Order of the British Empire in the Civil Division – she rejected it saying, 'There was nothing civil about it, I didn't sit behind a desk all day.' Years later she accepted a Military MBE, CBE, and a Legion of Honour, as people began to realise the impact these women had made.

Why is Emily a radio operator?
I was a Wren Radio Operator during the 'Cold War' and I was fascinated by wartime SOE 'wireless operators' who managed to transmit and receive messages in secret while trying to stay one step ahead of the Gestapo and the RDF's. They couldn't transmit from the same place twice and some citizens were willing to betray them for financial gain; so they couldn't trust many people. It was said to be a lonely life. I based my stories on women like Noor Inayat Khan an SOE wireless operator, who managed to survive for several months before a French national betrayed her to the Gestapo. She was executed as a spy in Dachau in September 1944.

Is there a book 2, a conclusion?
Yes. Once I got caught up in Emily's escapades I realised she had much more to do. D-Day is only the start of the end of the war. She must try to beat the Nazis, save her friends and resolve her personal issues. So I had to continue and conclude with Book 2…

If you enjoyed the books please give me a review on Amazon or contact me on my author page. Thank you!

You can contact me through my website (janinaclarke.com) and find me on Facebook.

Until next time…

Printed in Great Britain
by Amazon

84407078R00220